THE EMPRESS OF EVERNOW

BOOK THREE - THE KINGDOMS OF EVERNOW

HEIDI CATHERINE

SEQUEL HOUSE

For Tamar - with thanks for your magic touch

BEFORE THE EVERNOW

The woman stumbled, falling in the hot sand and crying out. She didn't call for help, for there was nobody else there. Instead, she cried out to her departed ancestors, asking them to ready the heavens for her arrival. She couldn't take another step.

A gust of wind sent sharp grains of red sand flying toward her, filling her eyes as it turned her skin raw. Her veil had long since been sliced to shreds and flown into the air in a red cloud of lost hope.

She covered her face with her hands and curled into a ball, her body unable to spare any tears. Her wait for death would surely not be long. She'd already lived over twenty-seven Shinings. Her time had been drawing near, whether she'd been released into the desert or not.

Her hands left her face, pulled to her belly as if by a magnetic force as she remembered the baby that'd just been taken from her. A daughter with a crumpled face, masses of black hair and a scream as certain as the horrors that lay before her as a child born in The Sands of Naar.

Her daughter would grow without a single touch from another human, until she reached her time. Then she'd be touched, except only in the very place she didn't want to be, not just once but every twenty-eight turns of the sand, until her purpose was served. If deemed worthy, she'd be allowed to live. If not, she'd be released.

The woman rolled to her back and spread out her arms wide. Let death take her quickly now and carry her into the sky that she could no longer see.

Something slid under her shoulders and her knees. She gasped, and more sand filled her mouth, causing her cracked lips to seek each other out to seal the gap.

As she was lifted into the air, she realized what had hold of her.

It was a man, cradling her in his arms, pressing her against his chest and covering her with a fine cloth to protect her from the sting of the sand.

She'd never been touched like this before. Never been fed by her mother or held by her father. Never been embraced by a lover or struck by an enemy. This woman cradled in the stranger's arms had never before been picked up when she fell. She was untouched.

Until now.

"Am I dead?" she called over the wind.

"No," the man shouted back. "You've just been reborn."

RANI

THE BEFORE

R ani stood at the window of her bedchamber and watched the sand falling, unsure if she wanted the grains to fall faster or for time to hold them still. She felt tooth against tooth as she ground her jaw, aware that the sand would continue to fall whether she was watching or not.

The Orbs of Time were her obsession. Two enormous crystal globes, sitting on top of each other, joined by a spiral that allowed sand to slip from one to the other as gravity exerted its mysterious force. When the moon reached its highest point in the sky, the last grain of sand would fall, and Rani would watch the timekeepers turn the orbs and the sand would begin its never-ending journey once more.

"I knew I'd find you here," said her father, coming into the room and seeing what held her gaze. "Why are you always staring at the orbs like that? I wish you wouldn't."

She shrugged, lifting her veil from her shoulders to cover her hair, as her father stood beside her to take in the view for himself.

The orbs sat in the center of a large circle of grass—the only blades to sprout in this brutally hot, sand-covered kingdom. The carefully tended lawn was ringed by tall stone buildings that defined the border of the part of the Capital known as the Round. Access was provided by a single archway that Rani had never once stepped through. She'd lived her whole life inside the walls of the Round, not just as one of the wealthiest inhabitants of the kingdom, but as the daughter of the wealthiest inhabitant of all. For her father was His Royal Highness, King Horus, the Emperor of The Sands of Naar. And Princess Rani was his heir.

"The Shining will be here soon," Rani said, not lifting her gaze from the orbs.

Approximately every three hundred and sixty-five turns of the sand, the sunrise would peek out from behind the dunes and shine through the archway at such a precise angle that the crystal of the orbs would glow, bathing the Round in multicolored beams of spectacular light. Rani would see her seventeenth Shining soon.

Her father snapped her shutters closed, robbing her of both the daylight and her view of the orbs.

"Sorry, Father," she said, bowing her head, and reminding herself why it was better when she didn't speak.

She wasn't sure why she'd mentioned the Shining, anyway. She knew they upset him. He'd seen his thirtieth Shining already, which meant he wouldn't see too many more. Soon, she'd take his place and be crowned Empress. A title that was as meaningless as it was frightening, for she was yet to produce an heir of her own. The pressure on her mounted with each turn of the sand.

Feeling her way through the dim light, she made her way to her chair and faced herself away from the window, waiting for her father to let the light back in.

Her father opened the shutters and she released a breath, welcoming the returning light as she adjusted her veil. She liked hiding underneath this layer of fabric.

Bringing her shaking hands together on her lap, she laced her fingers, imagining how it would feel to entwine hands with someone who lived in a body other than her own.

"Has your time come yet, my daughter?" her father asked, as he did more and more frequently these days.

"No." She cast down her eyes, letting the sleek black strands of her hair cover her face. Given that her mother had been released only moments after Rani's birth, her father took it upon himself to ask about these things. She didn't want to discuss such delicate matters with him.

"Are you pleased about this?" he asked.

Her gaze sprang up to meet his, as her dark eyes widened and she shook her head. "I'm afraid."

"The future Empress cannot be filled with fear!" He bent over her, careful not to risk the chance of an accidental touch. His face was so much like her own, with black eyes and skin the color of spun gold. A male version, not all that much older than Rani herself. He'd been a mere thirteen Shinings at the time of her siring. "Do you hear me, daughter? You're a Princess. Start acting like one. And stop grinding your teeth!"

"I'm sorry, Father." She stilled her teeth, let out a breath and searched for words to fill her mouth instead. None came. Words never came easily to Rani.

"The Board is concerned," her father said. "The Chairman thinks you're hiding your time from them."

"I'm not." She felt her teeth connect and dropped her jaw, not wanting to disappoint her Father further with this habit she knew irritated him.

"He wishes to inspect you, to see for himself. You must go to the Conception Center at even-time. He insists upon it."

The shaking of her hands spread through her body until it reached her legs. "Please, no. Plenty of girls my age haven't yet reached their time. I'm not unusual."

"Daughter! You're highly unusual. One day, you'll be Empress of The Sands of Naar. An heir must be produced. There cannot be a delay."

Rani knew she couldn't make her time come sooner any more than she could make the sand run faster. How to explain this to her father? She responded instead by turning and glancing back out her window.

"Daughter," he said again, only this time with a softer voice. "There's no choice here. Please, I don't wish to see you released."

"And I don't wish to be Empress." The words were out before she could stop them and this time instead of grinding her teeth, she bit down on her tongue.

Her father sighed, returning to the window and looking out as he gathered his thoughts. "It's the role you've been born to. It's an honor to rule our kingdom." He blinked at her with such sincerity that she almost believed him. Did he believe himself?

"We don't rule it," she said, crossing her arms, keeping her voice low. "The Chairman does. If we ruled it, we could change it."

Her father's eyes widened at this unusual display of defiance, and she saw the edges of his patience begin to fray.

"You're young, my daughter," he said. "I had these same ideas once and they led to nothing. You must accept the laws here."

"Can't Sharma inspect me? She's on the Board." Rani was pleading now but didn't care. There was nothing more to be lost. "Why does it have to be the Chairman?"

"He insists on doing the inspection himself." Her father ran his fingers through his slick hair, displacing a few strands that refused to go back in place. "You know he doesn't trust Sharma."

Rani ground her teeth as a sign of defiance more than the habit itself. The whole idea of having a woman on the Board was to represent the interests of the females in the kingdom. What was the use of that when they had no say?

Her father sighed. "It's beside the point, anyway, Rani. It's been decided. The Chairman will inspect you at even-time. Make yourself ready."

"Father! Tell him no. Please! I'd rather die than have him look at me." She locked eyes with him, pleading with her whole body, not just her words.

He shook his head. "You know I can't say no to the Chairman. He has the power to have both of us released immediately. I must protect you, my daughter."

"You're the Emperor. He won't release us both." She couldn't let this go.

"I have other children, as you know. Just because they're in the Growing Center doesn't mean they don't exist. We can both be replaced if needed. The inspection must take place."

She closed her eyes, imagining what an inspection by the Chairman might involve, and shuddered. There was no way she was going to let that happen.

Never before had her words been able to save her, which was why she used them so sparingly. But right now, they were all she had to put an end to this. She had to find the right ones, whether there was truth to them or not.

"Father, I lied to you," she said, which was a lie within itself. "My time came at sun-up."

She watched as one of her father's eyebrows shot up and he studied the serious expression she held to her face. She needed him to believe her. This inspection couldn't happen. It just couldn't.

"Is this true?" he asked, raising one eyebrow.

She nodded. "I was embarrassed to tell you. However, I see now how important it is that I tell the truth."

He studied her a moment longer, then a smile spread across his face, his joy blurring his ability to see her lie. She'd just told him the one thing he'd been waiting so long to hear.

"Excellent! You should have said so to begin with." He clapped his hands. "I'll have you added to the registry immediately. Congratulations, Rani. I'm so proud of you."

She offered him a weak smile, surprised he was this easy to fool. Her shaking hands steadied as the threat of the inspection evaporated.

"Don't look so afraid," her father said. "You have fourteen turns of the sand to prepare yourself for the siring. There's no need for you to see the Chairman at even-time. You can relax now."

She added strength to her smile, fueled by the small win she'd just had.

"I'll check in on you later," he said, leaving the room with far lighter footsteps than when he'd arrived.

Rani returned to the window, her eyes glued to the Orbs of Time once more. She felt exactly like that red sand, trapped inside the center of her kingdom with all eyes upon her, waiting for her time to run out. She had no more control over what happened to her than those grains of sand being pulled toward the earth. And when her life was done, and she was released into the desert, the sand would turn once more, setting the path of her eldest child in motion. The same path she was being forced down, as had all the generations before her.

It was no wonder The Sands of Naar was grinding to a halt. Population was dwindling. Life expectancy was shrinking. And misery was flooding the kingdom in a tsunami of grief. How could anyone be happy with their life here? It was almost a blessing that their lives were shorter than those who'd come before them.

In fourteen turns of the sand, she'd be violated in the second worst way she could imagine. The only thing worse would be an inspection by the Chairman. The vilest man she'd ever laid eyes on.

She had no choice. Just like she had no choice in whether or not she wanted to be the Empress of this evil kingdom. She was the sand, being pulled down by a force greater than herself.

The reason she was obsessed with the orbs was because she hated them. Just like she hated her life. Just like she hated herself for being too weak to change it.

THE CHAIRMAN

THE BEFORE

"*O*rder!" The Chairman brought down his gavel with a thud. The Board were being particularly unruly today, muttering under their breath like they thought he couldn't hear them. The sand wouldn't pause for their chattering to end. It flowed on regardless. It'd be even-time soon and he hadn't a moment to waste. He licked his lips at the prospect of what was ahead. He'd never seen a future Empress laid bare.

"She must be inspected," he said, running his finger the length of the gavel as he spoke. "It's the only way to be certain."

"You can't tell if her time has come by looking," said Sharma, the only female Board member, seated on the opposite side of the round table.

He shook his head and made a tutting sound. What a pathetic statement. Did she take him for a fool? He'd know if the Princess's time had come. This was his area of expertise, having observed countless sirings in The Sands of Naar. Princess Rani may be small and quiet, but he was certain she was hiding a blossoming womanhood underneath those long dresses she wore. He knew what to look for.

"Are you suggesting I don't know how to do my job?" he asked.

"No, Chairman." Sharma shrank back in her seat and placed a hand on her rounded belly, full with child. "Forgive me."

"Excellent." He put down the gavel and rubbed his hands together, admiring the slender length of his fingers. "I'm glad you agree."

He scanned the other nine Board members, to see if there were any further objections. They sat still, their mutterings of only moments before silenced.

It was his duty to the kingdom to see if everything was in order with the Princess. The heir *must* produce an heir of her own. The chain couldn't be broken. It was always easier when the heir was a male and there was no need to wait for any time to come. The current Emperor had been ready at an extraordinarily pleasing young age.

"The inspection will happen at even-time. The Emperor has been asked to ensure the Princess attends."

Ten dark-haired heads bobbed at him in response.

"Now, Registrar, we're ready for your report. Please commence."

The Registrar stood and cleared his throat, as he flipped open the large leather-bound book on the table in front of him.

"We have eight-hundred-and-seventeen females registered. If you recall, last Shining we had a little over a thousand. Numbers are falling. We're averaging thirty sirings for every turn of the sand—some turns more and some turns less—resulting in approximately three successful pregnancies per turn. If this continues, by next Shining, we'll have had over a thousand babies born."

The Chairman put down his gavel to dip a feather into an inkwell to make some notes. That was a lot of numbers to take in at once. A thousand babies was good news. Perhaps their fortunes may change, and the population would increase. It'd been a long time since that'd happened.

"How many releases have been recorded since the last Shining?" he asked, hoping to hear a number less than a thousand.

"One-thousand-two hundred," came the reply.

"Damn it!" The Chairman thumped his fist on the table, forgetting to set down his feather, which snapped in half with the force.

"Is it time to re-consider our rules on release?" asked Sharma.

She really did have a big mouth. The Chairman cursed the law requiring at least one female to take a seat on the Board. They could do this job far better without that inconvenience. She was getting too comfortable here, forgetting her place and the promises she'd made in her past.

"You mean relax the rules?" He smiled at her, luring her into his trap.

She smiled in return. "Yes, Chairman."

"No!" His smile dropped into a sneer. "Do you need a reminder of what happened the last time the rules were relaxed? Historian! Please enlighten us, once again."

The Registrar sat down as the Historian rose to his feet.

"The Sands of Naar wasn't always a kingdom of health and prosperity," he said by rote. "Our ancestors lived by few rules, touching each other at will and mating without record. Then a terrible disease spread across the desert. People fell ill and died, passing the disease to all they touched, threatening to wipe out the entire kingdom. Frightened for his people and overwhelmed by the task, the Emperor established a Board, granting them authority to rule as necessary to restore the population. Slowly, with much hard work and wise heads put together, solutions were found and the population stabilized. Today, the Board still exists, having eradicated the disease by maintaining strict control over the population. This control must be enforced, or the disease will return and the kingdom will be no more. Anybody who's deemed to have broken the law and thereby puts the kingdom at risk will be released into the desert."

"Excellent," said the Chairman. "Do you still wish to relax the rules, Board Member?"

"No, Chairman," Sharma said, although her eyes still said yes, which was irritating.

"How many turns of the sand until your child is born?" he asked her, wondering how soon he could consider her release. With the population in danger, the release of a pregnant woman would never happen. Perhaps an exception could be made this one time…

"Twenty-three," she said, bowing her head, and sinking back into her chair yet again.

He nodded, having made his point and needing to say no more to ensure her silence lasted this time.

The rules couldn't be relaxed. There'd be anarchy. And it would only be a matter of time before his position as Chairman came into question. The only way he could hold onto his power was with total compliance of each and every rule, including the Princess's obligation to produce an heir.

The door flew open and the Chairman rolled his eyes at the interruption, only to realize it was the Emperor. The Board stood and bowed, waiting to be told they could take their seats once again.

This protocol amused the Chairman. The Emperor should be bowing to the Board, not the other way around. However, this was part of their tradition and it was important to keep tradition in place. Their way of life depended on it. As did his position as Chairman.

The Emperor didn't tell them to take their seats. His eyes shone with too much excitement to remember something like that.

"Princess Rani's time has come!" he blurted out, his words running together. "In fourteen turns of the sand we can make haste to produce the heir."

A band of disappointment gripped the Chairman around the chest. He'd been looking forward to inspecting the Princess at even-time.

"We must call a special meeting to discuss the heir's parentage," the Emperor said. "A suitable sire must be found immediately."

"There's no need for that," the Chairman said, rubbing his chin as his disappointment was washed away by a wave of excitement at the opportunity to announce a decision he'd made long ago. "As you know, normally I observe the sirings, rather than participate in them myself. I've decided to make an exception this time. I'll sire the child myself."

The Chairman spun around, certain he'd heard a gasp. It was that woman again, he was sure of it. However, Sharma returned his glare with an impassive stare.

"We should meet to discuss this," said the Emperor, twisting his hands into a knot.

"No, we will not," the Chairman said, feeling a pleasant stir in his groin. "We'll take a vote. All in favor of me siring the Princess's heir, please raise your hand."

Nine hands rose into the air, including his own. The Chairman raised his eyebrows at Sharma, waiting for her to cast her vote. All votes needed to be unanimous to be passed. Just another problematic rule this Board had inherited.

Sharma's eyes darted to the Emperor, who was ineligible for the vote. This was a matter for the kingdom and he had no say in that. Did the stupid woman think the Emperor could find her a way out of this?

She looked back to the Chairman and raised a shaking hand in the air.

"It's been decided," the Chairman said, banging his gavel on the table. "The heir to The Sands of Naar will carry my blood."

Problem solved.

"The meeting's adjourned." He thumped his gavel once more.

He may have been robbed of his even-time inspection, but in fourteen turns of the sand, it was unanimous that he was going to have so much more fun.

SHARMA

THE BEFORE

Sharma left the Board meeting, incandescent with rage. Holding her tongue had been difficult, but she'd had to, just in case the Chairman decided her child was as worthless as he clearly thought she was. This was the only time in her baby's life when she'd be able to take care of it, and she was determined to do it well. She couldn't risk upsetting the Chairman to the point he had her released. She could help nobody from her grave.

Having seen thirty-two Shinings, she was aware this may be the last child she had. Hopefully, her name would be removed from the registry for good and she'd be allowed to live her final turns of the sand in peace.

She wound her way through the long corridors of the palace as she returned to her bedchamber. All Board members were required to live in the palace so they were available at short notice to attend to the needs of the kingdom. She was glad of that today as her legs were aching. The sooner this baby was born, the better. Although, right now, technically she was touching her child. Her baby was encased in nothing but her touch. Once it was born, it'd be carried to its crib with thick-gloved hands and cared for without any contact of skin. It was no wonder many failed to thrive. So, perhaps sooner wasn't better for this child to be born. Perhaps it'd be preferable if it stayed in her belly forever.

She closed her door behind her and went to her window to look out at the Orbs of Time. Almost half the sand had fallen from the topmost orb to the bottom one, which meant it was soon to be even-time. At least Rani didn't have to deal with the Chairman's inspection today. Although, what awaited her in fourteen turns would be inarguably worse.

An ill feeling pooled in her stomach that had nothing to do with her pregnancy and she pushed away images of the Chairman siring Rani's heir. Sharma had lost count of the times she herself had endured a siring. Every twenty-eight turns of the sand since her time had come, apart from when she was with child, which had been seven times before now. She wondered what'd happened to those children. Many children in The Sands of Naar didn't live to see their first birth-day. How many of her babies had survived? Had any lived long enough to leave the Growing Center and start lives of their own? Had she seen them in the Round staring up at the orbs and not even real-ized it?

There was a quiet tap at her door and she went to it, knowing who it would be. Sharma's room shared a wall with Princess Rani. They were close in ways that stretched beyond their physical proximity. Rani trusted Sharma, just as she trusted Rani. Without her, that poor girl would have grown up with only her father and servants for company.

She cracked open her door. "Come in. Quickly, before you're seen."

Rani slid past her and slumped in a chair by the window, her dark eyes drawn to the orbs, as always. It was hard to believe this skinny girl would be Empress one day. She seemed too small. Too quiet. Too kind of heart.

Although, from what Sharma had just been told at the meeting, she wasn't a girl anymore. Her time had come. Why hadn't she come to her to ask for help? Had the Emperor prepared her? Would the

Emperor even know what she had to do? One of the female servants must've gone to her aid.

"Did you hear?" asked Rani, crossing her arms.

"It had to happen eventually," said Sharma, as gently as she could. "You're almost seventeen Shinings now. Most girls have their time at thirteen or even less."

Tears slid from Rani's eyes as she turned to face Sharma, her teeth working hard to grind each other away.

Sharma sat on the bed near her and made soothing sounds, her hands itching to draw Rani close and offer her the comfort she clearly needed. She often wondered if others felt like this with their need to touch and be touched. Perhaps it was just her. She'd never dared to ask anyone else about it.

"What did they say?" asked Rani. "You took ages."

"Sorry, it was a long meeting. Your father came in at the end to tell us that your time came. He was most excited."

Rani shook her head, clearly not as excited as her father. She looked more like someone was about to die, rather than be conceived.

"What's wrong, Rani?" Sharma felt her baby kick and stroked her belly, comforting her child in the way she wished she could bring comfort to Rani. "We've talked about this before. You knew this was going to happen."

"I lied to him!" Rani sat forward in her chair, bringing herself unusually close to Sharma. "Sharma, my time hasn't come. The Chairman wanted to inspect me, and I had to think of something, so I told Father a fib."

Sharma's hands fell into her lap as an icy shiver ran down her spine. "Hold on," she said, wanting to be certain she understood. "You told your father your time came to get out of your inspection with the Chairman?"

Rani nodded and this time tears of Sharma's own escaped down her cheeks. How could she tell this poor child what'd been decided in the meeting? A siring was far worse than an inspection. The news would destroy her.

"Rani, I need to tell you what happened after the Emperor made the announcement. This isn't easy for me to say…"

"Just tell me," said Rani, blinking slowly.

"It's about the meeting to decide the heir's parentage." Sharma coughed and shuffled in her seat. "You see… there'll be no meeting."

Sharma noticed Rani's legs were shaking, her hands held together so tightly in her lap they had no chance to move. This poor girl was terrified.

"Did Father see through my lie?" asked Rani, tilting her head.

"No, my sweet girl," she said, wishing that was it. "He didn't. The Emperor believes you."

"What then?"

"The Chairman decided who'll sire your heir, without a meeting being necessary." Damn! Why weren't the words coming to her? What words could she use to soften such a devastating blow?

Rani looked at her and waited. "Who?"

Sharma stood up, the urge to put her hands on Rani stronger than ever. Where did that instinct come from? Perhaps it was because she knew her words wouldn't be enough to soothe Rani once she heard her fate.

She drew in a deep breath. "I'm so sorry, Rani. The Chairman wishes to sire your heir himself."

"No!" Rani leaped from her chair and stood before Sharma, leaving only a breath of space between them. "Tell me this isn't true. Please!"

"I wish I could," she whispered, looking down to the floor. Witnessing Rani's distress was too much to take. Her own heart felt like it'd been torn from her chest. She'd swap places with this girl if only she could. Her own innocence had been dragged from her body long ago now. She didn't wish the same for Rani. Or any girl in the kingdom.

"What am I going to do?" asked Rani, sitting back down and drawing her shaking knees to her chest as she wrapped her arms around them.

"I don't know," said Sharma, recognizing Rani's position in the chair. When her belly wasn't so big, she often sat like this herself, trying to draw comfort from arms that were her own.

"You have to help me," said Rani. "Sharma, please, we have to think of something."

Sharma nodded. She had fourteen turns to think of something. She owed Rani that much. But how could she save this poor girl from her inevitable fate when she couldn't even save herself?

RANI

THE BEFORE

The moment Rani learned who was to sire her heir was the moment her will to live died. If only her body died along with her will. She'd rather the Chairman release her into the desert than subject her to the horror that awaited her.

Now, when she looked at the Orbs of Time, she was clear she didn't want the grains to fall faster. She wanted them to hold still. For the universe to stop and keep her steady and safe in the Now. Sharma had told her once about something called the Evernow, where people claimed to be happy to live in the moment. Rani couldn't remember ever being happy in any moment, although given what lay ahead, then perhaps her life had been total bliss so far and she hadn't realized it. Sometimes the bad had to be experienced to appreciate the good.

Yet regardless of her wishes, the sand kept falling and each grain that slid from one orb to the other brought her closer to her doom.

Her whole life, she'd hidden herself away in the palace, complying with the laws and keeping her father and the Board happy. She'd never left the Round and could only imagine how the other people in the Capital lived, piecing together an image in her mind from the stories she overheard. Sharma didn't seem too keen on answering her questions about it. Rani could only assume the part of her life she'd lived outside the Round hadn't been happy. Which was sad because her life inside the Round didn't seem particularly happy either.

As the Emperor's first-born child, she was the only child in the kingdom not to be raised in the Growing Center. She was also the only child in the kingdom to know one of her parents. The Registrar kept detailed records of genetic lines for the purpose of avoiding sirings within families, but otherwise this information was considered completely unnecessary. If you weren't the child of the Emperor or Empress then what purpose was served by knowing who your parents were? This, of course, meant that there were no brothers or sisters or cousins or aunts, relationships that Rani knew existed just as she knew mammoths had once walked the dunes.

Being raised in the palace was supposed to teach her to be a good leader. This system was flawed for two reasons. How could she lead people she knew nothing about? And how could complying with the Board's every wish be considered leading at all?

Rani opened her shutters and sat on the wide stone windowsill in exactly the way she wasn't allowed to do. Usually, she only sat here at night when the Round was empty and nobody would see her. But more and more she'd come to think that nobody could see her anyway. She was an invisible girl. Her thoughts didn't matter. Her wishes were never heard. Her tears were never seen. She was timid and weak, too frightened to stand up for what mattered, yet even more frightened about what would happen if she stayed still.

She dangled her feet over the edge, thinking about how easy it would be to let herself fall. Her window was at the very top of the curved building. All she had to do was shuffle forward until she slipped. Then she'd feel the wind in her hair as she plummeted for a blissful few seconds, wiping out the certainty of the fate that lay ahead. Let the Chairman touch her body when it was cold and still. This kingdom would be better off without her, and she'd undoubtedly be better off without it.

She looked down and saw the upturned face of a girl staring at her from the grass below. They locked eyes and the girl shook her head, mouthing the word 'no'. Who was this girl who seemed to know what she was contemplating?

"No," the girl mouthed again.

Rani withdrew her legs from the windowsill and tucked them underneath herself, checking to see if the girl was still watching. But her eyes were directed at the orbs now and it was if she'd never looked up and the moment they'd shared had never happened.

The sand shifted through the orbs, reaching the point where half the sand from the topmost crystal had flown into the bottom. Eventime.

The girl stood up and Rani watched her walk to the Conception Center. Even from this distance, Rani could sense her fear. It was in the hunch of her back, the slowness of her steps, and the downward direction of her gaze. It was the walk of a body that was being dragged toward its fate.

Rani leaned forward, wanting to call out the word 'no' herself. The girl seemed too young and afraid to be forced into such an act. How could the Board have concluded that this was the solution to their population woes?

A shudder ran through Rani as she imagined herself walking into the Conception Center in fourteen turns and she looked back down toward the ground below, its pull on her greater than ever. She untucked her legs and let her feet dangle once more.

Just before the girl disappeared into the building, she stopped and turned her face upward once more to look at Rani. She held up her hand with her palm facing out.

"Wait," she mouthed.

Rani found herself nodding, retreating back into her room and throwing herself on her bed.

Who was that girl? And what did 'wait' mean? That letting herself fall from the window wasn't such a bad idea, yet now wasn't the time? Now seemed like the perfect time. Her life was over in fourteen turns anyway.

She sat up and ground her teeth so hard she winced.

Fourteen turns! Not now.

She still had fourteen turns to live the life she'd been robbed of. Fourteen turns to fill her eyes with the world that lay outside that curved arch. Fourteen turns to find her voice and talk and laugh and maybe even dare to touch. Fourteen turns to track down that strange girl and ask her how she'd known she needed her help.

It was like Rani had just been slapped awake. Her eyes were open, and she had fourteen turns to live an entire life.

And when her fourteen turns were up, she knew what she was going to do.

She'd wake up when the moon was high in the sky and sit on her windowsill with her feet dangling down and watch the timekeepers turn over the Orbs of Time.

Then she was going to let herself fall.

Instead of spending her remaining time afraid of the Board releasing her, it was time to release herself.

THE EMPEROR

THE BEFORE

*U*nable to settle after the Board meeting, the Emperor decided to volunteer at the Conception Center, not for concern of his kingdom's dwindling population, but because he needed some relief. A distraction from what'd been a most eventful and frustrating day.

Finally, Rani's time had come. It'd been such a long wait. For a while, he'd thought maybe the Chairman was right in thinking there was a problem with her. However, everything was in working order. Soon, an heir would be sired.

He cringed as he thought about who was to sire that heir and dreaded telling his daughter. She'd reacted badly enough when she'd thought the Chairman was just going to inspect her. With any luck, maybe Sharma would tell her first. He knew they talked. Sharma had saved him plenty of difficult conversations.

He walked out of the main entrance to the palace, nodding at the servants who held the door for him, and stepped into the hot sun. A guard followed him into the Round, keeping several paces behind to give him the feeling of being alone.

There were a number of people sitting on the lawn today, watching the time slip through the giant orbs as they ran their hands across the grass, marveling at the feel of it. Even the people who'd walked here together, sat alone, keeping a respectful distance.

Guards roamed the Round, looking for any contact or sign there'd been contact in the past, ready to release anyone who broke the law.

The Emperor walked around the circular lawn, quickening his pace as negative feelings built inside him. Rani was going to have to take these same steps in fourteen turns, although he imagined her steps would be far slower than his own. If only he could spare her from her fate, he would. But the Chairman had spoken and there was nothing that he could do, just like Sharma hadn't had a choice in how she'd voted.

He walked up the steps to the Conception Center, taking them two at a time and nodded at the workers who held the doors open for him. If they were surprised to see him so soon after his last visit they kept this well-hidden.

Volunteers were required to arrive at even-time, men taking the door to the left and women to the right, after signing in with the Registrar.

The Emperor tried not to notice the tear-stained faces of the women, preferring to concentrate on the men who were far more accepting of their duty to their kingdom.

He nodded at the Registrar, who made a note in his book.

"You just made it, Your Highness," he said. "I'm closing the book until the next turn of the sand."

"Many volunteers on the list?" the Emperor asked, even though the result was of no consequence to him. He'd be selected as a sire no matter how many other hopefuls were waiting.

The Registrar nodded. "I'll draw up the selection now. Please go ahead and await your call."

The Emperor went directly to the large reception room through the door on his left where a hundred seats had been generously spaced for the volunteers.

He took one of the last remaining seats and reminded himself why he was here. The relief of a siring would be beneficial today. An Emperor couldn't have too many children. Nobody had to know his needs were far more primal today.

It was a tediously long wait and the Emperor wondered if perhaps it was the men who were worse off than the women who were busy readying themselves, not staring at walls as they bored themselves to death. Surely an exception could be made for the Emperor? Did he really have to endure this long wait?

He yawned, his ears aching from the deafening silence. Speech was forbidden in here as they prepared their minds for the task ahead. Hopefully the selection wouldn't take too much longer. At least he was guaranteed to be called. How must this feel for the men who'd come here for nothing? He'd heard there were a few men who'd turned up for hundreds of sirings and never been called, with others deemed more worthy by the Registrar.

He needed to get this over with, so he could let go of some of his tension and move on with the task of informing his daughter of the outcome of today's Board meeting.

He rubbed his wrists, which were still sore from being bound behind his back during his last visit, only one turn of the sand ago. Surely the binding was unnecessary, especially with a Board member observing for any unnecessary contact? He'd change so many of these rules, if only he were given the chance.

After what felt like eternity, the Registrar came into the room and cleared his throat, ready to deliver his speech.

"We have twenty-seven sirings today. Thank you for serving your kingdom and volunteering your time. The list has been placed in the entrance hall. Please proceed in an orderly queue. His Royal Highness shall go first."

The men waited for the Emperor to stand and stride to the entrance hall, where he glanced at the top of the list to see the number he'd been assigned.

Nine. Hopefully that was one of his favorite women. The Registrar knew who he liked and had never disappointed him so far.

As he stared at the numbers on the list, all he could think of was that in fourteen turns of the sand his daughter would be a number. And the Chairman would be standing right where he was now, looking for his name next to her number.

All his needs of only moments before left his body, draining out of him like the sand in the orbs. Was he any better than the vile Chairman? Had any of the women he'd been assigned to in the past wanted their sirings? He'd never really stopped to think about it from their point of view before. Now that he brought it to mind, their faces had always been turned and their eyes remained blank.

But this was the way things had always been done. Well, not always. Ever since the Board had been appointed and the kingdom had been saved. Without this act, nobody here would've been born. There'd be nothing in the Capital except sand, blowing through on the hot winds of time.

He blinked as he tried to push away the image of Rani bound to a table, her body shaking as it was prone to do, and tears pouring from her eyes that were so much like his own. She didn't want this. She'd said she'd rather die than have the Chairman look at her. And now he planned to do so much more.

His daughter was about to become a very unwilling number.

Bile wound its way up his esophagus and he dry-retched, as the shame of his past actions became suddenly clear.

He *was* no better than the Chairman. And here he'd been worrying about whether everything was in working order with Rani when all the time it was him. He was never going to be in working order again now he had that image of her in his mind.

"Emperor, please proceed to room nine," said the Registrar, studying him closely with a furrowed brow.

"I've changed my mind," he said. "I'm going to head back to the palace instead."

"As you wish," said the Registrar, flipping open his book once more.

He did wish. Not only that, he wished for so much more. His poor, sweet daughter.

RANI

THE BEFORE

*R*ani dressed carefully, wrapping her veil around her head so only her eyes could be seen. She wore red, the color favored by most women in The Sands of Naar. Rani understood why now, more than ever. Blending in with the sand that surrounded them was a comfort. Who wanted to stand out in a kingdom like this?

She slipped out of the palace using the servants' door, not wanting the company of a guard today. Nobody gave her so much as a second glance. She could be anybody under her scarf and the long dress that swooshed around her ankles as she walked. Nobody would study her closely enough to notice the subtle yet intricate patterns woven through the fineness of her clothes, made from fabric fit only for a Princess.

She made her way out to the Round, stepping onto the lawn, rather than walking around it as she'd normally do. It felt soft underneath the thin leather soles of her sandals. So much nicer than the marble floors of the palace. There were dozens of people sitting alone on the grass, watching the sand fall. She carefully wound her way between them, finding an empty space close to the entrance of the Conception Center.

Rani had never sat on grass before. It felt cool and pricklier in places than she'd expected. She'd imagined it to feel like a cloud. When she fell from her window and got sent to the clouds, would they feel like this too? She hoped not.

The men had started to emerge from the Conception Center, some smiling, others lost in thought, but all with an air of satisfaction.

Bastards!

Rani surprised herself with the venom of this word as it raced through her mind. Except what other word was there for it? How could these men violate the females of their kingdom like that? Just because something was the law, didn't make it right.

Was her father one of the bastards? When she was young, she couldn't remember him attending regularly, but lately, she'd watched him from her window on a more and more frequent basis. What had changed and why would he continue to volunteer when he already had his heir and several spares in the Growing Center who'd be only too happy to take her place? Little did they know that soon one of them would get the chance to do exactly that.

It was hard to think badly of her father. His affection toward her seemed to stretch beyond obligation. There was love in his eyes. And a good amount of pity at times. Like he wanted to save her, only didn't know how. He was a good man, but like her, he lacked courage. Just because he was kind to her, did that make him a good person, if he wasn't so kind to others?

Soon the women would start emerging from the Conception Center. Rani knew they wouldn't carry themselves with the same sense of satisfaction as the men. Their footsteps would be shuffled as they cast their eyes down. Humiliated, bruised, and ashamed. Alive on the outside. The possibility of life growing on the inside. And everything else about them dead. That was never going to be Rani.

The first woman came out and adjusted her veil, the sleeve of her dress slipping down to reveal bruises on her wrist. Was struggling against her ties a reflex she couldn't resist, or had she actually thought she had a chance of escape?

As she descended the stairs, two more women followed, however, Rani didn't pause to study them. Her eyes were glued to the door, watching for the girl who'd told her to wait.

Three more women exited before she saw her.

She was younger than Rani. Her time must've come early, the poor thing. She was wearing a long yellow dress, with a matching veil that covered her hair but not her face.

Rani shifted her own veil to reveal a little more of her face, so the girl would recognize her. They made eye contact and Rani moved the veil back in place, certain the girl knew who she was.

She waited as the girl went to the grass and sat down near Rani, as close as she could without drawing the attention of the guards who kept watch over them all.

Her eyes were glued to the orbs just like all those who surrounded them. Wet tears were falling in time with the sand, tracing their way down her face, as they dripped onto her lap. She didn't make a sound or even move. The guards walking the perimeter of the Round would have no idea she was even upset. Not that there was a law against that. Yet.

"Are you okay?" Rani asked, keeping her eyes on the orbs and her energy on the sad girl.

"No," came the quiet reply.

Rani turned to the girl and shifted her veil once more, wanting to reveal more than just her eyes to this sad girl.

"My name's Rani," she said.

"I know who you are." The girl wiped away her tears. "You're the daughter of the Emperor. The Princess. I saw you at your window."

"What's your name?" asked Rani, not ready to talk about that.

"Azrael." The girl bit down on her bottom lip and tucked her hands together on her lap.

"How old are you?" Rani asked.

"Seventeen Shinings."

Older than she thought. The same age as Rani, and as different lives as they'd led, they were both facing the same ordeal at the same age.

Azrael glanced to the guards to see if they were being observed, then back at Rani. She pointed at the Conception Center. "It was my first time."

Rani's hand went to her mouth, which she realized was hidden by her veil. "Was it awful?"

Azrael nodded as a fresh set of tears burst from the corners of her eyes.

Rani shuffled closer, surprising herself by wanting to put her hand on Azrael's arm. But not only was that against the law, she doubted Azrael would want her touch. She'd been touched enough already.

"Will you help me?" Azrael asked, blinking away her tears.

Rani shook her head and Azrael looked away and clenched her fists.

"I can't help you," Rani said, heat rushing to her face.

"You mean, you won't." Azrael gasped as if unable to believe what she'd just said. "Forgive me, Your Highness. I wasn't thinking."

"Azrael, listen to me. I want to help you. Except I'm as powerless as you are. My own siring will take place in fourteen turns and there's nothing I can do to stop it. If I could, I'd help both of us. What's happening here is evil." She let out a breath, feeling good for having expressed herself like this. Had she spent her life with her words trapped between her lips simply because she hadn't met the right person to share them with?

"But you're the Emperor's daughter. You'll be Empress one day yourself. You must be able to help."

Did the people of this kingdom really still believe the royal family held any power? Did they really have no idea what slaves they'd all become?

"Why don't we help each other?" asked Rani, wanting to give this poor girl some hope to hold onto, despite it being one of the rarest commodities in the kingdom.

"How could I possibly help you?"

"I want to see the Capital," she said, feeling both brave and timid simultaneously. "Will you show it to me?"

Azrael's brows pinched together. "We're in the Capital right now. The Round is the very heart of it."

"All I've seen is the heart. I've lived in the heart my whole life. I want to see the rest of it before I die. Its arms and its legs and its brain and its stomach. The whole lot."

Azrael almost smiled. Maybe if she hadn't just suffered such a trauma, she would've.

"I've never so much as walked through that arch," said Rani, pointing over her shoulder.

"Who's stopping you?" asked Azrael. "You could walk through it right now. Nobody would recognize you if you cover your face."

Her voice dropped to a whisper. "I don't know what's out there."

"Why do you think so many people visit the Round each day?" Azrael asked.

Rani shrugged. "They watch the sand."

Azrael nodded. "And why do you think they want to watch the sand?"

Rani shrugged again. "It's peaceful."

"Looking at the sand reminds us that time continues on no matter what our hardships. It waits for no-one. The sand was running before I went into the Conception Center today and it was still running when I came out. My world may have stopped, but time didn't."

Rani knew this feeling well and was surprised to have it shared by someone else.

"Is that how you feel?" she asked. "That your world has stopped?"

Azrael nodded. "This is part two for me now. I'm at my own even-time. Everything that happened before is in the Before and everything that comes after is the After."

Rani liked this comparison, feeling like she was at her own even-time herself. Only her After was going to be much shorter than her Before.

"Do you believe in the Evernow?" she asked.

Azrael shook her head. "There's no Evernow for me. Or for you, by the looks of it."

Rani drew in a breath at the raw honesty of this girl who had so little fear, for everything had been taken from her already.

"Why did you ask me to wait?" asked Rani.

"You were going to jump," she said, as if it were self-explanatory.

"I wasn't." Rani realized she'd just lied for the second time that day, when this girl had offered her nothing but honesty. She deserved better than that. "Well, not yet anyway. You're right, I'll wait."

If the girl was surprised at her omission, she didn't show it. "I wanted you to wait for me, not wait to jump."

"Why would you want me to wait for you?"

"I can't explain it," said Azrael. "I was sitting on the grass before I went in, looking up at the sky, begging death to take me. Then I saw a movement, and it was you. You looked like an angel up there. I felt certain if I stopped you from jumping—if I saved your life—that somehow you'd save mine, too."

"I can't save you," Rani said, shaking her head.

"So you keep saying." Azrael stood up and brushed the grass off her dress, taking a step away from Rani before turning back to look at her. "Well, are you coming or not?"

"Where to?" Rani tilted her head.

"Through the archway of course. You said you wanted to go. What are you waiting for?"

Rani stood up and nodded. She was waiting for nothing and had no time to waste. "Lead the way."

AZRAEL

THE BEFORE

*W*hen Azrael had opened her eyes at sunrise, she'd thought she'd known what was ahead. Pain, humiliation, and fear. She hadn't realized there'd also be surprise. And not all of it bad.

Witnessing Princess Rani contemplating jumping from her window had felt like an experience her body had with her mind somewhere else. If only she could have organized for her mind to be somewhere else when her body had been in the Conception Center. She'd do anything to be able to wipe away the memory of that experience, but that was never going to happen. Some memories branded themselves in a way that was permanent without giving the choice as to whether they're wanted or not.

She wasn't sure why her gaze had been pulled away from the sky to see Princess Rani sitting on her window ledge. They'd met eyes and it was almost as if a cord was connecting them. The intensity of it had frightened Azrael and when she'd told Rani 'no' she'd meant it. She didn't want her to jump. She *couldn't* jump. Because if she did then it was all over, not just for Rani but for Azrael, too. For everyone. The intensity of this feeling had overwhelmed her.

And the Princess hadn't jumped. Instead, she'd come to find her and had sat on the grass waiting for her to walk out of the Conception Center, only to tell her that she couldn't save her. She was as mixed up about life as Azrael was. Not that she should be surprised by this. People who contemplated falling to their death weren't normally thinking clearly.

Princess Rani walked beside her now, an arm's length away in case their hands were to brush as they swung their arms. It made Azrael smile to think there was a Princess walking amongst the people and they had no idea. The Princess was smaller than she'd imagined, only a little taller than herself. Quieter too. She spoke with a soft voice that sounded like it'd never been broken in properly. She mustn't have cried enough as a baby. And there was a pretty face underneath that veil, with a striking resemblance to the Emperor's.

Azrael's hand went to her waist and skimmed her stomach, wondering if there were the beginnings of a baby in there and if it would grow to look like her. She hoped the siring had been successful. Not because she wanted to have a child, of course. It was because then she'd be taken off the registry while the baby grew. She'd been taught in the Growing Center about how the babies came out and although that sounded almost as bad as how they got in, it most definitely didn't sound worse.

They walked under the archway and out onto the red sand. The tall buildings that rimmed the Round didn't have windows facing in this direction, making them look more like a curved wall. This not only kept out the sand and heat, but the Round could be closed down and protected in an invasion. The last time Forte Cadence had tried to attack, their soldiers had been forced to retreat when access to the palace was unable to be obtained. That was many Shinings ago now. There seemed to be some kind of truce from Forte Cadence lately. It was a pity. Maybe they'd fare better under their neighboring kingdom's rule.

Azrael looked across at Rani, who was blinking silently, seeing the towering wall for the first time, and she tried to imagine what it must look like to her. She'd lived her entire life within that circle of stone. Walking through that arch must have felt like stepping off the edge of the world.

"Where is everything?" asked Rani, dragging her eyes away from the wall and scanning the desert from left to right. There was nothing except red sand as far as the eye could see.

"Men to the left, women to the right," said Azrael. "That's how the Capital likes it."

Rani crinkled her brow, not understanding.

"Come on, I'll show you." Azrael turned right, staying close to the shade of the wall, leading Rani away from the archway.

It didn't take long before the women's village came into sight. A collection of thousands of tents had been built up against the wall, seeking shelter from the wind and the sun when it came from at least one direction. They were lined up in neat rows, so the guards could patrol as necessary.

If they'd turned left instead of right, they'd have come upon the men's village, built in a similar way—or so Azrael had been told. Women were forbidden to enter the men's village and vice versa. The patrolling guards were an exception, of course, given most of them were male.

It took a few seconds for Azrael to realize Princess Rani was no longer following her. Her feet were planted in the sand and her veil had slipped away from her face, revealing her lower jaw working to grind her teeth. A boy in the Growing Center had a habit of doing that when he was afraid. Was the Princess really so frightened? Or was this a habit made from nerves?

"Cover yourself up," said Azrael, taking a few steps back. "Quickly, before someone recognizes you."

The Princess covered her face, leaving only her dark eyes, open wide, drinking in her surroundings. "These are your... houses?"

"Yes, although, I've only lived here for fourteen turns."

The Princess's lower jaw stilled. "Of course. You were in the Growing Center before then."

Azrael nodded. "Yes, Princess."

"Please, call me Rani. I beg you to. I don't want to be a Princess out here. I don't want to be one at all."

Azrael nodded, wondering if being a princess could really be so bad? Although if it didn't grant you an exemption from the sirings then perhaps it wasn't so great either.

She watched as Rani's eyes lit when an idea took hold. "Will you take me to the Growing Center? I've never seen a baby before."

"Really?" That seemed crazy. How could she have never seen a baby? Then again, the only babies in The Sands of Naar were in the Growing Center and if she'd never been there…

"What do they look like?" Rani asked.

"Like, well, they look like babies." She thought about how to describe them. "You know, small people with big eyes, bald heads, and fat little arms and legs."

Rani laughed. "No, what do they really look like?"

"It's true!" said Azrael, the relief of a smile crossing her face. She'd thought she was never going to smile again. "That's what they look like. How did you imagine them?"

"Like smaller versions of us." Her eyes narrowed. "You're joking with me, aren't you?"

Azrael smiled, trying her best not to laugh in return, as she imagined a baby with the same proportions to its body as a grown adult. Rani would find out soon enough. "Come on, follow me, I'll show you, Pri— Rani."

Rani nodded and fell into step beside her as they took one of the paths that separated two rows of tents. Azrael was glad she'd met Rani today. It'd been a nice distraction and she still felt that, despite Rani's protestations, she was going to save her. Perhaps not on this turn of the sand, but in a future one.

"Is the Growing Center far from here?" Rani asked.

"Beyond the tents. On the other side of the Round to the archway. If you made a hole in the palace wall, you'd probably look right down on it from your bedchamber."

"I've never thought about what was on the other side of the wall before," said Rani. "I've spent my life focused on the completely oppo-site direction."

Azrael wondered what'd driven Rani to find out about her kingdom now, if not before. She had so many questions for her. Why did she have no power over the kingdom if one day she'd be their ruler? Was it purely the thought of the siring that'd been driving her out her window, or was there something else bothering her?

There would be time for questions later. Being raised in the Growing Center had taught Azrael to be patient. Nothing was rushed in there. The pace was slow, and each turn of the sand had felt like a Shining of its own. She'd hated it in there. Being released into the village when she became a woman would have been exciting if only it didn't come at such a price.

They passed the tent Azrael had been assigned and she pointed it out quietly to Rani. It'd been made from animal hide, like all the other tents, each one dyed a different shade to help tell them apart. If it were possible to look at the village from above, it would look like some kind of upside-down rainbow, except instead of a pot of gold at the end, there was only misery.

Azrael's tent was blue, which she liked as it was the opposite to red. That was if a color could have an opposite. She was so sick of seeing nothing except red sand every day.

She shared the tent with an old woman who had to be at least thirty-five Shinings. New girls were always paired with the older ones. Azrael had even more questions for the woman than she had for Rani, but so far, she hadn't answered any, not even to tell Azrael her name, choosing to speak in grunts than actual words.

"How do you find your tent," asked Rani, breaking the silence, as they walked on. "They all look the same."

"Fifth row from the wall. Fifty-fifth tent from the archway."

"You counted?" Rani's eyes ran the length of the tents, as if she could count them with a scan of her eyes.

"Of course," said Azrael. "Don't want to come home to the wrong tent. Besides, I like numbers. They were my best lesson in the Growing Center. I can count on numbers."

Rani laughed. "You can *count* on numbers."

"Did you just make a joke?" Azrael laughed, seeing the tight line of tension slip from Rani's shoulders.

"Pretty sure you were the one who made the joke," said Rani.

"So, you're a funny princess, then? I had no idea." Azrael shook her head.

"Neither did I. I'm finding out a lot about myself right now."

The light dropped from Rani's eyes, leaving Azrael in silence as they made their way to the end of the village of tents.

It was here that the road opened out to the Growing Center—a large building made from the same stone as the city wall. They were on the other side to the city as the archway now and Azrael noticed Rani looking up, undoubtedly imagining her bedchamber on the other side of the wall.

"So, this is the Growing Center," said Azrael. "Just beyond is the Supply Center and beyond that is the men's village. If you were to keep following the wall you'd be back at the archway again."

"What's in the Supply Center?" Rani asked.

Azrael resisted the urge to roll her eyes. Princesses had no need to fetch their own supplies when they had servants to do it for them.

"It's where we go for our rations. Food, clothing, blankets, medicine. That kind of thing. There's a Washing Center in there too."

Rani let out a deep breath and shook her head.

"What's the matter?" Azrael asked, wondering what she'd said wrong.

"I know nothing about this kingdom!" said Rani. "Nothing! I may as well have lived my whole life on the moon."

Azrael smiled at this image. "Come on Moon Princess, let's go find a baby for you to look at. That'll cheer you up."

With any luck, Azrael would fall asleep later in her tent stifling her laughter at the look on Rani's face when she saw her first tiny human, instead of the image of that man as he'd hovered over her and her soul had filled with hate. It was easier to keep that image at bay for now, with Rani as a distraction.

Azrael beckoned for Rani to follow as she made her way down to the rear of the building where she knew the youngest babies slept in tiny cribs. She went to the window and eased open the shutters, hoping one of the carers wouldn't be there. Normally the babies would be left to cry. If they had a full belly and a clean bottom, there was nothing else they could possibly need. Babies cried to strengthen their lungs and develop their voice, not because they were unhappy.

Rani came up beside her. Close. So close. Azrael moved away slightly, feeling safer with a little more distance.

The two girls blinked as their eyes adjusted to the dim light inside. There was a crib right underneath the window with a baby wearing only a clean cloth between its legs. It was exactly the sort of baby Azrael had described. Bald and fat. Also, thankfully asleep.

Azrael pointed, although there was no need. Rani was already staring at the child with a look of pure horror. Her eyes were wide, and her nose crinkled as she pulled away, as if the sight of this strange small human was too much for her.

"You weren't joking," Rani hissed. "Why didn't you tell me you were being serious?"

"I did!" Azrael let out a laugh and the baby's eyes sprang open.

It took one look at the two girls at the window and let out a loud cry.

Rani leaped back from the window so quickly she fell on the sand, landing on her bottom.

"Sorry, little baby," Azrael said as she closed the shutters, which did nothing to drown out the volume of the screams. This one would have very strong lungs by the time it grew up.

"Azrael," said Rani, sitting up. Her veil had fallen away from her face and she was laughing. "Did we scare it?"

"Not as much as it scared you?" Azrael joined in the laughter, enjoying the light feeling that a moment of happiness brought her.

As with most moments of joy in The Sands of Naar, it didn't last long.

Two guards appeared at the other end of the Growing Center and quickened their pace to see two girls clearly up to no good.

"Quick!" said Azrael. "Get up! We have to run."

Rani scrambled to her feet and took off after Azrael, as they ran toward the Supply Center. If they could get there before the guards, they'd be able to blend in with the other women. Yet another advantage of the long dresses and veils.

"Come on!" called Azrael, willing Rani to quicken her pace. She wasn't used to running in the Round, she supposed. Perhaps she'd never run anywhere before. If the guards caught up to them, they were done for. They were getting far too close.

The temptation to leave Rani and save herself swelled in her gut, however, she couldn't bring herself to do it. They'd come here together. If the guards were going to release them into the desert, they could do that together, too.

"Leave me!" Rani said to Azrael, seeing the futility of their situation. She was puffing and clutching her side. "I can't do it."

Before Azrael had the chance to answer, a gloved hand took hold of her arm and squeezed it so hard she was surprised it didn't fall off. Her feet stopped running and instead, her heart picked up the pace. Rani was beside her, trapped in the grip of the other guard.

Their actions had forced the guards to touch them. The law had been broken and there was only one punishment for that.

Release.

RANI

THE BEFORE

*R*ani wasn't sure what hurt more. The pounding of her heart? The heaving of her lungs? The sharp pain piercing her side? Or was it the band of agony gripping her arm?

"Let go of us immediately," hissed Rani, pulling her veil away from her face with her free hand. "Do you know who you have hold of?"

"Princess Rani!" The guard released her arm.

"And the other girl," she said, lowering the pitch of her voice in an attempt to sound assertive.

The other guard let his hand fall and Azrael stepped aside.

As shocked as the guards were, Rani felt certain she was more surprised. Not that they'd been caught, but that the guards had listened to her. Sometimes it wasn't what was said, it was how it was said. Now that she'd found her voice, she intended to keep on using it. Who knew she had all these words trapped inside her?

She cleared her throat and prepared to hold her ground. If the people in The Sands of Naar believed she had power, then let that work for her.

"I could have you both released for putting your hands on me," she said, straightening her back and covering her face with her veil to hide her smile.

"Please forgive us, Princess," said the guard who'd held Azrael.

"Since there was no harm done, and no witnesses, I shall see fit to offer you mercy." She straightened her back trying to make herself taller. "Now, be on your way and speak of this to no-one and I will see that no harm comes to you."

"Yes, Princess." They bowed their heads and stepped back.

Rani nodded at Azrael, whose mouth had fallen open, and together they continued on.

"That was so impressive," whispered Azrael, despite nobody being close enough to hear. "I thought you said you don't have any authority in this kingdom."

Rani shrugged. "I don't."

Azrael stopped, turned to her and burst out laughing. "I've never cried so much or laughed so much in my life as I have on this turn of the sand. It's been both the worst and the best of my life."

"Same," said Rani, stopping beside her and shaking her head. She'd done more living in this one turn of the sand than all her other turns put together. To think that if she'd let herself fall from her window, she'd have missed out on it all.

"When the guards grabbed us, I really thought it was all over," said Azrael.

"Why didn't you run off like I told you? That was really dangerous!"

Azrael shrugged her boney shoulders. "Because that's not what friends do. Friends never leave each other behind."

Rani blinked back tears. Friends. She'd waited her whole life to have a friend. Sharma was more like a mother to her. If she'd known having a friend was like this, she would've left the palace many Shinings ago.

"Thank you," said Rani. Then with a shaking hand, she reached out and touched Azrael on the bare skin of her forearm, where the sleeve of her dress had slipped up.

Azrael jumped back as if she'd been struck by lightning. "What are you doing?"

"I don't know," said Rani. "I just wanted to..."

What were the words to make this right? To wipe the frown from her new friend's face? To explain what couldn't be explained? How to tell her that she'd been so drunk on the feeling of power and new experience that it'd gone to her head?

"I just wanted to know what it was like," she said, settling for the simple truth. "I'm sorry."

"Three times." Azrael shook her head. "All in one turn. First in the Conception Center. Second by the guard. And third by you."

"I really am sorry," said Rani, meaning it. She should've thought of Azrael here, too. It hadn't just been about her and what she'd needed at that moment. "I'm no better than whoever touched you at even-time."

"Don't say that," said Azrael, stepping back to her, a frown crossing her face like a black cloud to replace the lightning. "Please don't say that. It's nothing like the same thing."

"I should go back now," said Rani, her legs feeling weak as she noticed the sun getting lower in the sky. "If I'm not at dinner my father will look for me."

"But you didn't see the Supply Center. It's just there." Azrael's voice was formal, not the same as how she'd spoken before.

"Next turn of the sand?" asked Rani.

"Just a quick look," urged Azrael. "I'm thirsty and I haven't collected my full ration of water."

"As long as we're quick," said Rani, unable to resist the temptation of filling her eyes with more new sights.

As they set off, Rani cursed herself for ruining what had built between them. "Are you upset with me?"

"No!" said Azrael, throwing up her arms. "Please don't think that. You just took me by surprise."

Rani nodded, hoping she was speaking the truth.

Azrael led her into a large tent that made up the Supply Center, and Rani came to a stop, feasting her eyes on the sight before her.

There were tables lined up in rows, loaded with all kinds of supplies. Her mouth watered at the aroma of food and she realized she was hungry. She really did have to get back to the palace. Dinner must be soon. It was so hard to tell without having the Orbs of Time as a reference.

"How do you know what you're allowed to take?" she asked Azrael.

"See the people behind the tables? They have books controlled by the Supply Master. Everything you take is marked off. If you take more than your ration, you'll be released. No questions asked."

Rani thought she was starting to see why life expectancy was shrinking so rapidly in her kingdom. People were being released for the most minor offenses. Not only that, there had to be a growing number of people offending on purpose in order to be released from their misery. The oldest person Rani had ever heard of was forty Shinings, but Sharma had told her that people used to live until eighty Shinings or more. It was hard to imagine someone that old. Nobody had died from old age for many hundreds of Shinings now. When the body began to fail, it was released. Simple. Or perhaps not.

She followed Azrael to a table that held glasses of water.

"Where does the water come from?" she asked, having never thought about this before.

"We collect the condensation from the skins of our tents in the cool night air. And any rain that falls, of course. There's the river, only it'd be impossible to collect water from there and make it back alive."

Rani had never heard of a river before but didn't want to appear foolish by asking what it was. She'd embarrassed herself enough earlier with that hideous baby. She could ask Sharma later.

Azrael gave the worker her name and was handed a glass of water. She offered it to Rani first, but Rani shook her head. "No, I can have plenty at dinner. This is your ration." It felt wrong to take something from someone who had so little, despite how thirsty she felt.

"Your lips are cracked," said Azrael. "Have a sip at least."

Rani took the cup, seeing it as much as an act of forgiveness from Azrael as the gift of water itself. She drew in a sip, swishing the water around her mouth before swallowing and handing the cup back to Azrael. "Thank you."

Azrael drained the rest of the cup in one gulp and put it back on the table.

"I really have to get back," said Rani, worried about what would happen if her absence was noticed. She wanted to do this for all the turns she had left, not spend them locked inside her bedchamber. "Perhaps we can come again on the next turn."

Azrael nodded. "I'll walk you to the archway."

Rani smiled, pleased that Azrael genuinely didn't seem to be upset with her after the way she'd so thoughtlessly put her hand on her.

"Do you think it's true?" asked Rani as they stepped out of the tent into the setting sun. "You know, that touching causes disease?"

Azrael shook her head. "I don't think any of it's true. Every law in this kingdom is a lie."

"Me too," said Rani.

Despite what they'd just agreed, she decided never to touch Azrael again. It was like all the freedom she'd just experienced had gone to her head. If she was going to get the most out of her life for the next fourteen turns, she needed to be more careful than that.

Which made her sad. Because now that she'd just started living, she realized she didn't want her life to end. But what other choice did she have? The next fourteen turns were just going to have to be enough.

SHARMA

THE BEFORE

*S*harma had never felt so worried. Rani was missing. She'd been gone since just after even-time and now the sun was about to disappear from the sky. It wasn't like Rani. She never went *anywhere.* If the Emperor discovered her absence, he was going to be furious. If the Board discovered it, then it'd be even worse.

She paced the length of Rani's bedchamber, looking out the window at regular intervals, hoping to see her running across the Round as she hurried home.

When Sharma's legs began to ache, she sat down and rubbed her belly. This was her least favorite part of pregnancy. The part where she was unable to deny there was a child growing inside her. She could feel its tiny feet and fists as they pummeled her. Right now, the baby's head was pressing against her navel. A head she'd never touch that would grow hair she'd never comb.

The door opened, and Sharma turned quickly, letting her hands fall to her lap.

"Emperor," she said, bowing her head as she pushed down her panic. What was she to tell him?

"Sharma. How are you?" He looked at her with affection she didn't deserve. "What are you doing here."

"I'm well, thank you," she said, preferring to answer his first question.

"Where's Rani?" he asked. "She's late for her dinner."

"She's... not feeling well," said Sharma, pointing toward Rani's washroom. "Totally normal for a girl having her first time."

"Oh." The Emperor looked away and shuffled his feet, clearly not wanting to discuss this further, which was exactly as Sharma had hoped.

"Perhaps her dinner could be sent to her bedchamber, just this once?" she asked.

"I was hoping to discuss the heir's siring with her." He sighed, clearly not looking forward to that conversation.

Sharma nodded, wondering if she should tell him that Rani already knew. It seemed wrong to keep that from him.

"Have you seen her since the meeting?" he asked.

"Yes," she said, not wanting to lie.

He crossed his arms. "You told her, I suppose?"

She nodded, realizing she had no choice but to come clean. "She asked me about it. I apologize if you wished to do it."

"How could I wish to do that?" He raked his fingers through his hair and Sharma was shocked to see the makings of tears stinging his eyes.

"I'm afraid she didn't take it well," said Sharma.

The Emperor went to the door and closed it. "May I speak frankly with you?"

"Of course." She was surprised he'd even asked. He always spoke frankly with her.

He lowered the volume of his voice, glancing toward the washroom to make sure Rani wasn't about to emerge. "I'm not pleased about the Chairman's decision. It doesn't feel right. I've checked our book of laws and can't find a single one he's breaking."

Sharma nodded, having done the same thing after leaving Rani sobbing at the news of her fate. She wondered if she should tell the

Emperor about his daughter's lie. He'd have no idea her time hadn't come. However, it wasn't her place to tell him that. The best she could do would be to encourage Rani to tell him herself. Although, lying was a serious offense in this kingdom. Rani could be even worse off if she admitted to what she'd done.

"I apologize for my vote in the Boardroom," she said. "You know I had no choice."

"I know that."

"What can we do?" she asked, keeping her words brief.

"Nothing," the Emperor said. "The best we can do is try to convince Rani that this is for the best."

"Yes, Emperor," she said, despite knowing this was an impossible task. Rani would never see what was to happen as *best*.

"Will she be long in there?" he asked, tilting his head toward the washroom.

"Perhaps you're better to leave her in my care for the moment," she said. "I'll let her know you wish for her to seek you out at sun-up."

He nodded. "Yes. Perhaps you're right."

Sharma let out a breath, hoping Rani would return before then. If she didn't, then Sharma would be caught out on a lie of her own and this mess would become even worse.

The Emperor went to the door and opened it. "I'm sorry, Sharma. Really, I am."

She nodded, unsure as to which of his sins he was sorry for. Not that he was an evil man. The Chairman filled those shoes well enough on his own.

He left and her waiting resumed. Come on, Rani! Where could she be?

Sharma went to the window and leaned out, her eyes scanning the Round in the fading light.

The grass was vacant, with everyone having returned to their homes before nightfall. Nobody wanted to walk through that archway into the desert at night to find their way home. It was difficult enough to tell the tents apart when the sun was in the sky.

Sharma had grown up on the other side of that wall and had hated it. There was no greater way for a kingdom to express how little its people meant than to have them live outside the wall that protected all it held dear.

The Growing Center had been a tedious upbringing, with its never-ending lessons and rules. Life in the tents had been the complete opposite, as she'd tried to find her place in the village. Everyone had to find a way to prove their worth to the kingdom. If a woman was with child, then some compensation was generally granted. Everyone had to report in with the Job Master to be assigned a task, of which there were plenty. Women were needed to work in the Growing Center, distribute rations at the Supply Center, weave fabric, or collect water. There were hundreds of possibilities and all of them difficult. The men were required to tend to the animals who provided the bulk of their food, build new structures, and explore ways to grow crops in their kingdom's impossible terrain. And then there were the guards and timekeepers, chosen from the strongest and most loyal citizens. Everyone worked hard. And if they didn't, there was only one place for them.

The desert. A place of certain death.

It was sometimes hard to tell if this was a punishment or a reward.

A flash of movement caught Sharma's eye and she leaned out further from the window.

Two girls were running through the archway. One had her face covered, although she had no doubt it was Rani. Sharma knew the shape of her. But who was the girl with her? And what had they been doing on the other side of the archway?

The girl with Rani called out something Sharma couldn't hear, and Rani waved to her, as the girl turned around and went back out the archway.

Rani scurried through the Round, keeping her veil tucked over her face and Sharma let out a deep breath. She was safe. For now.

RANI

THE BEFORE

*R*ani opened the door to her bedchamber and tried to ease the clenching of her stomach with deep breaths. The sun had set and dinner would've been and gone. She had no idea what the fallout of her absence would be. Was her father angry? Worried? Or completely calm? She'd never missed dinner before to find out.

As she stepped into the room, she sensed rather than saw that she wasn't alone.

"Father?" She squinted in the dim light as her eyes adjusted.

"It's me," said Sharma, standing so Rani could see her heavily pregnant silhouette in front of the window.

"Oh, I'm glad." Rani went to her bed and fell onto it, while Sharma fiddled with a lantern, filling the room with soft light.

"Your dinner's here," said Sharma, pointing to the table.

Rani's eyes widened with pleasure and she scrambled to the table. Tearing off a chunk of bread, she dipped it into what looked like mutton soup and brought it to her lips. It was cold, but that was of little concern. It was food and after what she'd seen today, she knew how lucky she was to get so much of it.

"Are you okay?" asked Rani, noticing Sharma was wincing as she rubbed her lower back.

Sharma nodded and took the seat by the window. "I'm fine. However, I told your father you're unwell. Where were you, Rani? I was so worried about you."

"I went through the archway," she said, between mouthfuls of cold soup. There was no point in lying about this. The law didn't prevent her from leaving the Round.

"I know," said Sharma. "I saw you returning. Who was the girl?"

"That's Azrael. She's my friend." Rani smiled at this word. It was still hard to believe she had a friend.

Sharma sighed. "You're in a much better mood than when I saw you last."

"A lot's happened since then." Rani set down her bread and wondered how to explain. She trusted Sharma, but would she understand?

"I didn't know you had a friend." Sharma winced again as she shifted in the chair.

"I just met her." Rani picked up her spoon. "She took me to the Growing Center. I saw a baby! It was the most frightening thing I've ever seen. I can't believe you have one of those in your belly right now."

"Rani, you didn't... you didn't drink anything today, did you?"

"Just water... why? Oh! You mean... no!" Her spoon slipped from her fingers and clattered to the table. "Of course not. Where would I even get any of that stuff from? It was banned before I was even born."

"It's just that you're not yourself. This isn't you sitting here, telling me strange stories, talking with so many words." Sharma had her hand on her belly now and was rubbing it with circular movements.

Rani left the table and went to Sharma, crouching down in front of her. "Is your baby kicking?"

Sharma nodded. "I can feel its foot right here."

Rani reached out her hand until it was hovering over Sharma's stomach. Her need to connect was spilling over in waves now. When she'd touched Azrael, the world hadn't ended, despite how shocked Azrael had been. "Can I feel it?"

"Rani! Please step back!" Her voice was shocked. Harsh. "What's wrong with you?"

Rani fell back onto the floor, almost as if the strength of Sharma's words had pushed her over.

"I'm sorry," she said, refusing to allow the tears that were forming to fall.

"Tell me, Rani. What's happened to you?"

"You wouldn't understand," she said, tucking her legs underneath herself and folding her arms in case the uncontrollable urge to touch someone came once more. Sharma was right. She really wasn't acting like herself.

"You might be surprised what I understand," said Sharma.

Rani weighed up her options. If she told Sharma the truth then she may tell her father and he'd most likely board up her window, lock her in her bedchamber and drag her to the Conception Center himself. It was too risky. But how could she lie to Sharma? The woman who'd shown her more kindness than any other person in the kingdom.

"Rani! Talk to me. Please."

"I've decided to spend the next fourteen turns, well, thirteen now, living." This part was true. It didn't matter that she left out the dying at the end of it bit.

Sharma nodded, seeming unconvinced. "Why? What do you think will happen to you after your heir is sired? Do you think your life will be over? Do you think mine is over now? I survived it. You can, too."

She didn't think her life would be over. She knew it would be. At her own hands. The Chairman would never touch her.

"Please, let me feel your baby," said Rani, coming closer once more. "I touched Azrael on the arm today and it didn't fall off. The stories of disease are lies. Whatever it was that passed through our kingdom, has long ago died out."

"No, Rani. No." She shook her head, the serious expression on her face, as much of an answer as her words.

"Why? I know you don't believe it either."

"Because that's a dangerous line to cross." Her voice was cold as she tried to shrink back in her chair. Impossible with a belly as round as hers was now. "It starts with one touch of my stomach and then what? Before you know it, you'll be placing your hands on everyone. It's too dangerous."

Rani got up from the floor and returned to her even-colder soup. She didn't want to upset Sharma.

"You mustn't leave your bedchamber again, Rani. Do you hear me? No good will come of it. You had your taste of freedom today. Please? I'm worried about you."

"You're worried about me?" Rani surprised herself with the hard tone of her voice. Hearing the news of her fate had opened up a well of anger inside her and with each passing moment, the level of her fury grew. "I'm worried about me, too! And I'm worried about you. And Azrael. I'm worried about that baby of yours. I'm even worried about Father. This is wrong, Sharma. It's wrong! I can't live like this."

"You can, Rani. You can."

"I won't." She glanced at the window, reminding herself of the release it'd bring her. She may have just decided that she didn't want to die, but that didn't mean she wouldn't.

"We don't have a choice," said Sharma, dropping her voice to a whisper.

"Are you happy?" asked Rani. "Do you enjoy your life?"

Sharma shook her head.

"So, what are you doing about it? Obeying rules and waiting for the guards to release you?"

"Don't, Rani, don't. I have peace."

"You don't have peace! This isn't peace."

"I'm fed and clothed and have all my needs met."

"You're raped and threatened and have none of your needs met, Sharma."

Sharma hauled herself out of the chair, unable to hide the tears that streaked their way down her cheeks.

"I'm sorry," said Rani, realizing she'd gone too far. "Forgive me. If you're happy, then I'm happy for you. But this life isn't my happiness. Which is why…"

She looked to the window, unable to finish what she wanted to say.

"Rani," said Sharma standing before her so that her stomach was level with Rani's face. "Give me your hand."

Rani reached out her hand, trying to steady the way it began to shake.

Sharma wrapped her fingers around Rani's own, the feeling of skin on skin, the softness and warmth of this small gesture so unlike anything she'd ever felt before. It was like floating in a warm bath during the cool night air and being enveloped in comforting bliss.

Sharma placed Rani's hand flat on her stomach and let go. Then she felt it. The baby, moving beneath her hand, a tiny foot sliding across the inside of Sharma's skin and Rani gasped at the miracle of it.

"I may not have a happy life," said Sharma. "But in my life, there are moments of happiness. Feeling my child move inside me is one of those moments. Spending time with you is another of those moments. You mustn't do anything foolish, Rani. Windows are for looking from, not for falling from."

Rani let her hand fall and Sharma stepped back.

"How did you know?" Rani asked.

"Because you keep looking at the window like it's going to save your life, which tells me that you're planning to use it to end it. I know because I've thought about doing the same thing every single time I've watched the timekeepers turn the orbs."

"But you haven't done it," said Rani, wondering how she never knew this about Sharma.

She shook her head. "I haven't. And neither will you."

Rani bit down on her bottom lip to stop her words falling out. She had no intention of backing out of her plan now.

"You will not be falling from any windows."

Rani stood up to draw level with Sharma. "I will."

"No, you won't," she said, locking her gaze on Rani. "Because I have a better plan."

AZRAEL

THE BEFORE

*A*zrael went to the Round at even-time to wait for Rani, wondering what this new turn of the sand would bring. The last time she'd come here, she certainly hadn't expected events to unfold in the way they did.

As the sand slipped through the orbs, so did her hope. Rani wasn't coming out. Had she changed her mind, or had someone prevented her from leaving? She'd been awfully worried about missing dinner the previous nightfall. And it hadn't seemed to be the lack of food she was worried about.

She ran her hand across the grass and looked up at the Princess's window. Had meeting her been some kind of dream? Then she remembered the feel of Rani's hand on her arm and knew it'd been real. She touched her arm now, certain it was still warm.

Her reaction to Rani's touch had been one of surprise, not so much repulsion or fear. It'd caught her off guard. Never had she expected that. However, nothing about the Princess had been as she expected. Azrael didn't think she'd ever met anyone she liked better.

Just when she was about to give up, Rani appeared at her window, her eyes searching the lawn. Azrael raised a hand, then caught herself and pretended she was straightening her veil.

Rani was miming something at her, holding her two hands as fists, her right on top of her left, then turning them to put the left hand on top. Whatever did that mean? She pointed at the orbs, then the lawn, and made that strange action again.

Oh! She wanted to meet Azrael on the next turn. Something must've happened. Something important. At least she hadn't been released into the desert for missing her dinner.

Azrael nodded up at her, then looked away so as not to draw attention or suspicion. But nobody was paying attention to the skinny girl on the lawn. They were all too busy inside their own heads, worrying about their own lives. They didn't have time or concern for her.

She got up and decided that today was as good a day as any to report into the Jobs Master. It was widely believed he assigned the better jobs to those who came to him, rather than those whose selfishness forced him to seek them out. Adding that to the fact she'd *volunteered* at the Conception Center and there was a possibility of her being pregnant, she was expecting one of the lightest jobs of all. A weaver perhaps? She liked the idea of sitting in a circle with a group of women transforming simple yarn into fabrics to keep them modest and warm.

She joined the line to see the Master, who sat behind a table with a large book open in front of him. Much like the Registrar who'd recorded her name at the Conception Center. She shuddered at the memory. At least whatever the Jobs Master assigned her, wouldn't be as bad as the hell the Registrar had sent her hurtling toward.

As she got closer to the front of the queue, she could hear the conversation as people tried to negotiate a better deal, providing a list of reasons as to why the task they'd been assigned wasn't suitable. It didn't seem the Jobs Master had a lot of empathy. One by one, he turned them away with a wave of his hand, telling them everyone needed to do their bit.

The woman in front of Azrael reached the desk and Azrael fiddled with her veil as she pretended not to listen.

"Please, Master," the woman said, her voice cracking under the strain. "I'd like to respectfully request a new task. I beg it of you, please."

"Name," he said, barely looking up from his book as he flicked the pages, looking to solve the irritation standing before him.

She gave her name and waited as he found her record.

Azrael brushed some sand from her sleeve as she wondered what job could be so bad it would reduce this strong-looking woman to such a state.

"The Waste Center," the Master said, as his finger landed on her name.

Azrael grimaced. No wonder this woman wanted to change jobs. The Waste Center was the very worst place to work out of all the worst places. Carrying buckets of human waste out into the desert was necessary but not desirable by any means.

"Yes, Master," the woman said. "I've done it for many Shinings now and my back is aching from the weight of the buckets. I can't bear the pain. I feel I'd contribute more effectively to the kingdom in another role. Please, Master. I'm too old for this work now."

The Master looked her up and down, like he was inspecting a goat at the market. "You don't look old to me. I see you're still on the Registrar's books, not that you've produced a child for your kingdom yet. Request denied."

He dipped his feather in a pot of ink and made a note next to her name in his book.

"Don't send me back there." The woman dropped to her knees in front of the table. "Please. I refuse to go back."

Azrael held her breath as she waited to see what anger this desperate woman had evoked in the Master.

"Stand up!" he shouted. "Immediately. And return to your job or I'll have you released."

Two guards on either side of the table, stepped forward.

"Please Master. I've always done as I've been told. I've contributed. I've done my best. But I can't go back there. Please, assign me a new task and I'll work hard for the rest of my life."

The Master sat forward and screwed up his face as he sniffed at the woman. "You smell like your job. It's a stain on your skin. I cannot send you anywhere else. Return immediately or I'll have you released."

The woman leaned back on the heels of her feet, put her arms above her head and spat at the Master, her saliva flying directly from her mouth and landing on the open book.

"Release me," she said.

Azrael stepped back, almost bumping into the person standing behind her. She wanted to be as far away from this scene as possible. She turned to run and saw she was surrounded by people. Leaving in a hurry without touching anybody would be impossible. She'd only end up being released right next to this poor woman who'd rather die than carry buckets of excrement for the rest of her life. It broke Azrael's heart, making her realize that life in the Growing Center hadn't been so bad after all.

The two guards grabbed the woman with their gloved hands and dragged the woman away. She let her body fall limp to make their job as difficult as possible. Despite calling for her own death, she wasn't going to march toward it willingly.

They dragged her away until she was out of sight and the crowd dispersed, leaving the path in front of Azrael clear. She'd missed her chance to leave with them and was left standing there, exposed and uncertain. Would the Master treat her more favorably given she was certainly less trouble than the woman before her? Or would his patience have been stretched beyond its already impatient state?

"Next!" The Master glared at her, sending her footsteps forward, despite the wave of dread that washed over her. She should've taken her chance to run. She knew it as clearly as she'd known Rani was going to save her life. But she'd gone too far now. Please, just let the Master be merciful. The rest of her life would be impacted by the decision he was about to make.

"Name." This wasn't a question. More like a demand.

Azrael gave her name. "I'm not in your book yet," she said. "I've only just left the Growing Center and had my first siring."

"Don't assume you're not in my book," he said, with a sneer, revealing a set of yellow teeth. "Everyone's in my book."

"Sorry." Azrael forced a smile, becoming aware of the two guards who'd taken the former guards' place. "May I request a job as a weaver? I showed excellent promise in this field in the Growing Center and I hope to provide the kingdom with a baby soon."

She'd shown no such promise, but the Master wasn't to know this. He may have everyone in his book, however, he didn't know everything about them all.

The Master set down his feather and looked at her. "You're young. Healthy. Fit. And I have a job that opened recently. Very recently."

Azrael felt her legs go weak. No, please don't let him be speaking of the Waste Center. She held her head high and hid her fear, just as she'd done at her siring, glancing at the guards who were bracing themselves, ready to drag her away if instructed. The taller of the two guards looked familiar and she wondered if he'd been in the Growing Center with her. Sometimes it was hard to reconcile adult faces with the rounded innocence of the faces she'd grown up with.

The Master gave her a warm smile, picked up his feather and wrote something in his book. "Report to the Waste Center immediately. There's a lot of work for you."

Azrael drew in a sharp breath and went to protest when the guards stepped toward her and she realized where she knew the tall one from. He was a man she'd seen only once before and one she'd hoped never to see again.

She tore her eyes from him and stepped back, holding up her shaking hands to show she wasn't planning to cause any trouble. The guards resumed their positions and she breathed a sigh, nodding meekly at the Jobs Master, unable to stop her body from shaking. That guard may have stepped back, but he was still far too close to her. The other side of the kingdom would be too close.

She needed to do what the Master told her and go to the worst place of the worst. Because if she didn't, then the guards were going to put their hands on her and take her to the desert. And it wasn't the desert she was afraid of. It was the tall guard. The only person other than Rani who'd touched her with bare skin, for he was the volunteer who'd been assigned to her in the Conception Center. She was certain of it. And he wasn't going to touch her again. Not ever. Just seeing him again now was bringing back enough memories. She clasped her hands together to try to stop the shaking, but it was no use. Her legs were wobbling now, as if in sympathy, and she knew if she didn't get away soon, she was in danger of collapsing.

"Thank you, Master," she said, aware of the warm stream of liquid running down her leg as the contents of her bladder spilled out, puddling at the base of her long dress.

She walked away, hoping nobody had noticed and wondering if Rani would allow her into her bedchamber so she could throw herself from the window. Perhaps they'd jump together. Because the whole crazy idea of it suddenly seemed not crazy at all. It seemed like the best of all the worst ideas she'd ever had.

SHARMA

THE BEFORE

Sharma had seen the light flood back into Rani's eyes at the idea she had a plan, without Rani even knowing what her plan might be. That's what desperation does. It forces a person to clutch onto a straw, hoping it might save them from the sand that's threatening to swallow them whole.

She'd tested Rani by checking to see if the Emperor had been right to believe she could be convinced that what'd been decided was for the best. If Rani could only believe that then she could find moments of happiness and make the most of the life she had now. But she wasn't buying any of it. It was like the news of what the Chairman planned to do to her had woken her from a sleep.

"I knew you'd think of something," Rani had said, desperate to hear more.

"Rani," she'd said, lowering her voice, despite knowing that nobody could hear them through these thick stone walls. "I'm not sure if my plan's a good one. In fact, that's a lie. I know it's not a good one. It's a huge risk. If it'll stop you from taking your own life then I'm prepared to discuss it with you, but not now. Go and see your father at sun-up and tell him you were feeling unwell, however, you're better now. Then come to find me at even-time and I'll explain."

Sharma had wanted to think her plan through before sharing it with Rani. Once something as big as this was said, it couldn't be taken back. She had to get it right and be certain about the details. And there was somebody's help she wanted to ask.

And now, here she stood at her window, waiting for Rani to visit. The timekeepers had turned the orbs, the sun had risen, and she was no more certain about what she was about to say at even-time than she'd been at sundown. Rather than the night bringing her clarity, it'd confused her more.

A gentle tap at the door let her know Rani was here. She'd known she wouldn't be late.

She opened the door and stepped back to allow Rani to pass.

"I'm listening. Tell me everything. I haven't slept a wink," said Rani settling herself into a chair, the gentle grinding of her teeth evidence of her old self having returned, despite the lack of sleep. "I even put off spending time with Azrael for this. What's your plan?"

Sharma drew in a breath, deciding to use whatever words came to her first. Most stories were best when told from the start. "A few Shinings ago, I arrived early for a Board meeting. There was a map on the table. A map of all the kingdoms."

"What did it look like?" Rani sat forward. "I've never seen one before."

"Hardly anyone has. And given the way the Chairman snatched it away when he came into the room, it's clear he wants to keep it that way."

"Are we the biggest kingdom? The desert goes on forever."

Sharma shook her head. "We're the smallest of the five kingdoms."

Rani gasped. "How can this be? Why haven't we been invaded successfully before now if we're so small?"

"Invaded for what?" asked Sharma. "Who wants to own this wasteland for anything other than the glory of it? That, and the walls of the Round are too high and strong. No army has been able to figure out how to get enough men to survive the trek through the desert and arrive in such numbers and with sufficient equipment to scale our walls before they die from thirst. The environment we live in protects us just as much as the wall itself."

Rani nodded, taking this in.

"The point is that soldiers *have* made it to our walls alive," said Sharma. "Which means… we can make it alive back to them."

"But we've always been told it's certain death out there," said Rani, her eyes gleaming with possibility.

Sharma nodded. "Perhaps it's not really as certain as we've been led to believe. It's possible our kingdom that claims to value honesty above all else has been lying to us."

"Do you think one of the other kingdoms would offer us refuge?" asked Rani.

Sharma shrugged. "If we can make it there alive, I guess that's something we'll need to find out. Listen, Rani, I have to be clear with you. I don't think our chances are great. We'll dehydrate quickly out there."

"Azrael said there's a river out there somewhere that has water. What's a river, Sharma?"

Sharma smiled at how little this girl who was supposed to rule the kingdom knew about life. "It's a long stretch of water that flows across the land."

"I want to see it. I want to see a river. I want to see everything." Rani looked out the window as if she could see it all now.

To think Sharma had suspected Rani had stumbled across some mead when she'd returned at nightfall, when she was clearly just drunk on life. How could she deny her the chance to see more of the world they lived in, even if it led to the possibility of their death?

"Do you think others have made it to the river?" Rani asked. "Ones who've been released."

"I don't think so. Without food, water, and shelter, survival would be impossible. We're going to need to carry many things on our backs if we go through with this. It may still prove to be impossible, even with supplies on hand. But Wintergreen is on the other side of the river. If we can make it safely across, they might help us."

"So there's a chance," said Rani, her face more alive than ever. "A small chance, yet a chance, nonetheless."

Sharma had to agree. There was a chance for Rani to escape the Chairman and live. And chance for Sharma to keep the last of her babies, hold it in her arms and let it suckle from her breast. They could die seeking happiness or they could live a hollow and miserable life. Although, as much as she and Rani could make the decision to take this risk for themselves, was it fair of her to make this decision for her baby? This was the part she was struggling with.

"There's just one problem," said Rani, the smile falling from her face.

"There are many problems with this plan," said Sharma.

"I can't leave without Azrael," she said. "She's my friend. And friends never leave each other behind."

"Who told you that?"

"Azrael did. And she didn't just tell it to me. She proved it when the guards were chasing us."

"What?" Sharma's eyes flew open. "The guards chased you. Why didn't you tell me about this?"

Rani waved her hands around like this was a minor detail. "It's okay. I sorted it out. Apparently, I can be quite scary when I want to be."

"Oh, Rani."

This latest revelation only made Sharma more certain the time to run had come. If Sharma didn't save Rani now, then it really would be too late. She was taking far too many risks.

"So, can she come?" Rani asked.

"If she wants to," said Sharma, feeling the weight of yet another life sitting on her shoulders. "But I can't make any promises about her survival. And she'll need to carry her own supplies."

Rani nodded, smiling widely, seeming to be under the very false impression that this adventure was going to be fun.

Sharma knew otherwise. Whatever happened out there, it wasn't going to be fun. The novelty would quickly wear off as thirst and hunger took hold. The sand would sting their skin and the heat would zap their energy. And she was going to have to give birth to this child out there.

The likely scenario was that they were all going to die. Then she remembered what Rani had said about none of them being alive inside these walls anyway, and she gathered her strength, willing it to chase away her fear.

They could stay where they were, dead while they were alive, or they could take a chance and find out if there was something more out there.

A chance. No matter how small, they had to take it.

RANI

THE BEFORE

*R*ani and Sharma crept through the Round, as silent as they were scared. The sacks they carried on their backs were heavy and in the moonlight Sharma looked like the shadow of a monster with a hump on both her back and her front.

Rani carried two bags, each cutting into one of her shoulders. Soon she'd only have the burden of one. Because she was certain that Azrael would choose to make this journey. It seemed impossible she'd say no.

It was obvious Sharma hadn't wanted Azrael to go with them, but Rani had to insist. She couldn't leave those sad brown eyes behind without the chance of escape. Friends never left each other behind. Azrael hadn't abandoned her when they'd run from the guards, and she wouldn't abandon her now.

They walked through the archway and turned right, keeping their black veils tucked across their faces, hoping not to be noticed by the night guards.

Rani dared a glance back at the palace before it disappeared from sight, imagining her body falling from the window as she'd planned.

That plan had been certain death and Sharma's new plan was... well, it was almost certain death. Which meant it had a much greater chance of success, even if that chance was small.

She felt no sense of sadness that she'd never see her home again. It was the way it had to be. She'd been driven from it and had no intention of spending the rest of her life pretending to rule her kingdom. Her only regret was for her father. He'd never understand. But it was different for men. He hadn't been tied to a bed and been forced to endure a siring. He'd done the siring himself, which was something the men didn't seem to mind at all. She pushed these thoughts from her mind, not wanting to think of her father like this. This wasn't his fault. He had other children who could take her place as heir. Children who'd be happy to do it and would make far better Emperors or Empresses then she would have.

"Are you okay?" asked Sharma, keeping her voice low, as they walked away from the archway into the darkness. "It's not too late to change our minds and turn back."

"I'm fine."

She really was fine. Because they had a plan. And she was no longer alone.

They continued on until the shadow of the village of tents came into view and Rani took the lead, hoping she'd remembered the location of Azrael's tent correctly. Fifth row, fifty-fifth tent. She hadn't known when Azrael had told her that she'd need this information so soon.

Counting tents wasn't that easy in the dark and Rani found herself retracing her steps and counting again when she got confused. She'd had lessons in numbers, however, it seemed perhaps Azrael had paid more attention to hers.

"Azrael!" she whispered, as loudly as she dared, when she was certain she was close.

"Shh!" Sharma came up beside her.

"I can't find her. I keep losing count."

"We'll have to go without her," whispered Sharma.

Rani shook her head in the darkness, not caring if Sharma could see her or not. Her answer was no. She couldn't leave Azrael behind.

She ran back to the start of the row and counted slowly this time, concentrating on each number until she reached what she was certain was the fifty-fifth tent. It was hard to tell in the darkness what color it was, but it did look right.

"Azrael," she hissed.

Instead of her friend's innocent face, she was greeted by a face that was far from innocent. A woman much older than Azrael with hair that stood up in every direction and a body so tall it was surprising she fitted in such a small tent. She was glaring at Rani and grunting something she couldn't understand.

"I'm sorry," Rani said, her heart thumping. "Wrong tent. Go back to sleep."

"Rani!"

For a moment she thought it was Sharma calling her, until she realized the voice came from beyond the grunting wall in front of her.

The woman stepped back, and Azrael took her place.

"Quickly," said Sharma, from behind her.

"Azrael," said Rani, keeping her voice low. "I'm leaving. I don't have time to explain. You can come with me or you can stay. I can't promise you safety. All I can promise is a very small chance of escape. You will likely have a longer life if you stay, but—"

"I'm coming." Azrael reached out and took Rani's hand, squeezing it gently.

Rani's mouth fell open, both from her sudden decision and the unexpected contact.

"Quickly," said Sharma again, more urgency in her voice this time.

Rani stepped away from the tent and handed Azrael one of the bags.

"Thank you," said Azrael.

"Friends never leave each other behind," said Rani.

"Never," said Azrael, slinging the bag over her shoulder.

The hum of whispers from within the other tents echoed around the village as the women wondered what the commotion was all about. Sharma was right. They needed to hurry.

Together the three of them ran into the night. Into the desert. Into a future that held no certainty, other than the promise of hope.

AAROW

THE NOW

"Aarow! Are you coming, or not?"

Aarow twisted his scarf around his head to cover his crop of sleek black hair and checked that his eyes and hands were the only parts of him exposed. The combination of sand and sun in such extreme quantities were unforgiving, even with his dark copper skin.

"I'm coming," he shouted back through the thatched door of his family's quarters. "I'll meet you in the supply room."

"Be careful," his mother said, rubbing Aarow's baby sister on the back. Bindi was fast asleep, lying across her chest, having just fed from her mother's breast after a restless night.

"I'm always careful." He laughed at the way she worried and stooped down to kiss her on the cheek, something that was easier before he grew so tall.

She reached out and squeezed his hand. "How many are you going after today?"

"Three females and an infant," he said. "By the river. It's been a long time since we brought any back from there."

"An infant? Are you certain?" Her eyes shone with what that might mean for the kingdom.

He nodded. "That's what Spector said. He spotted them this morning."

"That's... incredible. What a brave mother. I wonder how she managed it." He noticed her clutching Bindi to her chest just a little tighter.

"I suppose we'll find out soon enough. If they're still alive when we reach them, of course." He didn't want to add that Spector had reported they weren't in good shape.

"Who's going with you?" she asked. "Was that Jinn calling for you just now?"

"Yes. We'll be taking Toran, too."

She smiled, and he knew she was reassured his two best friends would be by his side. Especially Toran who was twice his size, despite the hard layer of muscle that lined Aarow's lean body from the hours he spent training for a battle that may never happen.

"Hurry then," she said, stroking Bindi's forehead. "It's no place for a baby out there. I'll gather the healers and make the preparations for their arrival."

Aarow left his mother and made his way through the labyrinth of underground tunnels, heading to the supply room nearest the entrance. He'd lost count of the number of rescues he'd made in the dunes, but this one was different. River rescues were rare, however, rescuing an infant was unheard of. Something serious must be up in the Capital if babies were being released now. It was no wonder his mother had such hope shining from her eyes. Maybe it was just as well he was prepared for battle.

His steps inclined as he approached the supply room and he braced himself for the heat that was soon to come. Stepping out onto the dunes was like falling into a giant bowl of hot soup.

"Why don't you walk a bit slower?" said Jinn, stepping from the supply room and thumping him playfully on the back. "It's not like we were waiting for you or anything."

Toran appeared like a mountain behind Jinn and threw Aarow a waterskin. He slung it around his neck and reached out for the fabric that came flying through the air next, catching it with ease. He looped that over his broad shoulders, wondering who he'd be wrapping it around to shield from the elements. They selected a thick animal hide each from a pile near the entrance and tied them with a rope to their belts to drag behind them as stretchers.

"So, what do we know?" asked Aarow, keen to get the details right before they stepped into the heat. No unnecessary energy could be wasted out there, talking included.

"Spector went to the river at sun-up," said Toran. "Wanted to take a bath under the blue sky apparently."

The three friends laughed with affection. Spector was thirty years old, which was ten more than they were, but behaved as if he were ten years younger. Aarow's father said Spector had been blessed. Childhood was the happiest time of anyone's life and Spector got to live his forever. Had he been born in the Capital, he'd certainly have been released by now. However, here he lived as a cherished member of the Colony, valued for his differences rather than exiled for them.

"What did he see exactly?" asked Jinn, furrowing his brow. Despite the way he liked to joke, he took the task at hand very seriously. Lives were at stake.

"Three females," said Toran. "One was sitting up, holding an infant. Spector thought the other two might be dead already. They're under the Joshua tree to the west of the river bend."

"Did they see Spector?" asked Aarow.

"Nobody sees Spector." Toran laughed. "Unless he wants them to."

"And they meet the criteria?" asked Jinn.

"Without a doubt."

The criteria were simple enough. Before a rescue could take place, two things needed to be established. One—the person to be rescued must be peaceful, posing the Colony no harm. Two—the person must believe they were about to die. The second sounded cruel, but it had long ago been established that it was essential. If a person was to let go of the life they had before, they needed to have reached the point of certainty that it was gone already. It was only then that they could fully appreciate the second chance they were being given.

"Let's go then," said Aarow, keen to get on with it.

"You get to carry the baby," Jinn said, tossing Aarow a grin.

"And why's that?"

"You're good with them. You've had practice with your sister. I could hear her screaming right through the walls last night."

Aarow punched Jinn gently on the arm. "Her stomach gets upset sometimes. I've heard you scream often enough when you're not feeling your best."

He didn't mind rescuing the baby. He liked babies. He just hoped they got there in time to save it. It would break his heart to have to bury a baby in the sand.

"I've never screamed in my life," said Jinn, trying to hook Aarow in a headlock and failing when Aarow deflected in time. It didn't help that Aarow was at least a foot taller than him.

"Cut it out, you two," said Toran. "Kara wants me back by sundown."

"Oh, Kaaaaaaara," Jinn chided, holding his hand to his lips and making kissing noises. "Kiss me, Toran, kiss me!"

"Jealous," said Toran, refusing to take the bait.

Aarow adjusted his scarf, agreeing that Jinn was indeed jealous. He was desperate for a girlfriend, but it seemed no girl was desperate for him just yet. As for Aarow, things were more complicated than the love lives of both his friends put together, however, he didn't have time to think about that right now.

The three men formed a circle and held out their hands. They knocked their fists together and released their fingers to splay their hands dramatically.

"Boom!" they shouted together, laughing at this handshake they'd used since they were children. It never ceased to amuse them, no matter how foolish it was. The handshake bonded them, reminding them of their long-standing history. Important to remember as they headed out into a situation that was no-doubt dangerous. Working as a team was key to a successful rescue, along with strength and endurance.

Toran pulled back the thatched gate at the entrance to the caves and Aarow squinted as bright sun scorched his eyes. He tucked his scarf a little lower over his brow as the seriousness of what they were about to do washed over him. It didn't matter how many rescues he went out on, saving a life would always be a privilege.

The three friends began their long walk, knowing there were many thousands of steps between here and the Joshua tree. At least there was a river at their destination as a reward. Today they'd all take a bath under the blue sky, just like Spector.

The sun was burning, as always, and the wind blew, as always. Hot grains of red sand flew at them, getting into their eyes no matter how much they squinted.

With only his mind to amuse him as the monotonous scenery passed by, Aarow found himself thinking of the story he'd heard his mother whispering to Bindi during their restless night, trying to lull her to sleep. It was her favorite story and one she'd told him when he was a child.

As Aarow pushed his footsteps forward he told himself the story, practicing how he'd tell it to his own children one day.

Once there was a Prince whose parents wished for him to marry a princess. A trail of women came to the palace, all claiming to be princesses in the hope of becoming his bride. The Prince found fault with each of them, asking his parents how they could possibly be real princesses when they were so far from perfect. He was convinced that when he found a real princess, he'd recognize her with his heart as well as his eyes. Otherwise, what would be the point in marrying her? He didn't want a marriage without love.

One night, a terrible storm blew up, with thunder and lightning and pelting rain. Aarow pictured the storm now, trying to let the cold of his imagination filter through to his body that was burning up in the sun, but it was no use. Sweat continued to trickle down the curve of his spine and the fabric of his clothes remained plastered to his skin.

However, in the story, it was cold and stormy, and the King was surprised to hear a knock at the palace door. He opened it to find a girl standing there, dripping wet and begging for shelter. Despite her disheveled appearance, the girl claimed to be a princess, who'd traveled far, looking for her prince.

The King ushered the girl inside and led her to the fire, while the Queen had her servants make the girl a bed, piling a dozen soft mattresses on top of each other and placing a single pea underneath them all.

It's at this point in the story when the Prince sees the girl for the first time. She was by the fire, wrapped in a blanket, eating a bowl of soup as her clothes dried out. He stopped to watch her, aware of his heart beating wildly as it tried to leap out of his chest and he knew his Princess had found him at last.

But before the Prince had a chance to talk to her, the Queen whisked her away to sleep in the bed she'd made up for her, keeping a close watch nearby as the girl tossed and turned all night.

In the morning, the Queen asked the girl how she slept, and the girl complained it was the worst sleep of her life, as there was a giant hard lump in the bed that bruised her all over. The Queen knew this must be a real princess, for who else could be so delicate as to feel a single pea through a dozen mattresses? So, the Queen presented the Princess to her son, who married her immediately and they lived happily ever after.

As Aarow walked on, he pondered this story, wondering why his mother liked it so much. Was she giving him a message? Because the truth was that if the Colony had queens and kings, Aarow would indeed be a prince. His father was their leader, having taken over from his father, and it was intended that Aarow would take over from him one day and be leader of the Colony. A position affectionally known as the Colonel. This was what complicated Aarow's love life. The woman he chose to stand by his side would need to help lead the Colony. He had to choose carefully and so far, nobody had seemed right, despite the many girls who'd made it clear they were interested. Just like in the story, he was waiting to recognize her with his heart.

But there were no princesses in the desert for him to marry. He didn't even want to marry a princess. If he ever fell in love, it would be with someone who was filled with courage and strength, not a woman who was so delicate she could feel a tiny pea underneath her bed. Was this why his mother told him this story? To give him hope that one day he'd find the woman he was looking for, no matter how difficult the search seemed?

Pushing this story from his mind for now, Aarow made his way up to the top of a steep dune with his two friends by his side, their footsteps slowing with the effort of the climb. The river wasn't far now. It was all downhill from here—quite literally.

They paused at the summit and took a long sip from their waterskins.

Aarow squinted at the Joshua tree, unable to make out the clumps of spiky branches he knew were there. It was just a dot on the landscape. A dot that they'd been told had four human lives sheltering beneath it.

"Let's do this," he said to his friends.

"Hope we're not too late," said Jinn.

They brought their fists together, squinting as a gust of wind sent a sheet of sand in their direction.

"Boom!"

RANI

THE NOW

*R*ani felt herself slipping. Not her body from the ground, but her mind from her reality. She was letting go. Little by little, despite the fight that was taking place inside her to hold on.

Sharma's child was cradled in her arms. To think that no so long ago, she'd never seen a baby and now there was a tiny human depending on her for survival. It was a boy, as evidenced by the strange body parts dangling between his fat legs.

She lifted her waterskin to her lips and took in some liquid, then rubbed some on her fingertips for the baby to suckle. He was letting go, too. Sleeping more and crying less. Needing milk from his mother and taking water from Rani's fingers instead, sucking on them and screwing up his pink face when they didn't provide the sustenance he was looking for.

Sharma's depleted body lay to one side of Rani, and Azrael's on her other. Rani adjusted their veils to cover their faces, the wind determined to keep them exposed.

No matter how desperate Rani's situation, she couldn't bring herself to regret her decision to come here. Her only regret was dragging Azrael with her. Friends may not leave each other behind, but sometimes taking them with you was worse.

More than fourteen turns had passed now. She'd counted sixteen of them with the rising and setting of the sun, wondering why they needed the Orbs of Time to do a job that the giant ball of fire in the sky seemed to do perfectly well by itself. If she'd stayed behind, she'd have thrown herself from her window by now. So really, running into the desert *had* extended her life.

The Chairman's hopes to have violated her would've also been dashed by now. It gave her great satisfaction to imagine his face when he discovered she'd disappeared. It seemed he didn't have quite as much power as he thought he had. Not everything could go his way, no matter how much power he insisted he had.

Rani's life in the Round felt like something that'd happened to someone else. Everything about it was foreign. This was her life now. Sand. Sun. Hunger. Thirst. Fatigue. Despair. Diminishing hope.

The three of them had run into the desert in the middle of the night thinking they knew what they were doing—what risk they were taking—when in fact they knew nothing. They knew nothing about life in the desert, each other or themselves. Survival out here wasn't one sunrise at a time, it was one breath at a time.

They'd walked until they ached, they'd talked until they were hoarse, and they'd slept until they never wanted to wake up. The food they'd packed had soon been eaten without sating their hunger and the water gone without quenching their thirst. And the skins they'd packed to use as a shelter were being slowly shredded by the sharp grains of sand that never ceased flying at them.

They'd reached the river and fallen in the water, exhausted and barely alive, but elated to have made it. However, their joy hadn't lasted long when Sharma stood in the water, bent over and announced her baby was coming. Azrael had gone to the sand and laid out what was left of the torn pieces of the skins and told Sharma to lie down, but Sharma had shaken her head and birthed her son in the river instead. There had been blood and howling and the use of many forbidden words, and when the screaming baby was lifted from the water, Sharma had crawled to the edge of the river and held him to her breast, claiming it to be the happiest moment of her life.

Rani had watched on in horror and fascination with tears pouring down her cheeks as she stood witness to what she was certain was a miracle. Her hands had rested on her own stomach as she felt a tinge of sadness that she'd never experience this miracle for herself.

Even though time seemed to stand still as this child took his first breath, the cruel wind did not, and Azrael soon urged them to seek shelter under the Joshua tree. They pressed themselves against the wide trunk and waited, unsure what exactly they were waiting for. They had water, but no food. They had freedom, but no escape. They had each other, but all hope was lost.

Sharma was the weakest of them all, with her hungry son slowly suckling away what little remained of her strength. She was weary and had fallen into such a deep sleep that she'd slipped back onto the sand and Rani had just managed to scoop up the baby before he rolled from his mother's arms. The sun set and rose two times and still Sharma slept. In this time, Rani watched Azrael grow weaker, her small frame growing smaller and the spark drifting from her eyes.

"I'm sorry," Rani had told her, over and over.

"I would still have come with you, had I known," Azrael had insisted. "Staying behind wasn't possible."

It hadn't been long until Azrael had slumped down on Rani's other side and fallen into a deep sleep of her own.

And now Rani sat here, trying to make peace with a life that had no such thing.

The wind blew the veil from Azrael's face again and she readjusted it, checking on Sharma and doing the same. They'd had no privacy in their lives and it seemed nothing would be different in death.

Except they weren't dead.

Yet.

Rani despised that word and the inevitability attached to it.

For one thing remained certain in her mind. They would die here under this tree. None of them had the strength to cross the river and make it to safety in Wintergreen. If safety in that kingdom were even a possibility. Rani had no idea how they lived there and what kind of people they were.

A movement on top of the tallest dune on the horizon caught Rani's eye and she leaned back on the tree, wondering what strange animal had learned to survive out here. She'd heard there were coyotes in the desert, but they hadn't seen any yet.

She squinted, trying to bring the shape into focus. Perhaps she was dreaming? Or perhaps she was already dead?

Her eyes closed and she forced them open once again, only for her eyelids to fall, losing the fight.

"I'm sorry, little baby." She brought the small child closer to her chest and gave in to the temptation of a deathly sleep. Let the coyotes end it all. She no longer had the strength to care.

AAROW

THE NOW

*a*arow, Toran, and Jinn undid the ropes from their belts, freeing the animal hides that dragged behind them. They placed them on the ground and sat down, gripping each side tightly.

They smiled at each other, despite their faces being covered by scarves, their dark eyes doing the smiling instead of their mouths. After one quick nod from Aarow, they kicked off from the top of the dune, each determined to reach the bottom first. Toran always won the race, being the heaviest of the three, but this never deterred his two friends from trying.

Aarow felt his stomach drop as the initial burst of speed gripped hold. There was no turning back now. To let go or slip from the hide now would be deadly. The sand would shred the skin from his body and the force would break his bones. The only option was to hold on, feel the intense rush of the wind and… scream!

"Yeeeeeee haaaaaar!" he called at the top of his voice, feeling so alive it almost hurt.

Toran hurtled in front and Aarow hunched the broadness of his shoulders and brought down his head, which sent him cutting through the air, his speed increasing as he edged in front of his friend.

His smile was wide underneath his carefully secured scarf and he hunched a little more as he slid across the sand at even faster speeds. This was what it would feel like to fly, to be a bird soaring across the sky without a worry in the world. Any trouble or concern he'd had for his future or his past vanished, blown from his mind by the movement of air. Nothing and nobody mattered except the rapid descent of his body down the dune.

The slope began to even out as he reached the bottom and he willed himself to keep his momentum going, determined to be victorious this time. Just as his speed slowed, Toran came hurtling past him with one hand dangerously punching the air as he overtook him.

"Hold on, you fool!" cried Aarow, caring more for his friend's life than his win. The ride itself was prize enough, no matter what place he came.

He watched in horror as Toran slid from his animal hide and tumbled over and over, landing in a heap, stretching out on his back and lying still.

Aarow waited a few heartbeats for his speed to slow just a little more, and he tipped himself from his hide, somehow landing on his knees and bringing himself to his feet as he ran to Toran's side.

Jinn did the same, right behind him.

"Toran!" they both called, squatting beside their friend and shaking him gently. He was still breathing at least.

Toran's eyes sprang open and he gave them a wide grin. "I won!"

Jinn cursed and slammed his fist down on Toran's stomach, not with all his strength, just enough to extract a groan. "You scared us."

"Don't tell Kara," he said, rolling to his side, then sitting up.

Aarow sat down beside Toran and willed his heart to slow down. The fun of the ride, then the scare from his friend was enough to finish him off. Jinn sat beside Aarow and they stared ahead of them, the Joshua tree close enough now to clearly make out three figures beneath it.

"Are they dead?" asked Jinn, still trying to catch his breath.

"Maybe," said Aarow.

The cry of a baby echoed across the sand, sending them all to their feet and running. However had a baby ended up out here?

Toran may be the fastest when it came to sand sliding, but Aarow had always been the fastest on his feet, his lean muscular frame an asset for propelling himself with speed. He shifted his scarf from his face as he ran, having discovered long ago that strangers were far less startled when you greeted them with your face instead of just your eyes.

There was a girl sitting slumped against a tree with a baby pressed to her chest. Two people lay beside her, covered by veils. It was more than possible this baby was the only survivor here. Although, the other thing Aarow had learned after countless rescues just like this one, was that sometimes death was a ruthless impersonator. Toran had proven that just now.

He reached the tree and knelt down before the girl, lifting the baby gently from her arms. He wrapped it in the folds of the scarf around his neck, using it as a sling, as he'd done with Bindi many times. Bending back down, he reached for the girl's wrist, as Toran and Jinn squatted beside him.

"Check the other two," he said, not hopeful they'd survived.

Cradling the girl's hand in his own, he pressed down on the inside of her wrist, searching for a sign of life. Her skin was warm, and he noticed the softness of her hands. Normally the people they saved showed signs of having worked hard their whole lives. These weren't the hands of a worker. Her clothing was different too. It hadn't torn to shreds in the wind, seeming to be standing up well to the elements. There was a fine floral pattern woven into it that he hadn't seen before, and it looked like it'd taken an extraordinarily long time to make. He didn't need a pea under a mattress to tell him there was something very different about this girl, even if she couldn't possibly be a princess. No princess would run with a baby into the desert.

He felt the faint beating of a pulse in her wrist and his own heart rate quickened in response.

"She's alive," he said.

"And this one," said Toran.

"This one, too," said Jinn.

Aarow had been certain at least one of them would be dead. To find all four of them alive was completely unexpected. Now came the difficult task of getting them back to the Colony in the same state.

"Let's try to get some water into them," said Aarow, shifting aside the girl's veil to press his waterskin to her cracked lips.

He tipped it back and water flowed across her mouth. She coughed, and her eyes opened and locked on his.

They were large, dark eyes, rimmed by long black lashes. He fell into her gaze in a way he didn't recognize. The confusion and longing he felt, together with a good dose of fear, took him a few heartbeats to explain. He was frightened of her not making it. Of those eyes turning dull and losing all focus. Of never finding out her name. Was this what it felt like to recognize someone with your heart?

He shook his head, pushing away such foolish thoughts.

"Hi," he said, certain his tongue had turned to stone.

Her eyes widened, and she looked to her lap, her hands searching the emptiness. "The baby?"

"I have your baby here," he said, shifting his scarf aside so she could see. "She's alive."

"A boy," she said, closing her eyes once more and her head lolling to the side.

"Wake up," he said, patting her gently on her cheek. "Don't go back to sleep. Have some more water."

He tipped his waterskin to her lips once more and this time she drank willingly, taking in the liquid in large gulps until it ran dry.

"I'm just going to get some more," Aarow said, setting the baby back down on the girl's lap. "You have to look after your son. Don't go to sleep." Hopefully, the motivation of keeping her child alive would be enough to keep her awake while he refreshed his water supplies and himself with enough strength to get her back to the Colony safely.

His two friends nodded at him, their own waterskins upside-down and empty.

They went to the river, keeping their footsteps brisk as they spoke in hushed voices about their chances of saving all four of these souls.

Throwing themselves into the water, they ducked underneath the surface and Aarow closed his eyes enjoying the cool relief as he let himself sink to the riverbed, the weight of his clothing pulling him down.

When he emerged, the walk home would begin. A walk infinitely more difficult than his journey here, as he'd have the weight of the girl and the baby in his arms. He couldn't possibly drag them behind him on the hide as they usually did. For some reason that just didn't feel right.

He pushed back up to the surface and filled his lungs with both air and determination. He could do this. He had to.

And when he did, he was certain this girl had a story to tell.

THE COLONEL

THE NOW

The Colonel paced the hot sand outside the entrance to the caves. Where was Aarow? He should've been back long before now. The sun was getting low, which meant the coyotes would be out soon. Maybe he should gather a search party and see what the problem was?

He kicked at the sand as he shook his head. No. There'd be no search party. Aarow was his son. The future leader of their community. It was important he experience the world and gain the respect of the Colonists. Being rescued by your father wasn't a good way to do this. Besides, Aarow was extremely capable, otherwise, he wouldn't have allowed him to go on rescues. He and his friends had saved dozens of lives now. They had youth and strength on their side. Important when facing such a harsh environment.

Alerted by a noise behind him, the Colonel spun around to find Spector hovering. He must want to talk, otherwise, he'd have kept himself hidden.

"Good work this morning, Spector," the Colonel said, offering him a smile.

Spector puffed out his chest just a little. Praise seemed to be what he'd come seeking. "I found them, Colonel."

"You did. And it was a great job. You're a real asset to the Colony."

Spector beamed through his dark waves of hair that frequently fell across his face and the Colonel resisted the urge to brush them away. He was a grown man.

"Can you tell me again what you saw?" the Colonel asked. "Three women and a baby, is that right?"

"A little baby." Spector grasped each elbow and rocked his arms. "Under the Joshua tree."

"How many of them were alive?"

Spector shrugged. "Maybe one. Could be more. Maybe less by now. The baby was alive. It was screaming."

If all four of them had survived, it could explain why things were taking so long. But what were the chances of that?

"Can you please do me a favor?" the Colonel asked, patting Spector on the arm. "Can you find my wife and ask her to come out here to see me, please? I don't want to leave here in case Aarow returns."

Spector brushed the hair from his eyes and nodded. He loved nothing more than running errands to please his Colonel. He tried not to abuse this power, although a simple task like this didn't seem too much to ask. He really did need to speak to Freya and he couldn't leave his post, waiting for Aarow. They couldn't be far away now.

Spector disappeared, and the Colonel pictured him winding his way through the tunnels to find Freya. Or *the Colonel's wife*, as Spector insisted on calling her.

They'd built a whole city underground, expanding their network with the arrival of each new citizen. Some of their population were borns and some reborns, and they all thrived, living in harmony. They had thousands of Colonists now. It was strongly suspected their population had exceeded the Capital. Of course, this was hard to be certain about. The reborns had no concept of the Capital's population, but it did seem their numbers were falling, while the Colony's continued to rise.

Something was definitely up in the Capital. A baby had never been released before. Their dwindling population made their young too precious to let go of. They had to squeeze some work and offspring out of each person before they were dispensed with.

Population was of little concern in the Colony, as long as their people were happy and life was peaceful. Two values that didn't seem to mean much in the Capital.

If Spector's report was correct, then something had shifted. Could it have been a baby goat he'd heard crying? No. Spector may be different to the others in the Colony, but he was no fool. He knew the difference between the cry of a goat and a baby.

"Miro, my love."

He turned at the sound of his name. Freya was the only person who called him Miro. Although, she could hardly call him Colonel. That would be too strange. He held out his arms to his wife, embracing her gently, their baby daughter nestled between them in a scarf looped around Freya's neck.

"Where is he?" Freya whispered, letting go of him and scanning the horizon.

"Should be back soon." The Colonel rested his arm around her shoulders.

A coyote howled in the distance and he felt Freya's back stiffen.

"He'll be fine," the Colonel said. "He knows what he's doing out there. He's lived in the desert his whole life. It's different for him."

Freya nodded. As a reborn, she'd never fully understood what it was like to grow up on the dunes. Her childhood had been spent in something called a Growing Center as if she were a tree, not a human. But she'd been a rebellious tree, being released into the desert when she was twenty-seven years old, only moments after giving birth to her first child. Pregnancy had never come easily to Freya, which lowered her value in the Capital. They were only too happy to release her when she reached for her child, desperate to hold her newborn in her arms.

He'd found her in the desert, wandering the dunes with a determination that he'd never seen in any of the reborns before. She hadn't accepted her fate, nowhere near ready to die. Technically he'd been supposed to leave her there for that reason. But he couldn't. And thank goodness he hadn't. He couldn't imagine his life without her.

She'd become a wonderful mother to young Aarow, who'd still been crying for the mother who'd birthed him, only to lose her life herself. With time and healing, she'd also become a wife to him, helping him recover from the pain of losing his first wife. Then eventually she'd become a mother to little Bindi, despite the fact she still so deeply mourned the child she'd left behind in the Capital. A child he was determined to get back for her one day. A gift he'd promised her, and one he intended to deliver.

"The healers are ready," she said. "If they return alive, we'll bring them back to health."

"Let's hope they're alive then," he said.

As much as Freya had added to the Colonel's life personally, he couldn't deny that what she'd brought to the Colony as a whole had been of far more worth. Freya had discovered the ability to sense the balance of a person's energy by placing her hands on them. She could restore that balance, leaving them feeling better in body and mind. She'd trained other healers and together their small team worked to ensure the Colonists lived in peace and health. The Colony had never lived longer, been stronger or experienced such harmony.

"Spector said you wanted to talk to me." Freya joined him in scanning the horizon for their son.

"No, I said I wanted to see you. You may be able to give people strength by placing your hands on them, but all I need to do is look at you." He tipped up her face to drink in her gaze.

Her hair may be streaked with gray and the lines around her eyes had deepened, but she was more beautiful than ever. He liked seeing signs of her aging, knowing that without the Colony, she'd never have had the chance to grow old. Just like his first wife, whose premature death still pained him greatly. She'd been beautiful, too, but in a different way to Freya. There was no comparing these two great loves of his life, so he made a point to try not to.

Freya put her arms around him again and rested her head on his chest. He kissed the top of her head and reveled in the closeness. She'd been so frightened of his touch when he first plucked her from the desert, recoiling at even the slightest contact. To begin with, little Aarow was the only person she'd allowed near. What those bastards had done to her inside that curved wall of hell made his blood boil. It'd taken years for her to trust him as a man who'd been betrayed by his gender.

The only comfort he had was the revenge that was being plotted. And if that baby in the desert meant what he thought it did, then maybe it was finally time. They'd been training for this battle for years and had the strength, the passion, and the determination. Did they finally have the numbers? They had one chance to overthrow the Capital. Once they revealed themselves, they had to be victorious. For if they failed, then life as they knew it would be destroyed. Failure was no option, which was why the time had to be right.

"They're here," said Freya pointing.

"Where?" He squinted into the fading light, unable to see whatever it was that'd alerted Freya.

"I can feel them," she said. "They're close."

He knew better than to laugh at this. If Freya said they were near, then he didn't doubt it.

Some familiar figures appeared on the crest of the dunes.

"There!" she said. "They're back."

"Do you think the baby made it?" he asked.

Freya nodded. "I think they all did."

The Colonel let out a deep breath. It was time, at last, to make things better. It was time to put an end to this. It was time to bring Freya's daughter home.

RANI

THE NOW

*R*ani was aware of being carried through the desert in the same way she was aware of her dreams. She knew what was taking place and it felt like it was happening to her, but she had no control over any of it. She was just a participant, floating along with the tide.

A man was carrying her, cradling her in his arms and Sharma's baby was sleeping across her chest. They'd been walking for a long time. He'd draped a veil over her, including her face, which meant she couldn't see anything. But she could feel it all.

She could feel the strength of his arms underneath her legs and shoulders.

She could feel the rise and fall of his torso as she rested her face against his firm chest.

She could feel his breath on her face as she drew in the manly scent of him.

She could feel the beating of his heart.

There was no way to tell where he was taking her and if his intentions were good, but there was also no way to resist him.

From time to time, he'd speak to his companions. Not long conversations, just short words about pace or direction. His voice was deep and soothing and she wondered if he always spoke that way or if he was trying not to disturb her.

The wind whipped her veil from her face and she saw one man dragging Azrael behind him on some kind of animal hide. Another larger man pulled Sharma along as if she weighed nothing at all. These three men were strong. Let their hearts also be kind.

The gentle way the man held her, told her more about him than words ever could. His heartbeat was like watching the Orbs of Time from her bedchamber. The constant rhythm reminding her of the passing of time.

"Nearly there," the man said, and she was uncertain if he was speaking to her or his companions. "We'll take good care of you and your baby."

She tried to tell him it wasn't her baby, but expected they'd figure that out soon enough.

His footsteps quickened in time with his heartbeat and soon there were two more voices. Another man and a woman.

"Is the baby alive?" the woman asked.

Rani held her breath as she waited, unsure herself if the baby had made it. He was awfully still in her arms.

"He is," said the man who held her.

"I'm proud of you, son," the new man's voice said. "Good work, Toran, Jinn."

"Quickly, bring them through," the woman said. "We're ready for them."

These people sounded like good people. The impossible seemed to be happening. They'd been saved. Not just from the desert but from the brutality of their former lives.

Rani felt a change in atmosphere as they stepped into what she assumed must be the home of these people. It was cool and got cooler still with every step the man took. The relief from the oppressive heat was beyond anything she could describe.

She moved her face from left to right until the veil fell free and she saw they were in a series of tunnels with torches lighting their way. Were they underground? She'd heard some people believed if you had sins to atone for when you died, that you were sent deep underground to a place of pain and fire. Had she died and was on her way to such a place now? But what was her sin? Wanting a better life was surely not so terrible a crime.

The man turned into a small room where two women stood waiting with their hands clasped. There were three beds dug into each of the walls. The man placed Rani gently on one of the beds and a woman lifted Sharma's baby from her chest.

Rani groaned, immediately missing the weight of the child as if she'd suddenly lost one of her limbs. How must it have felt for Sharma when her other babies had not only been taken from her belly, but taken from her life? Had Rani's own mother felt like this when she'd been taken from her?

She felt a new closeness to this mother she'd never known. How awful it must have been for her to have lost her child, then be released into the desert shortly afterward. Rani's heart bled for her as much as it bled for her own loss.

A new possibility lit her mind as she felt one of the women begin to unwrap her layers of clothes. What if her mother had been rescued just like this? Had Rani run from her father only to find her mother? That seemed too good to be true. She'd already had one miracle. It would be foolish to wish for another.

"I'll come back to check on you later," the man said to her. "The healers will take good care of you."

She nodded, not wanting him to leave, but knowing there was nothing she could do to keep him with her. He'd done his job by bringing her here. It was now up to the women he called healers, as to whether or not she'd live to see him again.

She watched him leave, wishing she'd had the strength to ask his name.

A cry from Sharma jolted her thoughts back to the room.

"My baby," Sharma said, her weeping muffling her words.

"Oh, it's this one's baby," one of the women said, leaving Rani's side.

Rani heard the ruffling of fabric, then the familiar sound of the baby trying to feed.

"We made it," Rani heard Azrael say, as her eyes closed and sleep beckoned.

They had made it. But where exactly had they made it to?

AAROW

THE NOW

"I'll come back to check on you later," said Jinn in a sing-song voice, digging his fingers into Aarow's ribs. "Did you fancy that one, did you?"

Aarow rolled his eyes and looked at Toran for support. But Toran's eye had been caught by Kara who was running down the corridor with her arms outstretched.

"See ya, fellas," Toran said, slapping them both on the back, knocking the wind out of them. Aarow was no lightweight, but this guy had no idea of his strength sometimes.

"Seriously," said Jinn. "What was so special about the girl you carried? You looked like you were under some kind of spell."

"She has a baby," said Aarow, not wanting to reveal his suspicions about the girl just yet, in case he was wrong. "The kid needs her."

Jinn seemed to accept this as an answer and together they headed off to the freshwater pools, not needing to ask if this was where they needed to go. They were filthy.

Their ancestors had dug out steps, deep into the earth until they hit water. How they'd known an underground river flowed beneath them, Aarow wasn't sure. But it'd been genius, meaning the Colony could be built well away from both the Capital and the actual river, far lessening their chance of being discovered. The pools provided them with fresh drinking water and a place to bathe.

Unless you were Spector, who liked to bathe under the blue sky.

"Just as well Spector found them this morning," said Aarow, stretching his aching arms. The combined weight of the girl and her child hadn't been much, however, after such a long walk, he'd felt it. "They wouldn't have survived another day out there."

"Let's just hope they survive now," said Jinn.

"They will." Aarow nodded as if his words could make this a certainty.

They got to the pools, not bothering to strip off their filthy clothes, and waded in. The cool water worked its magic on their sore bodies.

"Hope Spector doesn't take any more trips to the river any time soon," said Jinn, splashing Aarow as he came up for air. "I'm exhausted."

Aarow turned to his back and stretched out his legs. "There are other rescue teams."

He had no intention of going out again. Not until he figured out who it was they'd just retrieved and why a baby was with them. He knew his father was just as desperate to know. But they'd have to wait until the women were well enough to talk. There'd be no getting any sense out of them right now. They'd be nursed back to health all in good time.

"Check them out," said Jinn, pointing to the other end of the pool where Toran and Kara were locked in an embrace.

Aarow laughed, aware of a strange emotion seeping through to his gut. He flicked the water from his hair as he stepped to dry land and tried to identify what he was feeling, blanching as he realized what it was.

Envy.

He was envious of Toran and Kara and what they had together. His parents had a close relationship like that and it'd never affected him. Was that because they were his parents and Toran was his friend?

Or was it because for the first time, he'd finally laid eyes on a girl who'd sparked his interest? Because as he'd carried her through the desert with her baby on her chest, he'd felt an uncontrollable urge to take care of her. He'd also felt rage. If she was running from the Capital with a baby in her arms, then she must've been violated in the way he knew happened there. He wanted to kill anyone who thought it was acceptable to steal someone's innocence like that.

He squeezed the bulk of the water from his clothes and shook his hair, watching the water droplets fly into the air. He felt better than he had all day, despite his aching muscles. If his mother had any time later, he'd ask her to do a healing on him. Something told him he was going to need to be in top form in the coming days.

"See ya," he called over his shoulder to Jinn, who raised a hand in the air, seeming in no hurry to leave the pool.

He went back to his family's quarters, hoping his father would be there. He really needed to talk to him about getting assigned his own quarters. He wasn't a child anymore and if the community was going to start to see him as a leader, it was important he show them how independent he was. But that discussion wouldn't happen tonight. They had far more serious issues to address.

"Aarow." His father was pacing the room. Bindi was asleep in her crib nearby.

Aarow didn't have to ask where his mother was. She'd be in the Healing Room for most of the night. She had important work to do. The women they'd rescued didn't just have broken bodies. Their spirits had been crushed as well. Healing them would be quite a task.

"Father." He slumped into a seat and propped his feet on the table. All their furniture was molded out of the compacted sand as each room was dug out. There weren't enough resources in the desert to build furniture and it saved hauling extra sand up to the surface. He'd been told the Capital had acquired furniture from other kingdoms many generations ago, but he found chairs and tables made from trees hard to imagine. Did they still have the leaves attached?

"Tell me more about the new reborns." His father sat beside him. "Was there anything else unusual? Did any of them speak to you?"

Aarow nodded, intending to tell him everything, apart from his confusion of feelings toward the girl he'd carried.

"Well, as you saw there were three of them. That for a start was different. And a baby. That's never happened before. And the girl I carried. Well, I could be entirely wrong about this but… I suspect she comes from wealth."

"How could you tell?" His father leaned forward, keen for his response.

"It was her hands. They were… perfect. Unscathed by work. Like they'd never been used. And her hair had a fragrance that'd been so ingrained I doubt she could ever wash it out. Like she'd been bathing in some kind of perfume. And her clothes were made from fabric like none I've ever seen before. They had a richness about them. Nobody in the Capital wears clothes like that. Or here."

"Shall we put a pea under her mattress?" his father joked, having heard his wife tell this story countless times.

"Maybe." Aarow refused to laugh. "I mean it, Father. If it weren't so impossible, I'd really think she could be a princess."

"Why's it impossible?" his father asked.

"Because a princess would have no need to run. And surely, they wouldn't release an heir to the throne. Let alone an heir with a baby."

His father let out a slow breath. "I'm not as sure as you about that. We don't know if she was released. Maybe she ran. Did they have any belongings with them?"

"They did!" Aarow slapped his forehead, feeling foolish for having overlooked this detail. When people were released, they walked into the desert with nothing except the clothes on their back. "They had a torn animal hide and a bag with a few empty waterskins and other useless belongings. Toran carried them back. He can show them to you."

His father nodded. "From what you've just told me, we likely have someone very important in our Healing Room tonight."

"What would it mean if she's a princess?" Aarow asked. "Especially if she's a princess who ran away."

"It means...everything, my son. It means the Capital is ready to fall. It means it might be time to seize it and set the people free."

This thought made Aarow nervous. Their life was so perfect in the Colony. Risking it to topple a kingdom that was slowly destroying itself seemed unnecessary. Then he thought of his mother and the way she yearned for the child she'd lost. Life wasn't so perfect for her. And what about the fragile girl he'd just carried from the desert? Clearly her life wasn't perfect either. There'd been enough suffering already. Maybe his father was right. Maybe it was time to set the people free.

FREYA

THE NOW

Freya was relieved her son was home safely but glad of an excuse not to go back to her family's quarters just yet. Miro and Aarow needed some time to talk and she wasn't sure she wanted to listen in. More and more lately, their talk had been of a revolution and overthrowing the Capital. Which frightened Freya in ways she found hard to explain.

Because as much as she'd hated growing up in the Capital and wanted to see it brought down, it was filled with people she cared about.

The carer in the Growing Center who'd risked her life to pull her free when she had her arm stuck in a wheelbarrow and was screaming as it pinched her skin.

The woman at the Supply Center who always gave her double rations, pretending not to have noticed she made a mistake.

The boy she'd sat beside in her lessons, who later grew into a man who refused to touch her when he was assigned her number in the Conception Center.

But most of all, her child. The one stolen from her before she was released into the desert. The child Miro was determined to get back for her.

Her beautiful daughter who she'd glimpsed only once, burning the memory of her deep into her soul. A daughter who'd be grown now and probably had a child of her own stolen from her by now. Repeating the pattern of evil. A pattern that had to be broken.

She looked down at the girl Aarow had carried from the desert, running her hands across her depleted energy field. There was so much healing to be done, as well as the more primary needs to take care of. This girl needed fluids, she needed the sand cleaned from her eyes, she needed aloe rubbed into the blisters on her feet.

As she tended to her needs, she wondered what this girl would have to say when she woke. Would her words spark the revolution that seemed so close? As much as she wanted her daughter back, she was aware that revolutions took their toll on the innocent as well as the guilty. What if breaking the pattern of evil, also broke her daughter? Then she wasn't sure it'd be worth the price. Not for her anyway. She needed her daughter back. A younger sister for Aarow, an older sister for Bindi.

For Aarow may not be the child of her blood, but he was still her son. She was the mother to him that he'd lost. He was the child to her that'd been stolen, each one filling a part of their hearts that'd been ripped from them without their consent.

She glanced across at the other two healers she'd trained, who were tending to the other two females. The baby was still feeding from his mother's breast, although Freya doubted there was much milk in there. It seemed to be comforting the baby to try. Or perhaps he lacked the energy to complain. With time, she was confident they'd restore these reborns to good health. They'd need to be patient.

Miro had been the one to teach her patience. He'd been far more patient with her over the years than she was sure most men would've been.

When he'd plucked her from the desert, her body and spirit broken by the Capital, he claimed to have fallen irrevocably in love with her. She'd tried to dissuade him, telling him that she never wanted to be touched by another man. She could never be a real wife to him. He said that didn't matter. He could wait forever if he needed to.

She'd thought his heart was just broken after the tragic death of his wife and he was looking to replace her, but it soon became clear that wasn't the case. He could have any woman in the Colony, however, he seemed to only want her.

But it was Aarow who won her heart before Miro. He took an instant liking to Freya and would latch onto her with his chubby toddler arms and hold his face to hers in a way that made her both deeply uncomfortable and deeply comforted at the same time. Before long, it was her reaching for him and pressing his little body to her own, drawing comfort from the love he had to give. She'd close her eyes and breathe in the baby smell of him and pretend he was her own until he really did become hers. Their bond was as close as any mother and son. It didn't matter that they weren't related by blood, they were related by their hearts.

And when Bindi was born, she knew for certain it made no difference if she'd birthed Aarow or not. Bindi and Aarow owned an equal third of her heart, together with the child she'd been forced to leave behind.

She dipped a soft cloth into some clean water and gently wiped the sand from the girl's sleeping face. She was a lovely looking girl who exuded strength despite her frail state. It was no wonder Aarow had seemed so taken with her. Even he'd been able to sense she was someone special. Or had he fallen in love with this girl in the same way Miro had with her? It was more than possible, she supposed. If that were the case, she hoped Aarow had his father's patience.

Miro had earned her trust slowly and waited for her to come to him. Slowly, she'd started to feel comfortable placing a hand on his shoulder or brushing knuckles as she passed him something. It wasn't until Aarow grew older that she began to crave something more from Miro. She'd come to depend on human touch and wondered what it might be like to embark on a more intimate relationship.

This hadn't been easy either and it'd taken many years until she'd allow Miro to be with her in the way a husband yearns to be with his wife. It never stopped triggering memories she was trying to suppress, but she found that slowly they dulled, and she began to think of being touched in this way as an expression of love rather than power.

Pushing these thoughts from her mind, she concentrated on the girl who lay before her, placing the palms of her hands on her energy centers as she swept away the bad and revitalized the good.

This poor girl's spirit was broken. But by the time she was finished with her, she was going to be ready to take on the world. Perhaps Aarow wouldn't need as much patience as his father had displayed. Respect and understanding may be enough.

RANI

THE NOW

*R*ani's eyes opened and she blinked, adjusting to the light in the room. She felt so much better for having had rest and water in the cool of this underground haven.

She turned her head to see Azrael in the bed adjacent to hers, sitting up and grinning.

"It's about time," she said. "I thought you were never going to wake up."

"You're obviously feeling better," said Rani, noticing her voice was croaky.

"There's water on the shelf next to you." Azrael pointed.

Rani reached for the cup and drank deeply, certain that never again would she quench her thirst from the desert.

"Go slowly," warned Azrael. "You don't want to be sick."

Rani sat back in bed. "Where's Sharma?"

"She's gone to wash," said Azrael. "And before you ask, her baby's fine. He's gone, too. I don't think Sharma will be letting him out of her arms for a long time yet. Maybe ever, which might be interesting as he gets older…"

Rani smiled to see her friend full of so much chatter. It seemed they'd all made a miraculous recovery. How was that even possible? They'd all been so unwell when they'd arrived here.

"I told you that you'd save my life one day," Azrael said, not seeming to be bothered by Rani's lack of words.

Rani cleared her throat. "I didn't save your life. I almost killed you."

Azrael wouldn't hear of that and shook her head. "You almost killed yourself, planning to jump out that window. Bet you're glad I stopped you."

Rani didn't know how to reply to this. She was glad to have a second chance at life. Although, she still wasn't certain what that second chance entailed. And what about all those people back in the Capital? She was supposed to grow up to be their Empress, and instead she'd chosen to abandon them, leaving them to fight their own battles for themselves.

"Rani," said Azrael, leaving her own bed to stand beside her own. "You look upset. Why? It's okay. We've been saved. Everything's going to be fine."

Rani forced a smile and nodded.

"Remember when I told you I didn't believe in the Evernow?" asked Azrael, not pausing for an answer. "One of the older girls in the Growing Center told me it was the time when you don't wish for your past or future, and instead live for what's happening right now. And I didn't think that was possible. But now I know it is and I think that's where we are. I don't really care what's in my future for it can't be worse than my past, but I'm excited to find out. I'm excited about today. I'm excited about right now. We did it, Rani. You came and got me. You saved me when you said you couldn't, but I knew you could. You're the bravest, most wonderful friend in all the world."

Rani choked on more tears that wanted to escape, trying to hold them back, and failing wildly.

"I need to apologize to you, Rani."

She shook her head, not believing for a moment that Azrael had anything to apologize for.

"You touched me on the arm the day we met, and I leaped back as if you'd caused me physical harm. The women who've been caring for us have been putting their hands on us and look what's happened. We've gotten stronger, not weaker. You were right about that too and I'm sorry I reacted in the way I did."

Azrael sat on the edge of Rani's bed with only the fabric of the blanket separating them. She reached for Rani's hand and held it. Now it was Rani's turn to feel strange and she resisted the urge to pull away. Not because she didn't want this hand of friendship, but because it was so foreign to her.

"And by the way," said Azrael. "I think the man who carried you here has fallen madly in love with you."

Rani laughed, breaking her silence at last. "What would make you say that?"

Azrael giggled with her. "He's been in here twice, staring at you like the world will end if your eyes didn't open. I tried to tell him I was perfectly fine, and he was polite about it, although, honestly I'm not sure he really cared."

Rani remembered what'd passed between them as he'd carried her from the desert. It was the opposite to interactions she'd had with people in the Round, which were filled with plenty of words and no touching. With the man in the desert, she'd been pressed against his chest with barely a word spoken.

"He asked me a lot of questions about you, but don't worry, I didn't tell him anything. If you want to tell him who you are, then that's up to you. I pretended to fall asleep in case I said too much."

"Where do you think we are?" Rani asked, taking another gulp of her water, noticing there was a plate of flatbread beside it. She tore off a small piece and nibbled on it.

"It's called the Colony," said Azrael. "There are thousands of people living here under the ground. The tunnels go forever in twists and turns and there's a spring with fresh water and—"

"Hold on!" Rani held up her hand. "How much longer than me have you been awake?"

"I woke at sun-up, not that we can see the sun from here. And I think it's nearly sundown now."

"And you've had the strength to explore all of that?"

"I needed a wash. If you don't mind me saying it, you do too."

Rani laughed, and her tears of moments before dried on her face. "Maybe you should keep your distance then."

Azrael went back to her bed and flopped down. "I'm happy, Rani. I'm really happy. I know we have no idea where we are or what's ahead but I'm happy. It's a good place. I can feel it."

Rani smiled at her friend, willing the universe to let this innocent girl remain happy. She'd asked for nothing in life. Let her have this one thing.

Then the door opened and the man returned. The man who'd plucked her from the desert and apparently looked at her like his world depended on it.

She sat up and pulled the blanket to a modest level, hoping Azrael had exaggerated her need for a bath.

"You're awake," he said, his smile confirming the truth in Azrael's assessment of him. For his eyes were unmistakably filled with love.

AAROW

THE NOW

*A*arow stood beside the girl's bed, not wanting to frighten her away by getting too close. Her eyes were open and she was sitting up. She looked tired, with lines under her dark eyes and sand stuck to her hair. None of that mattered. The important thing was that she was awake.

"Hello," he said, coughing to cover his awkwardness. He didn't normally have trouble speaking to people.

"Thank you for rescuing us." Her voice was soft and gentle, yet her face so much more animated than when he'd carried her from the desert.

"Of course," he said. "You needed help and that's what we do here. You must have a lot of questions."

He noticed her friend in the next bed turn to her side and pretend to sleep, her eyelids fluttering in a way nobody did when they were really asleep. He tried to recall her name, fairly certain it was Azrael. Yet still, he didn't know his princess's name, despite having asked Azrael for it several times already and being told he'd need to ask her himself.

The girl nodded, making him wonder if she was always this quiet. Azrael hadn't had the same issue earlier, chatting away to him until she seemed to have realized she was saying too much and closed down.

"I have questions for you, too," he said. "Starting with your name. My name's Aarow." He smiled, not putting out his hand, having learned long ago that didn't go down well with reborns.

"Aarow," she repeated, studying him for a moment, before color raced to her cheeks and she looked away, smoothing her hair down with her fingertips.

"You look fine," he said. Well, better than fine if he were truthful, but he sensed this wasn't the time to tell her this. She might crawl even further into her shell than she already had.

"And your name is?" He ventured forward to squat beside her bed, leveling their faces, but when she shrank away, he shuffled back to give her space.

She seemed to be deciding on whether to tell him her name or make one up and he wondered how he was going to know the difference.

"Rani," she said, her dark eyes locking on his own.

He was certain this was the truth, mainly because he knew the Emperor's daughter was called Rani. He didn't need his mother to put a pea under her mattress. Her name proved what he'd already known. Just like in the story, he'd already recognized her with his heart. This had to be the princess.

"Rani's a beautiful name," he said, deciding not to let on that he knew who she was. Allow her to adjust to her surroundings a bit first. Something didn't fit, though. The most recent of the reborns had told them that Princess Rani had failed to produce an heir.

"Where's your son?" he asked, noticing there was no sleeping infant in the room. The woman from the other bed was missing too.

"With Sharma," said Rani. "His mother."

"Oh." It was now his turn to fall silent and he cursed himself for jumping to conclusions, just because she'd been the one to hold the child when he'd found her. This new information convinced him even more that she was indeed who he thought she was. It also gave him hope that maybe the Capital hadn't broken her in all the ways he was afraid they had.

As if on cue, Sharma and her baby returned to the room, followed by two healers.

One of the healers went to say something to him and stopped herself.

He rose to his feet. It was clear Rani needed more time to recover before he spoke to her, and this healer was too afraid to stand up to the future Colonel by asking him to leave. It pleased him that people recognized his future leadership, but he didn't want to be the sort of leader people were afraid of.

"My father and I need to speak to Rani when she's feeling better," he said. "Can you please send for us as soon as that's possible?"

The healer looked at Rani and crinkled her brow as if wondering why her patient had attracted such attention. To her, she must just look like any of the reborns plucked from the cusp of death.

"Who's your father?" Rani asked him, finding her voice at last. "Why does he need to speak to me?"

"He's the leader of the Colony," said Aarow, noticing the look of surprise on her face. It was a shame he'd had to tell her this. He'd have liked to have seen how she treated him without this piece of information first. Although to a princess, being the son of the leader of a Colony probably wasn't all that impressive.

"I'll be fine to speak with you and your father on the next turn." She propped herself up on her elbows and he smiled to have heard such authority in her voice. He'd known there was so much more to this girl hidden beneath her quiet demeanor.

The healer stepped between them to straighten Rani's already smooth blanket. Her hint couldn't be more direct.

"We call them days in here, not turns," the healer said to Rani.

Rani nodded, not seeming to mind being corrected.

"I'll leave you to rest," said Aarow, reluctantly taking the healer's hint, finding it hard to tear himself away.

"See you on the next day," Rani said, and he tried not to laugh at the way she'd used this new word.

"I think you'll be happy here," he said, taking a step away, much to the relief of the healer.

At these words, Rani offered him her first smile. Her whole face lifted and glowed as her appreciation spread from her lips to her eyes.

"We're already happy here," said Azrael, no longer pretending to sleep.

"I'm glad," he said. "Rest now, and my father and I will be back to speak with you in the morning." His eyes landed on Rani as he said this and he turned toward the door.

"Are you planning a battle?" Azrael asked, stilling his footsteps.

He turned slowly, wondering how she could possibly know about this.

"What did you ask?" He was suddenly more interested in Azrael than he'd been before.

"Never mind," she said, falling silent.

"You asked about a battle," he prompted. "Why?"

"I dreamed of one," she said, fiddling with her blanket. "It was only a dream. Forgive me for mentioning it."

He nodded, weighing up whether or not he believed her. Were these three women spies sent from the Capital? Had the Colony spent all this time believing they had the advantage of surprise when the Capital knew of their existence this whole time? Why else was a princess here? And why would this girl ask him about a battle? In all the rescues he'd ever done, not once had this question ever been asked.

"See you at sun-up," he said, trying not to look at Rani. It was unbearable to think she might be lying to him when he'd only just decided she was telling him the truth. "Thank you for your time."

He closed the door behind him and rested his back on it for a moment, drawing in a deep breath.

They had to tread carefully here. He needed to think with his head, not his heart. All their lives were at risk.

RANI

THE NOW

"How do we know when it's sun-up?" Rani asked in a whisper, unsure if either Azrael or Sharma were awake. "There are no windows." The Orbs of Time would be useless in a place like this.

"I have no idea," came Sharma's whispered reply. "Horus isn't awake, so it can't be too late."

"Who's Horus?" asked Azrael, saving Rani the question.

"My son," said Sharma. "I named him last night."

"That's my father's name," said Rani, confused.

Azrael turned on a lamp and soft light filled the room.

"Your father's a good man," said Sharma. "What happened wasn't his fault."

"He's a weak man." Rani sat up. "He did nothing to save me."

"He did everything to save you." Sharma rose from her bed and perched on the edge of Rani's bed. "Who do you think organized our bags of supplies?"

"You?"

She shook her head. "It was a risk, but I went to your father and talked to him. I apologize for not telling you this before now."

"You didn't, Sharma!" She sat up in bed and searched Sharma's face for any hint that she was making this up. "You could have ruined everything. He'd never let me go."

"Listen to me," she said. "He did let you go. He organized our supplies. He told me which direction to run to reach the river. He wanted us to go to Wintergreen and tell them who you were. He seemed certain they'd help us."

"You're lying to me." Rani shook her head and inched away from Sharma in her bed. "My father loved me. He couldn't be certain of that. He wouldn't give me his blessing."

"He did it *because* he loves you."

"No." There was no way she could believe this. It couldn't be true.

"It's true," said Azrael, joining the conversation.

"How would you know?" snapped Rani. "You never even met my father. And don't tell me you dreamed it."

Azrael fell silent for once and looked away. Rani would need to apologize to her later.

"Rani," said Sharma. "He was almost as upset about the Chairman's plans for you, as you were. He was sick over it. I wasn't the only one who noticed your obsession with your window. Your father knew he had to either watch you die or give you a chance in the desert."

Regret punched Rani in the gut. If this were true, she shouldn't have left her father. He father loved her. Why was it only now that she realized that she loved him too?

"Why didn't he say goodbye?" she asked.

"Because if you knew you'd had his blessing, it would've made it harder for you to leave. He didn't want that for you."

Rani slid her teeth across each other in a familiar grind, annoyed that Sharma was right.

Sharma reached out a tentative hand and touched her fingers to Rani's cheek. "Don't do that with your teeth," she said. "I'm sorry I didn't tell you earlier. He made me promise not to. He'd be furious if he knew I'd told you now."

Rani pulled away, not wanting her touch. Not wanting anyone's touch.

"So, why name your son after him?" she asked, slipping from her bed and crossing the room, breathing a sigh at the return of her personal space.

"Because without him, I'd never have laid a hand on my son. I'd be stuck in the Capital waiting for the Chairman to release me into the desert with no hope of survival. Only a very small number of people have made it to safety here. It was because of the Emperor's help that we're all alive today. Now my son can grow to be the true man he's meant to be and I get to watch him do it. I couldn't think of a better person to name him after than your father."

Rani nodded, grateful for the new perspective on the man who'd raised her, but heartbroken at the feelings this stirred to life.

"It's a lovely sentiment," she said. "I'm sure he'll do my father's name proud."

"Can we call him Horrie?" asked Azrael, venturing back into the conversation. "He doesn't look much like a Horus."

Sharma laughed. "I'm sure he won't mind. Horrie suits him. It's kind of cute."

Horrie woke with a cry and flapped his little arms in the air.

"I'm really not sure if that's a protest or a sign he likes it," said Azrael.

"Hush, my child," said Sharma, going to Horrie and scooping him up to hold against her chest. His tiny lips smacked together as the intensity of his cries increased. He was one hungry baby, determined to make up for lost time.

Sharma pressed him to her breast and he suckled, groaning through his cries now that he was getting rewarded for his efforts at last.

A healer came into the room, clasping her hands as if ready for business. It was the healer who'd tended to Rani, only this was the first time she'd had a proper look at her and Rani had to try to hide her shock. This woman was so...old. Her hair was gray, and her face was lined. How was it possible she was even still alive?

"I see someone's awake," the healer said, not seeming to notice Rani's reaction. "Did the baby wake you all?"

"I think we woke him," said Azrael. "His name's Horrie. Do you like that?"

The healer's eyes opened widely as her lower jaw fell just enough to provide an answer without words.

"It's very unique," she said, fussing with Rani's blanket.

Azrael shot Rani a quick glance and poked out her tongue, causing Rani to burst out laughing having never seen such a gesture before.

"How old are you?" Azrael asked the healer.

"Azrael!" Sharma scolded. "This woman is here to help us."

"It's okay," the healer laughed, going to Azrael's side. "I'm forty-four."

Rani's eyes widened. She hadn't realized people could live so long.

"How old are you?" the woman asked Azrael, perching on the side of her bed.

"Seventeen. And I'm sorry if I was rude just now."

"Not at all," the woman said. "I like your honesty. My name's Freya, what's yours?"

"Azrael. I like your hair. It's sparkly, like your eyes. Can I touch it?"

"Sure."

Azrael reached out to put her hand on Freya's hair and Rani wondered what it felt like. Did gray hair feel the same as black? She'd have to ask Azrael later.

"How did the color run out?" Azrael asked.

"That's what happens when you get older." Freya took hold of Azrael's hand and squeezed it.

Rani decided that she liked this woman and the gentle way she was treating her friend.

"I've never met anyone as old as you," said Azrael.

Freya laughed. "I said older, not old. There are plenty of people older than me in the Colony. You'll see."

"That's incredible," said Azrael. "The water in your pools must be enchanted."

"Perhaps it is," Freya said, smiling.

It seemed Azrael had enchanted Freya with her blunt honesty, just like the water in the pools.

"Well, I'm pleased to see you're all feeling better," said Freya, rising from the bed and looking at Rani and Sharma. "Shall I send for the Colonel and Aarow?"

"The Colonel?" they all asked together.

"Yes, that's what he's called around here. I should probably tell you that he's also my husband."

So, if Freya was married to the leader of the Colony, she must be Aarow's mother. Rani would never have picked that. They didn't look at all alike.

"The Colonel's our version of the Emperor," Freya continued. "Only he actually has a say in our fate."

Rani winced, although what Freya said was true. Her father had no power, even if he did have a far kinder heart than she'd given him credit for.

"Is that a yes?" asked Freya, directing her question at Sharma. "Shall I send for them now?"

It was Rani who answered. "Just give us a little time to clean ourselves up, then yes, please send for your husband. And Aarow."

She felt a flush rise to her cheeks, saying his name aloud for the first time and wondered why she felt such an affinity to him. Was it because they were both the child of a leader? Both who'd been allowed to go out into the desert. One in the hope of returning swiftly, the other in the hope of never returning again.

Or was it because of how undeniably handsome Aarow was? No, she didn't want to think like that. The perfect structure of his face and powerful lines of muscle on his body meant nothing to her. It was the kindness of a soul that made someone handsome. Regrettably, this seemed to apply to Aarow, too.

She sighed. Moving forward with her future would be so much easier without the cloud of confused feelings Aarow stirred to life in her. She had to push all that aside and concentrate on the questions he'd said they had for her. How much should she tell him and how much should she leave buried in the sand?

It seemed she didn't have long to figure this out.

SHARMA

THE NOW

Sharma fed little Horrie with her eyes glued to him. It felt like a miracle to be able to sustain this perfect human with milk she produced all by herself. How had her body known how to do this? She remembered all the other times she'd given birth and the women in the Birthing Center had milked her with their thick gloved fingers like she was a goat. Why couldn't they have just let her babies feed from her then? It was obvious to her now that nurturing a baby from her breast was about so much more than just feeding them with precious milk. It was about feeding them with love. Running a thumb across feathered eyebrows. Drawing an index finger down the bridge of a tiny nose. Holding out a finger for a small hand to grasp.

Her bond with this child was strong, but it did nothing to diminish the bond she felt for the children she'd never been allowed to hold. If anything, it strengthened this feeling, making her miss them even more.

Azrael had taken Rani to the pools to freshen up before they talked to the Colonel and his son and she was glad of some time alone with Horrie. Her body was still aching, her lips cracked and her head pounding. But slowly, she was recovering and able to take in just how lucky they'd been. The healers had been working wonders with them. They should all be feeling far worse than they were.

Running into the desert had been a foolish gamble. The fact the gamble paid off might make it seem less foolish but the decision was still the same. Rani had saved Horrie's life, keeping him alive when she'd become too weak to do so herself. This made her love Rani even more, if that were even possible.

There was so much she needed to tell Rani now they were free. The promises she'd made to keep secrets from her didn't seem valid outside the Capital.

She'd started by telling Rani the truth about the Emperor's involvement in their escape and had been surprised by the strength of her reaction. It was like she'd wanted to leap right up from her bed and run straight back to the Capital.

This had made Sharma nervous about everything else she had to reveal to her. Secrets far more shocking than that. Rani had no idea about the extent to which she'd been lied to over the years. And as much as Sharma wanted to protect her from the truth, it had to come out. The time for secrets was over.

Horrie's lips released their grip on her and his head lolled back.

"Wake up, little man," said Sharma, jiggling him gently, wanting to see his dark eyes sparkle as he tried to focus.

There was no waking him. He was so fast asleep she had to put her hand on his chest to make sure he was still drawing breath.

She hadn't slept well the night before. Azrael had been talking in her sleep, saying something about lights and Shinings. Every time Sharma had managed to drop off, Horrie had woken her, wanting another feed.

She wondered where they'd be allowed to sleep once they left the Healing Room. It was hard to know how things worked underground and just how many rooms had been dug into the sand. The parts of the Colony she'd seen so far were expansive with twisting tunnels that seemed to go for miles. It was extraordinary, leaving her wondering why the Capital had been built above the ground instead of under. It made so much more sense to hide from the harshness of the sun and wind down here.

The thatched door opened, and Azrael and Rani appeared. Rani looked like a real Princess once more, now that she was clean and dressed in fresh clothes. It was a shame she'd never be Empress in the way her ancient ancestors had intended. Or maybe it wasn't. Because there was no doubt that ever since she'd left the Capital she was better for it. Even when they'd sat dying underneath the Joshua tree she'd been better for it. Because the fear in her eyes and the grinding of her teeth had been replaced by freedom and there was great dignity in that.

"You look beautiful," she said to Rani.

"What about me?" asked Azrael, spinning in a circle.

"You cleaned yourself up yesterday," laughed Sharma. "Yes, you look beautiful, too."

Rani and Azrael took a seat at a table off to the side of the room. Just like the beds, the table and chairs had been made from hardened sand. They were surprisingly comfortable. Sharma settled Horrie on her bed and tucked some blankets around him, joining the others at the table.

"What's happening out there?" asked Sharma.

"Not a lot," said Azrael. "A bit early yet."

"How far away do you think the Colonel and Aarow will be?" Rani crossed her arms, losing the light smile that'd held her features only moments ago.

"Not far, I'd say," said Azrael, smirking.

"What's that look for?" asked Sharma.

"I'll let Rani explain."

"There's nothing to explain!" Rani threw up her hands.

Sharma remained quiet, looking between the girls, waiting for one of them to tell her what she'd missed. Most likely Azrael, who found it far harder to hold her tongue than Rani.

"The Colonel's son has fallen for Rani's beauty."

Rani shook her head, a pink color rising to her cheeks. "Not true! Azrael just has a very vivid imagination, that's all."

"Are you blushing?" asked Azrael, the smile falling from her face.

"Of course not." Rani brushed at her cheeks. "It's just a little warm in here."

Sharma suppressed a smile. It was nice and cool down here. Blaming the temperature was a stretch.

"Do you…like him too?" asked Azrael, positively frowning now.

"I've hardly even met the man!" cried Rani. "Please!"

"But you thought he was handsome?" Azrael pressed.

"Of course," said Rani, rolling her eyes. "I'm not blind."

It was true. Aarow was extremely handsome, but Sharma hadn't noticed what Azrael clearly had. She really needed to start paying more attention if she was going to learn to survive down here.

Azrael folded her hands in her lap and sat back in her chair.

"Now, now," said Sharma, trying to figure out what'd possibly just soured the mood in the room so much. Had Azrael hit a nerve? Although it seemed to be her own nerve she'd hit. Was it jealousy? Perhaps she liked being Rani's only friend.

Relationships were so complicated, and they were all still tired and unwell. It would be foolish to think life would make more sense now that they'd escaped the Capital. Something told her life was about to get a whole lot more complicated.

The door opened once more, and two handsome male complications stepped through. She couldn't even begin to guess what they might have to say.

AAROW

THE NOW

*A*arow followed his father into the room and suppressed a yawn. He hadn't slept a wink and this time it wasn't because of Bindi. He and his father had been up all night talking about how to handle this meeting.

"Are we boring you already?" Azrael asked him.

The three women had risen from their beds and were sitting around the table in the corner of the room. They looked so different to the last time he'd seen them. It was amazing what some food, water and rest could do to restore the body. The healings had no doubt sped up this process. Rani was impossibly more beautiful, and he averted his eyes as he'd do with the sun. Some beauty was hard to look directly in the eye.

"Not bored," Aarow said. "Yet."

Azrael laughed and Aarow couldn't help but think how well she'd get along with Jinn. They had the same lighthearted approach to life. He'd have to ensure their paths crossed to see if a friendship would blossom.

His father shot him a stern look and Aarow wiped the smile from his face. This was a serious matter. It'd never been more serious.

"Father, this is Azrael," said Aarow, clearing his throat and showing he knew how to take charge. "And Rani and Sharma."

"Pleased to meet you," his father said, taking a chair. "You may call me Colonel or Miro, as you wish."

Aarow liked this about his father. He had no illusions of grandeur, just as happy to be called by his given name than the title he'd worked so hard to earn, by merit as well as birthright. Although, the only person Aarow had ever heard call him by his first name was his mother. Even Aarow sometimes thought of him as the Colonel.

The women nodded politely and Aarow took the vacant seat next to his father.

"Well, this is familiar," said Sharma.

"What's familiar?" Aarow watched his father's brow furrow as he analyzed her words.

"Nothing," said Sharma, her smile doing little to cover the panic in her eyes at having let something slip. Aarow just wasn't sure exactly what that something was.

"There's a round table in the Capital, I hear," said his father. "One that the Board sit around. Only it's made from timber, not sand."

Sharma nodded slowly, her expression giving nothing more away.

"We have no secrets from you," said Rani, folding her hands on the table. "We owe you our lives. Honesty is the least we can offer you."

"I'm glad to hear that," said Aarow, catching her gaze, holding it, then letting it go, afraid of how it might feel to keep it for too long.

"We know your names, but what positions do you hold in the Capital?" his father asked, sticking to their plan of getting this information without delay.

The three women looked to each other, as if deciding who would speak. Rani nodded and the other two bowed their heads in return. Even if Aarow hadn't worked out who she was, gestures like this would give it away. She may not be the loudest or the oldest of the three, but clearly she was their leader.

Rani directed her gaze at the Colonel as she swallowed as prepared to speak.

"I'm Princess Rani, eldest child of the Emperor of The Sands of Naar."

Aarow let a long breath slide from his lungs. Despite having already figured this out, it felt like a revelation to hear it said out loud. A revelation and a relief that Rani had been honest with them.

"This here beside me is Sharma," she continued. "The only female to sit on the Board of our kingdom. Her son is Horrie, the child the kingdom wished to take from her. And this here is Azrael, a girl forced to live in poverty outside the walls of the Round."

Aarow and his father glanced at each other, neither of them having expected such immediate transparency. This would make everything so much easier.

"I can see why Sharma and Azrael took their chances in the desert," said Aarow. "But why would the future Empress do something so risky? Were you taken prisoner?"

Rani laughed. "Hardly! Taken prisoner by the only friend I've ever had and a woman who's been like a mother to me? I can assure you, I left of my own free will."

"Then why?" Aarow asked.

The joy fell from Rani's eyes and a sadness took hold, making him regret pushing her on this point. However, he had to know. If they were going to invade the Capital, they had to know exactly what they were up against. This was crucial.

"How much do you know about the laws of the Capital?" Sharma asked, deflecting attention away from Rani.

"We're very well informed," said the Colonel. "Many of our population are reborns."

"A reborn?" asked Sharma. "You seemed to know more about our lives than we know of yours."

"Sorry," he said. "It's what we call someone who was born in the Capital and rescued by us and brought here to start again."

"I like that," said Azrael. "I definitely feel like I've been reborn."

"You still haven't answered our question as to what the Princess is doing here," Aarow pointed out, directing his words at Sharma. Rani would step in when she felt comfortable.

Sharma looked at Rani for permission and received a gentle nod in return.

"The Board believed that Rani's time had come," said Sharma. "You understand what that means?"

Aarow and his father nodded and Aarow hoped he'd managed to keep a flush from his cheeks. This wasn't a comfortable conversation to have with three women he'd just met.

"The Chairman of the Board wished to sire the kingdom's heir," Sharma continued. "Rani didn't share his wishes."

Aarow winced, feeling like he'd just been punched in the gut. With full force. By Toran. How dare the Capital violate their women like this! Especially the woman they were supposed to hold most dear. The woman who was their future Empress. He'd heard plenty of stories about this Chairman, and not one of them had been good. It was no wonder Rani had taken her chances in the desert.

He looked at the three faces across from him. One woman risking her life to keep her baby. Another to keep herself from poverty. And the other to keep hold of herself.

"This has to end!" Aarow slammed his fist on the table, causing all three women to jump.

"It does," his father said, shaking his head, then directing his gaze to Rani. "You must be informed that we wish to invade the Capital and seize power of the kingdom."

Aarow watched as Rani's jaw fell. "Invade the Capital?"

The Colonel nodded. "We've been waiting for the right time. Training for this moment and monitoring the Capital to maximize our chance of success. We only get one shot. Once we've revealed ourselves, we'll no longer be safe in the Colony. We have to win."

"I knew you were training for a battle," said Azrael. "I knew it was more than just a dream."

"You did," said Aarow, not judging her for this. He knew better having been raised by a woman who healed people with her hands.

"You're planning a battle?" asked Rani, still seeming to be struggling to take all of this in.

"Is this news distressing for you?" he asked, concerned they'd caused her too much pain too soon.

She shook her head. "I'm surprised, but not distressed."

"Will it be a peaceful invasion?" asked Sharma. "There are many good people trapped within the Capital."

"We'll do our best to make sure nobody gets hurt," said the Colonel.

"But you've been training for battle," said Azrael. "How can nobody get hurt?"

"We've been figuring out ways to overpower people without hurting them," said Aarow. "We don't wish to cause any further pain. Our goal is the opposite. You've suffered enough already. Someone has to do something. The other kingdoms aren't used to the desert. The conditions are too harsh and they have to travel too far. All their attempts have failed. It has to be the Colony to do this. We're your only hope."

"And why is the time right now?" asked Rani.

"We've been told the population has dwindled," the Colonel said, taking over. "Is this correct?"

"Yes," said Sharma. "People are being released for the most minor offenses. Not following the law, growing too old, being too weak. It's reached crisis point, only the Chairman isn't willing to make any changes to ensure our population is maintained."

"Why do you think that is?" asked Aarow, genuinely curious.

"The people in the Capital aren't used to change of any kind," said Sharma. "My guess is that the Chairman is afraid if rules are amended, then it's only a matter of time before people start to question his position. One change could lead to many. His power depends on total acceptance of the rules."

"I never thought about it like that," said Azrael. "But I think you're right."

The Colonel nodded. "So, to answer Rani's question, with the population falling, and morale within the Capital at an all-time low, we believe our chances right now are stronger than ever. Especially with the three of you on our side. You can give us an insight none of the other reborns have been able to. But you have to want this as much as we do. You have to trust us."

"We trust you," said Rani, looking between Aarow and his father. "And you're right. Someone has to do something. Everyone is suffering, apart from the Chairman himself. There will be no Capital to invade if things are left much longer."

"So, will you work with us?" asked the Colonel.

Rani sat forward on her seat. "Will you promise me the safety of my father?"

Aarow swallowed hard, hating to make promises he wasn't sure he'd be able to keep. Taking the Emperor down was a key part of their battle plan. Whether or not he was harmed depended on how he reacted. If he fought back, it'd be almost impossible for him not to be hurt. Although, nobody would have rated the chances of these three women making it here alive. Sometimes the impossible was possible.

The Colonel lay his hands on the table. "As I said before, we'll do our best to make sure nobody gets hurt. This includes the Emperor."

"What do you think?" Rani asked her two friends. "Should we trust these men? Will we work with them?"

Sharma nodded. "I don't think we have much of a choice. This seems our best chance to bring change to the Capital. As long as nobody gets hurt."

"The Colonel said we'll do our best," said Aarow, wanting to make things perfectly clear. "We can't promise nobody will get hurt. All we can do is promise to try."

"And what do you think, Azrael?" asked Rani. "What have your dreams told you?"

Azrael pulled her shoulders back and nodded at Rani. "It needs to happen."

Rani looked eyes first with Aarow and then his father. "Then we will work with you."

"It really is just like my dream," said Azrael.

"Did your dream have an ending?" asked Aarow, curious to hear more.

She shook her head. "No dream ever has an ending. They end when you wake up."

Aarow thought about this for a moment. "Then let's hope we wake up smiling. It's time to go to war."

SPECTOR

THE BATTLE

Spector flapped his arms to make his feet go faster. The Colonel had told him not to go far, which was difficult as he was used to flying at his own speed. He was an eagle—a lone bird—not a sparrow drifting with a flock in the currents of the sky. However, he was an eagle who wanted to please, so he made sure he listened to the Colonel, swooping back every now and then so he didn't get too far ahead.

He hadn't thought he'd be allowed to play the Battle game when he'd heard the grown-ups talking about it. Then the Colonel had reminded him that he was a grown up and said he could come. Father agreed, but Mother didn't, and his parents had a big fight about it. Eventually, Father convinced Mother and here he was now. Ready to play Battle.

The Colonel needed him. He was fast and strong and brave. Best of all, he knew how to stop being an eagle and start being a coyote. He could watch someone from the dunes, as if stalking his prey, and they'd have no idea he was even there. The Colonel said he'd saved lots of lives doing this. He was an important member of the Colony.

He'd even saved the life of a Princess. And a baby. Even if it was an annoying baby who never stopped crying. He had a stupid name too. Horrie the Horrible. Spector didn't tell anyone he called him that. People didn't like it if you said mean things about a baby. It wasn't *nice*. And Spector tried to be nice as much as he could. He couldn't help it if sometimes a not nice thought got stuck in his head. He asked Mother about this once and she said it didn't matter so much if you had a bad thought, what counted was what you did with that thought. And he'd always done good things with his thoughts.

He pushed his hair back off his face and glanced back to the flock, realizing he was getting too far away, so he turned to swoop back. There were over a thousand birds behind him. Men birds and women birds. Everyone in the Colony who was fit to travel had come. Only the young and old had stayed behind. Spector had always wondered why life was like that. You got born hopeless, like Horrie the Horrible, then slowly you got good at things, then you ended up hopeless again. It didn't seem fair. He planned never to get hopeless. Eagles soared until the day they died.

The Colonel had said it'd take all day and some of the night to reach their rest spot. Spector didn't want to rest. They'd done a lot of training for the Battle game. This was mainly breaking up into groups and pretending to fight each other. It seemed like a bit of a waste of time. Surely there weren't people out there who'd hurt each other on purpose? Mother always said there was nothing like a good cup of black sage tea and a chat to sort problems out. He'd asked the Colonel if they should try that first, but he said no, which was disappointing. Then again, Mother had lost the argument with Father about him playing Battle, so perhaps tea didn't always work. Better to do the training just in case, he supposed.

Sometimes, instead of training, the Colonel would talk to them, asking them questions and having ideas so he could figure out how to win. Battle sounded like a fun game, except the Colonel never smiled when he spoke about it. Aarow talked sometimes too. Spector liked Aarow. He was just like the Colonel with more smiles on his mouth. He'd be a good Colonel one day, too.

The Princess talked to them sometimes as well. She had a quiet voice, although the more she used it, the more it came out loud. The last time she spoke it was almost like a shout and everyone had clapped and whooped and cheered, making Spector wish he'd listened to her words put together, instead of how each one sounded when it came out.

She knew a lot about the Capital and Aarow said they were lucky to have her on their side. She was a special part of the Battle game. Spector had a secret bad thought about the Princess, too. He wondered if she was a little slow in her brain, because she didn't realize that if the Capital no longer ruled the kingdom then she wouldn't be a princess anymore. Spector had never heard of anyone who wouldn't want that. All the girls in the Colony followed Aarow around, keen to be a princess. Not that the Colonel's wife was technically a princess, but it was the closest they got to it in the Colony.

The older woman he'd spotted in the desert with the Princess had stayed behind at the Colony. She didn't want to, but Battle wasn't safe for Horrie the Horrible. It was hard to play at fighting when you were holding a baby. You'd lose that part of the game for certain.

The other girl was here with them, walking next to the Princess and talking like she was worried there'd be no words left if she stopped. Everyone thought the girl was younger than the Princess, but Spector knew she wasn't. He was good at guessing ages. This girl was the same age as the Princess, her face just hadn't caught up to her years. She was like the opposite of him.

Because as much as people thought Spector didn't know he was different from the rest of them, he did know. He knew that, as well as everything else he needed to know in life. Mother said the world needed lots of different people. She said he was perfect. There was no need for a cup of tea to convince him of that. He was a perfect eagle.

Spector raced off ahead, giving his wings an extra flap, keen to get started with the Battle game. They were going to win, for sure, for certain. And he had an important job to do as part of it. This was the happiest day of his life.

RANI

THE BATTLE

*R*ani huddled beside members of the Colony, no longer flinching when their shoulders bumped, or an outstretched foot tapped her on the knee. These were her people now. When the Colonel had referred to her as a reborn, she hadn't realized just how significant this was. She *had* been reborn. Or perhaps just-born would be even more appropriate, as she felt like she'd never lived before now.

Sitting in the dark at the bottom of a dune holding Azrael's hand felt like the most natural thing in the world. But in the last few turns —days, she reminded herself—she'd become aware of just how different this innocent gesture could be, depending on whose hand it was you held.

Once, in training, she'd been paired with Aarow and when she'd tried to fake punch him in the stomach, he'd caught her hand, firmly yet gently, and threaded his fingers through hers. It was no different to how she held her friend's hand now, yet it was nothing the same. Azrael's touch brought her calm and comfort. Aarow's touch sent every one of her senses into meltdown. She'd heard her lungs pull in a deep breath and hold it. She'd seen his pupils widen, turning his brown eyes to black, making her wonder if hers had done the same. She'd smelled his masculinity as his heart rate picked up a beat. And she'd tasted metal as she realized she'd been biting her bottom lip so hard she'd drawn blood. And in this way, she'd felt his touch, not just with her skin, but with her soul.

He'd let go of her hand and stepped back, choosing to partner with someone else on the next round and she wasn't certain if it was because her touch had meant the same to him or because it hadn't. She didn't know a lot about love and desire and how to pull them apart.

It was quiet in the dunes, given how many people lay in wait. The Colonel had been very clear about this. Not a sound could be allowed to rise with the wind, alerting the ears of the Capital. Surprise was one of their secret weapons.

The other was touch. For they'd brought no weapons with them other than their hands. If all went well, Rani also hoped to touch the people with her heart.

The moon was sliding slowly toward the dunes as night threatened to turn to day. The lower it got, the higher Rani's anxiety rose, and she felt her teeth grind, a habit she thought she'd left behind, along with her old life.

What she was about to do felt so much bigger than anything she'd done before, including running into the desert, for that had affected the lives of only four people, whereas this affected the lives of the entire kingdom, both in the Colony and the Capital.

The Colonel had said failure wasn't an option and he was right. If they revealed the existence of this hidden colony and failed to seize power, then their peaceful life was over.

Rani couldn't see how that could happen. They had the numbers. They had the strength. They had the determination. And they were working for the good. Surely that had to count for something? Azrael had said it didn't. Bad things happened to good people all the time. A darkness had crossed her eyes when she said that, and Rani's own eyes had filled with tears as they did whenever she was reminded how her friend had suffered in the Round. Aarow's friend, Jinn, had been paying Azrael a lot of attention since their arrival and Rani had watched her recoil from him, not because he wasn't a good person, but because he was a man and Azrael needed time to heal.

The only thing to be thankful for in that situation was that Azrael's time came again not long after their arrival, which meant there'd be no child to remind Azrael of what had happened to her. Not that Rani thought she'd ever be able to forget.

Rani's own time came, too. For real this time and she'd run to Sharma for help. It was like her body had been waiting until she was as far away from the Chairman as possible before it turned her into a woman.

Her thoughts were interrupted by the cry of an eagle, so realistic that Rani wondered if in fact, a real eagle had flown overhead rather than the imitation call they'd been told Spector would perform. That man had quite a talent! Rani had warmed to Spector immediately, but was puzzled by the strange way he looked at her when he wasn't hiding behind his hair. Like he wanted to ask her a question and didn't know how to phrase it.

Azrael squeezed her hand in the darkness and Rani could sense her fear through their fingers. She squeezed back to tell her she understood. It was the only way she could communicate right now.

The eagle cry came again and the Colony adjusted their scarves to cover their faces. They were dressed like anyone else in the Capital. Blending in would be the easy part. Taking control would be harder.

But greatness couldn't be achieved without hard work and risk. The Sands of Naar was entering a new phase in its history. There was no turning back now.

Let the battle for freedom begin.

AZRAEL

THE BATTLE

*A*zrael clutched Rani's hand, knowing it was time for her to say goodbye. This was where the Colony would divide into two groups. The borns and the reborns. Rani was the exception, as she'd been for most of her life. She'd be facing this battle alongside Aarow and the Colonel for reasons Azrael was yet to fully understand.

Never did Azrael think she'd willingly return to the Capital. Then again, never did she think she'd be part of a revolution, set to overthrow it. But she was returning as an enemy, not a friend. Actually no, that wasn't right. She was the friend. The Chairman was the only enemy here. It was important to remember that.

The reborns rose and stretched the cramps in their limbs as they sipped on their waterskins. Their job was different to the borns, but the Colonel had stressed it was no less important.

Azrael let go of Rani's hand and stood with them, ignoring the twisted knots in her stomach. Were they from nerves or excitement? Probably both. There was only one other time she remembered feeling like this, and that was in almost this very same spot, as she'd fled her former life in the Capital.

It was still dark and she couldn't see Rani's face, so imagined she was smiling at her. She smiled in return, wishing she could say good-bye. But not a sound was to be made. She was here to help, not to ruin everything with her inability to keep quiet.

Azrael headed with the reborns toward the Round. Before they could be spotted under the soft light of the clouded moon, the women turned to the left and the men to the right, making their way to the tents that once they called home.

There were probably only a hundred of them, but the strength of the energy that passed between them made it feel like there were a thousand. They may have left the Capital alone, but they were returning together.

Azrael was near the rear of the group and watched the shadows of the others divide once they entered the women's village. As much as they were working as a team, they each had an important role to play on their own.

She counted the rows of tents to be certain it was the fifth row she took. Then she counted the individual tents, searching for her own.

Would the woman she'd shared it with remember her? She wasn't sure. All she'd ever done was grunt at Azrael. She'd never even said a word. Perhaps it didn't matter if she remembered. As long as she listened to what she had to say. Ears always worked better when mouths were kept closed.

"Fifty-one, fifty-two, fifty-three, fifty-four…fifty-five," she counted under her breath.

There it was. The tent. Her tent. Or perhaps someone else slept on her mat now.

"Hello?" she whispered as she pulled back the animal skin and stepped inside.

If only this could be done in the daylight it'd be so much easier. She had no idea if there was even anyone inside.

"Hello?" she tried again. "It's me. Azrael. Do you remember? I shared this tent with you for a time. I need to speak with you."

She heard the ruffle of fabric and a soft glow filled the tent as a lantern sparked to life, the flame kept low so only the softest light was emitted.

There was a young girl, sitting on what had once been Azrael's mat, holding a lantern in front of her, the shadow of the flame dancing off the walls of the tent with the shaking of her hand. The grunting woman was staring at her from her mat, her expression neutral as if Azrael's sudden appearance was the most uneventful thing in the world.

"I remember you from the Growing Centre," the girl said, drawing Azrael's attention away from the woman.

Azrael nodded, although she struggled to recognize the girl in return.

"They said you were released. Where have you been?" she asked.

"We don't have much time," said Azrael, speaking quickly. Now that she had their attention, she had to get on with what she'd come here to do.

"Time for what?" the girl asked.

"I wasn't released," said Azrael. "I ran away, with Princess Rani and Sharma who once sat on the Board. We ran into the desert, hoping to cross the river and find a kingdom that treated us with respect." She paused to gauge how they were taking this news. The girl was wide-eyed and the woman had propped herself up on her elbows, finally deciding what Azrael had to say might be interesting.

"Why would the Princess leave?" asked the girl. "She was supposed to be our Empress one day."

"Because even she wasn't immune to the cruelty of the Chairman. She had no other choice."

"None of us have a choice." The girl set down the lantern and crossed her arms.

"We do!" Azrael crept closer to her. "We do have a choice. I don't have time to explain everything to you right now, so please just listen to what I have to say. We ran into the desert, making it as far as the river, and no further. The conditions were far more brutal than we'd ever imagined and we thought we were going to die. But just before death claimed us, we were rescued and brought to a Colony that thrives under the desert sand. The Colony is ruled by kindness and respect, instead of hatred and fear. Touch isn't evil, it's used to heal. Nobody must endure a touch they don't wish to receive and the touch of a loved one is welcome. People can marry and raise their babies, forming bonds that last forever."

The more Azrael spoke, the more the girl's eyes lit up. Her words hadn't just hit a nerve, they'd set her whole body alight with the possibility of escaping the misery that was her life.

"I want to go there," the girl said.

Azrael smiled. This was exactly the reaction she'd hoped for. "You don't have to go. The Colony has come to you. They want to overthrow the Board and set all of us free. Under their rule, we'll be able to live just as they do in the Colony."

"No more Conception Centre?" the girl asked.

Azrael shook her head. "Absolutely no more Conception Centre. That will be the first thing to go. It's been promised."

A grunt came from behind Azrael as the woman cleared her throat.

Azrael spun around to look at her, wondering if at last she was going to speak. She was sitting up, her eyes filled with tears.

"Talk to me," said Azrael.

The woman blinked slowly, staring hard at Azrael. "Will we be reunited with our children?" Her voice was soft, far more feminine than Azrael had expected.

"Yes." Azrael reached out to comfort her, then thought better of it, remembering how much time she'd needed to adjust to human touch. "You had a child?"

"I had many children," the woman replied, her voice breaking from not having been used for so long. "All taken from me at birth. I..."

Her voice trailed off and Azrael realized she'd judged this woman without understanding her story. If Azrael had babies torn from her, she doubted she'd want to get close to anyone else either. What was the point in a kingdom so cruel?

"What do you need us to do?" asked the girl, leaping to her feet.

Azrael stood beside her and waited as the woman joined them. She held out her hands, one to each of them with her palms facing up. "Please, take my hands. I promise nothing bad will happen. The stories you've been told about touch are a lie. It's time to release your fear. This is the most important thing you can do to change your lives."

The girl slipped her hand into Azrael's without a moment's hesitation, grinning broadly at the contact.

"I've always wanted to do that to someone," she said. "Your hand is so warm!"

Azrael waited as the woman glanced around the tent as if a guard may jump out any moment.

"You're safe," said Azrael. "Please, trust me."

The woman nodded and took hold of Azrael's hand, gripping it tightly. She held out her other hand and took the hand of the girl so they formed a circle.

"What do we do now?" the girl asked.

"We go and talk to the others," said Azrael. "I need your help. I haven't come here alone. Right now there are dozens of women just like me in the tents they once lived in, talking to the women they were never allowed to touch. In the men's village, the same thing is happening. We need to reach everyone with our message, and we need to do it quickly. Will you go to our neighbors and spread the word? We need everyone on our side if we're going to succeed."

Both the girl and the woman nodded, promising to help.

"What do we tell them to do?" the woman asked.

"Nothing. Tell them to do nothing. Not yet. Just stay outside the Round for now. The Board and any guards who choose to fight won't be able to defend the Capital on their own. Your job is to wait. And when the battle is over, your lives will become better than you can imagine. I promise you this."

"Thank you," the woman said. "I'm sorry I—"

"Please!" Azrael cut her off. "No apologies. You've done no wrong here. Quickly now. We have no time to waste."

They released their hands and left the tent, each of them choosing another that was dark and quiet.

The plan was working. Azrael just hoped the other reborns were having as much success as she'd just had. She hoped for so many things she felt like her chest might explode.

Desperation did that. Sometimes it consumed every ounce of your hope and other times it turned hope into the only thing you had left.

AAROW

THE BATTLE

Spector made the final eagle call and Aarow searched for Rani in the darkness. When they entered the Round, he needed to be by her side. It was going to be chaos and he had to protect her. It was his job to keep her safe. If she weren't such a key part of their plan, he'd have tried to convince her to stay behind in the Colony with Sharma. Although, he knew she'd never have agreed to any such thing.

He found her, the familiar shape of her small frame illuminated in the fading moonlight. She reached for his hands and clasped them. The breath rushed out of his lungs. When he'd tried to hold her hands in training, she'd had a strong reaction that he'd been certain was negative. It was only later when Jinn teased him about it that he realized he'd totally misread the situation. She felt what he felt. She just didn't know what to do about her feelings. Now that he thought of it, neither did he. He'd never met anyone like Rani before.

He fought the urge to ask if she was okay. Nobody was allowed to speak right now. It wouldn't look good if the son of the Colonel was the first to break this rule.

So, instead, he let go of her hands and brought his fingertips to her cheeks. She wasn't crying. He let his hands slip to her shoulders. She wasn't shaking. He put the palm of one hand gently on her chest to feel the rate of her heart. She was nervous, but she wasn't afraid.

She was okay. What she couldn't tell him in words, he could tell with his hands.

Before he could take his hand back, she reached for it and brought it to her lips, trailing a kiss across his knuckles and a message across his heart. And he knew without doubt that he'd die for this girl if he had to.

The Colony stepped forward, ready to swoop, jolting Aarow back into reality. They had a job to do and a battle to win.

He went to the front of the crowd with Rani by his side and the curved shadow of the giant wall loomed ahead of them. Aarow longed for the sun to rise so he could see it properly. It wouldn't be long now.

As they approached the archway that marked the entrance, Aarow felt his gut drop in the same way it did after kicking off down one of the dunes. There was no turning back. Forward was the only way to find his way through this, no matter how scared or exhilarated he was. The decision had been made and the time to back away had passed.

By now, hopefully the reborns had gathered the support of the people. It'd only take one of them to alert the guards and ruin their element of surprise. The reborns had reassured them this wouldn't happen. They said everyone was as desperate for change as they were. Life couldn't get any worse. They wouldn't ruin their one opportunity to break free from the rule of the Board.

They walked silently toward the Round in one large group. Their timing had to be perfect and Aarow was confident they had it right. It'd been Azrael's suggestion the battle take place on this exact day. She'd seen it in one of her dreams. Dreams that she said were getting more vivid since she'd arrived at the Colony. They were also dreams that made an awful lot of sense. It had to be today.

Because when the morning sun rose above the dunes and shone

through the archway, its rays would hit the Orbs of Time and fracture into a billion shards of shining color.

Today was the Shining.

The people would be gathered. The guards would be distracted. The Board would be standing around the orbs with the Emperor by their side—Rani's father who she was determined must be kept safe.

This was why the people had to be kept out of the Round. If they didn't, then it would overfill and the guards would be alerted that something was up. It was important they think this was just a Shining like any other. Besides, if the people panicked there'd be mayhem and if they wanted to take control peacefully then they needed everyone to remain calm. Everyone except the Board, that is. There'd be no peace for them.

The guards at the archway paid no attention as they walked through with their scarves tucked tightly around their faces and their eyes cast down. They looked just like any other citizen of the Capital here to witness the Shining. There was no reason for alarm. It was expected that people would gather here today.

There were lanterns placed at intervals around the lawn, casting a dim glow across the circular space. This was Aarow's first time in the Round and even though it was exactly as had been described to him, it felt strange to be here for himself. Everything was bigger than he'd imagined, making him feel like a small child. The Orbs of Time were spectacular, and they weren't even shining yet. He could see why they were prized as such a wonder. Who had made them and known exactly how many grains of sand were needed to be encased inside? Rani said nobody knew. Just as nobody knew how the blocks of stone had been dragged to the middle of a desert to create the walls of the Round. It just was.

The Colony spread out once they were inside, some seating themselves on the grass and others hovering around the edges. The reborns had described the Round in such detail that Aarow really did feel like he'd been here before. They all knew what to do.

Rani had told him the guards would close access to the Round when enough people had filed in. If it got too crowded, it'd be impossible to ensure that no shoulders were accidentally bumped. By their calculations, just about all members of the Colony should make it inside the walls. Those who didn't would need to stand outside the Round and watch the sparks of light pour out over the top of the walls into the morning sky.

Aarow and Rani intended to see the Shining from another vantage point altogether and he followed her now, around the curved path that hugged the lawn, to a doorway on the opposite side of the Round to the archway. It surprised him that accessing the palace could be so easy. With Rani's face covered, she could be anyone. Did these people live in such fear that even the thought of them doing anything wrong was unimaginable?

It was strange to be inside a building and still know he was above the ground. It wasn't cool inside, like in the Colony. And there were windows. It made him dizzy to be able to see the sky while having a roof over his head.

There was some furniture scattered around the entryway, the sort made out of trees and he resisted the urge to stop and touch it. It looked so smooth and shiny, not at all like the bark of a tree.

He followed Rani through a corridor to a staircase, not carved into the earth like the stairs at home but built from stone and curving in a spiral up and up and up. Did everything have to be made from circles just because they called this place the Round?

It was all so foreign to him. He could understand now why the reborns looked at the Colony with such wide eyes.

They got to the top of the stairs only to find a guard at the top, about to make his way down.

"Stop where you are!" The guard held up his hand.

Aarow waited quietly, ready to take on the guard if required. Passing him in peace was a better plan, if possible, and they'd already decided if this happened, then Rani would take the lead. This didn't sit well with Aarow's protective instincts, but he'd reluctantly accepted it was the way it needed to be for now. When he'd found her in the desert, they'd been on his territory. However, life within these stone walls was far more familiar to her than it was to him.

Rani unwound the veil from her face and the guard held up his lantern to get a better look at her.

"Princess Rani!" He shuffled back a step, his hand flying to his throat. "We were told you'd been released."

Rani straightened her back and tipped up her head, locking her gaze on him. "Well, as you can see, that's incorrect. Now, please step back and let us pass. The Shining is almost upon us. We don't have time for this."

The guard pressed his back to the wall.

"There's no need to tell anyone you saw me," said Rani, as she passed. Her voice was firm and unlike any tone Aarow had heard her use before. "Do you understand?"

The guard nodded and scurried down the stairs.

"Impressive," said Aarow, removing his scarf, needing relief from the warmth of the air. Rani had an authority about her that came only from being born into a role like she had. She didn't need to use volume or threats to get her way. It was the confident look in her eyes and level tone of her voice. She'd been right to insist he let her take the lead.

Rani went to a door at the end of a hallway and opened it, motioning for him to follow. This must be her bedchamber. The place she'd told him she'd spent almost her entire life, sitting at the window, watching the sand fall through the Orbs of Time. This room represented her past. He only hoped that he himself could be what represented her future.

For the more he'd gotten to know Rani since she'd arrived at the Colony, the more he'd felt a pull toward her. As the eldest child of the leader of her people, she understood him like nobody else had before. However, it was so much more than that. He'd watched her thrive in the Colony, like a flower that'd been deprived of water and now found itself standing in the middle of a river. At first, she'd been overwhelmed, but now she'd adjusted to her surroundings, she was in full bloom.

As he went to step into the room that held so much history for Rani, she came to such a sudden stop in front of him that he walked straight into the back of her.

"What's wrong?" he asked, restoring the distance between them as she backed out of the room.

She turned to him and stood on her toes, so she could speak directly into his ear. "There's someone sitting at my window."

The hair on the back of his neck stood up, both at the warmth of her breath on his skin and the words she spoke.

"Who?" And more importantly, how would this person affect their plans. They had no backup. A hiccup like this hadn't been allowed for.

"It's a boy," she said. "I think he might be my brother."

RANI

THE BATTLE

*R*ani stepped into her bedchamber to face the boy she was certain must be her brother—her father's second eldest child and new heir to the throne.

His eyes weren't focused out the window now. Instead, he'd turned to face her, waiting for her to return, the startled expression on his face revealing he knew exactly who she was.

Aarow touched her gently on her back, letting her know he was there and offering her the only crumb of comfort he could.

"Hello," she said to the younger, male version of herself. Did all her father's children resemble him so much?

He squinted at her as his forehead wrinkled and she decided he looked about fifteen Shinings old.

"I think I might be your sister. My name's Rani and this is my friend, Aarow. Are you the Emperor's son?"

"Rani," he said. "They told me you were released."

It was only when he spoke that she noticed he was shaking, his dark eyes blinking rapidly.

"You're scared," she said. "Please don't be scared of me. We're here to help you."

"My name's Taavi. They want to make me Emperor. I'm to stand at the window and Father will announce it after the Shining."

Rani wanted to run to him and throw her arms around his shaking shoulders, but she held her feet firm on the floor. She may have started to desensitize with all this touching, although Taavi wouldn't have. She didn't want to scare him away when she'd only just found him.

"You don't want to be Emperor?" she asked.

He blinked at her, not answering her question.

How foolish she'd been to assume her siblings would leap at the chance to take her place. All she'd done by running away from her troubles was transfer them to someone else.

"Taavi," she said, taking a few steps toward him. "I need you to trust me. And Aarow. He's here to protect me. And you now." She looked back at Aarow who was nodding his head in agreement, the kindness in his dark eyes shining through.

"What's going on?" Taavi asked, keeping his words simple.

"Something's about to happen in the Round. Aarow's people are going to take control of the kingdom. They're good people. He lives in a place called the Colony and has rescued hundreds of people who were released into the desert and given them a new and peaceful life. Right now, those people are returning to the homes they grew up in outside the Round and explaining exactly what I'm telling you now. The more of them who join us, the better the chance we have of over-throwing the Board."

"There's going to be a revolution?" Taavi asked, his eyes widening.

At these words, Aarow stepped forward. "Nobody should live in fear. We need to change all of that."

Taavi went back to the window and looked out. "What's your plan?"

"It will all be clear very soon," said Rani, standing beside him and looking out at the sky. "Don't worry. You don't need to do anything."

The Shining was about to burst into life, the tip of the sun just visible over the dunes.

"Aarow, come to the window," she said. "It's happening."

He joined them and they stood in a line. She let her hand fall and reached for Aarow's, hearing him draw in a breath of surprise at the contact. He enclosed his hand around hers, the size of his hand making her feel like a young girl.

But she wasn't a young girl. She was a woman now. A woman about to do something that would go down in history. She was grateful to have Aarow's support. And that of her brother, who she vowed to protect at all costs.

She looked down and could see the Board marching out of the palace to assume their positions, the eleven of them standing evenly spaced in a circle around the Orbs of Time, leaving a space for the Emperor. They all faced the archway, which meant they had their backs to the three silent observers, watching them from above.

If the Board had paid more attention and treated their people like individuals instead of numbers, they might have noticed the difference in the sets of eyes that surrounded them. It seemed that so far, nobody was any the wiser.

Sharma had been replaced on the Board by a woman Rani had seen around the palace. Rani hoped she'd switch her loyalties to the Colony easily. If indeed her loyalties lay with the Capital right now. It didn't seem fair that she'd only just stepped into this position and was about to face her first fight. Although, nothing in the Capital was fair. As long as she didn't fight back, then no harm would come to her.

Rani shuddered as she watched the Chairman walk to his position at the point of the orbs directly facing the archway, thankfully obscured from her view once he was in place. She didn't need his ugly soul to ruin possibly the last Shining she'd ever witness.

"Is that him?" asked Aarow, having heard what evil this man was responsible for.

"Yes," she whispered, swallowing hard as he gripped her hand tightly.

The Emperor came out of the palace next and took his place at the rear of the orbs. If he were to turn around and tilt up his face, he'd be looking directly at his eldest two children. Rani sent him a silent message of apology and love, thanking him for trying to save her from a future that spared nobody. She wanted him to know she was alive, to relieve his burden of guilt, but his eyes remained fixed straight ahead, his posture one of a man who thought he'd failed her.

"There it is," said Taavi, pointing, as the first ray of daylight hit the orbs and shattered into a thousand smaller rays of colorful light, bouncing off the stone buildings and back to the orbs where it splintered again.

More light came pouring through the archway, and soon the entire Round was bathed in color as the rays dazzled and sparkled, turning everything into some kind of magical land.

"Have you seen it from inside the Round before?" Rani asked Taavi.

"Never." He shook his head without lifting his eyes from the spectacular sight before him.

It was Rani's seventeenth time witnessing this miracle, created by her ancestors and performed by nature, not that she could remember her first few, of course. However, it was Aarow's first time and she shifted her attention to him now.

He was still squeezing her hand, the fingers of his other hand gently touching his parted lips as his head shook slowly from side to side.

Rani wasn't sure what was more beautiful. The Shining that she'd always cherished, or the enraptured face of this man who'd unexpectedly woven his way into her heart.

There was an eerie silence, with speaking banned during a Shining, as well as touch. This miracle of light was to be respected, and not a murmur was permitted.

As she cast her eyes back to the Round, she looked not at the light, but at the people, noticing members of the Colony getting into position, two of their strongest fighters assigned to tackle each Board member. The rest had their focus on the guards. The Colonel had been assigned to the Emperor and he stood close by, ready to ensure no harm came to Rani's father as the power of his kingdom was swept from under his feet.

"When does the revolution start?" asked Taavi, his voice a whisper as if he could be heard from the pit of silence below.

"Any moment," Rani said. "There'll be an eagle call and we'll swoop. Everyone is ready now. We need the element of surprise. Nobody is expecting this."

Taavi leaned out of the window, squinting his eyes as he tried to see who was ready and how.

Rani smiled at her brother and his keenness to play a part in over-throwing this kingdom.

"See there," she said, keeping her own voice low as she pointed to two men inching closer to one of the Board members.

Taavi's dark eyes widened, as if the reality of what was about to happen just dawned and he leaned further out the window.

Rani squeezed Aarow's hand and released it, feeling awkward in front of her brother, who hadn't seemed to notice their contact yet. Just as her hand broke away from Aarow's, a noise echoed across the Round, taking Rani a moment to realize it had come from her own brother's lips.

"Beware!" he shouted, waving his arms wildly. "An invasion's upon us! Beware!"

Rani's world spun faster than ever before, as several things happened at once.

She saw her father turn and look up at the window, his mouth falling open as he locked eyes with her.

She felt Aarow push past her as he grabbed hold of Taavi and placed his palm across his mouth to silence him.

She heard the eruption of noise in the Round as people moved and pounced and screamed and ran.

She smelled the fear as Taavi twisted from Aarow's grasp and put space between them in the only way he could find.

The window.

He climbed onto the windowsill, telling Aarow to keep his hands off him.

Aarow raised his palms as a sign of peace, but even this simple movement caused Taavi to panic and lose his balance.

He toppled, and Rani reached out and grasped his shirt, but the fabric tore in her hands and down he fell, his arms flailing and his legs kicking as he fought against the pull of gravity as it raced him to his death.

And once again she locked eyes with her father who stood frozen, the only body in the Round not in motion apart from her brother, who was never going to move again.

Their element of surprise was ruined and the peaceful revolution had turned to panic. To think that of all the people in the kingdom and the person to betray them had been standing right by Rani's side. She'd failed her kingdom in the worst possible way.

Her confidence in the revolution's success lay in pieces alongside the broken body of her brother—the person she'd failed the most.

This was anyone's war now.

AAROW

THE BATTLE

*A*arow looked at the giant Orbs of Time wishing there was a way to draw the sand back up and reverse time.

Rani's brother had fallen from the window and was unmistakably dead. And it was all his fault.

"Taavi!" Rani called out. Her eyes locked on her father, who was still staring up at the window.

"I'm so sorry," Aarow said, drawing her away before she leaped from the window herself.

"He's dead," she said, as if saying it out loud would help her believe it.

"I know. I really am very sorry." He felt his shoulders drop as if the weight of holding them up was too much with all the guilt piled on top.

"Oh, Aarow," said Rani, turning her back to the window. "Please don't take the blame for this. You were only trying to keep him quiet. He could so easily have ruined everything. If you hadn't grabbed him, I'd have done the same."

He was glad it hadn't come to that. There was no way he wanted

Rani to carry this burden for the rest of her life. This was something he alone was going to have to learn to come to terms with himself.

"Why did he do it?" Aarow shook his head, trying to shake the image of the falling boy from his mind.

She put a hand gently on his arm. "I'm no expert on people, but I think he was scared."

"Of my touch or the revolution?"

"Both," she said. "He seemed scared of...everything."

The noise in the Round took on a new level and they went back to the window, knowing there wasn't time to discuss this now.

People were moving in all directions, screaming with both excitement or fear, depending on which side of the battle they were on.

Aarow's eyes went straight to Taavi's body and he saw the Emperor standing over him, trying to protect him from being stepped on, but not seeming to know how to do this while avoiding touch, both of the people and his son.

"He needs help," said Rani.

"Colonel!" Aarow called from the window, trying to get the attention of his father who was busy calling out orders to his people, directing them to bring him the members of the Board.

"I have to go to Taavi," said Rani. "This isn't right. We need to move him out of the way."

"No," said Aarow firmly, knowing she was safer up here, but also that she was right. Ensuring Taavi's body was treated with respect was the least he could do given he was responsible for the life having just flowed out of it. "I'll go."

"We'll both go," she said, her eyes lighting up.

He shook his head. "You're needed here. It's part of the plan. You know that."

Perhaps he shouldn't leave her. His part in the plan was to protect her. What would happen if the people stormed the building? Everyone would want a piece of the princess. What if the Chairman broke free? He couldn't risk anybody getting their hands on Rani, whether they were the Chairman or not. Things could turn very quickly in situations like this.

"Aarow, we have to hurry!" Rani pointed to the archway. The gates had been forced open and people were pouring into the Round now. Soon, it'd be impossible to fight his way from the palace doors and reach Taavi before his body was trampled.

He had to make a decision. And fast.

"I'll only go if you promise to stay here," he said, taking a step toward the door. The only thing riskier than her staying behind was having her out there in the chaos in the Round.

"I want to come with you," she said.

He shook his head. "We need you here. Please. I'll just go to Taavi and then I'll be right back."

"Then go!" She seemed to know he meant what he'd said. He wouldn't leave if she insisted on coming with him. "Hurry."

"Don't move from this room. Do you understand?" He looked deep into her eyes, hoping he could trust her on this.

"I'll be right here," she said. "You'll be able to see me at the window."

He had no choice but to believe her. He had to get to Taavi's body. It didn't matter how badly he'd betrayed them. He was only a boy. A boy who'd been raised in one of the most brutal and confusing places that could ever be dreamed up. He could hardly be blamed for his actions. He hadn't deserved to die for what he'd done.

Aarow looked at Rani one last time, swearing that when he returned to her safely, he was never going to leave her side again.

He closed the door behind him and heard her slide some kind of lock into place. They didn't have locks in the Colony as their doors were made from thatch. They didn't see the need for them either. Although, right here, right now, a lock was an excellent idea.

Stepping out of the palace into the battle was even more of a shock than stepping from the Colony into the hot sun. This wasn't just like hot soup, it was a whirlpool of boiling determination and rage.

Aarow's eyes swept the Round. Men and women alike were taking hold of the guards and Board members, grabbing them with bare hands as they shrank back in terror, not accustomed to being manhandled.

When this kingdom had been attacked with arrows or cannons, they'd successfully defended themselves from a distance. But the Colony had known that hand-to-hand combat was their weakness, with the simple placing of a hand on a shoulder seen as an assault. Lack of touch was supposed to be what saved their kingdom, only right now it was their downfall.

All this time, the Shining continued, casting rays of light across the Round, bringing the faces of the people into sharp focus. More people were running into the Round, impossible to tell which side they were on, for they were all dressed the same, until they revealed themselves with the fearless way they touched anyone who stood in their way.

Aarow looked up and scanned the windows for Rani, seeing her leaning out as she searched for him in return. She saw him and pointed to her brother, urging him to hurry.

This side of the Round wasn't as crowded as the entrance and he spotted Taavi's small body with the Emperor bent over him. His own father was standing a mere few paces away, too caught up issuing instructions to be of any assistance. Or perhaps not seeing much need at this point. He wouldn't even know who Taavi was or why it was important to bring his body to safety.

Aarow ran toward the Emperor, only to be forced to grind to a halt when a guard stepped in front of him and held up his hands.

"Stop!" the guard said. "Nobody touches the Emperor."

The guard was a tall man. Broad too. Not the sort of man anyone would choose to pick a fight with. Aarow guessed he did his job as a guard well. Until now. Because Aarow was determined to get past him.

"Move out of my way," Aarow said, taking a step. "Nobody needs to get hurt."

The guard waved his two gloved hands like a flag. "Stop! Now!"

Aarow really didn't have time for this. The Round was filling with more people with every moment that passed. He had to move Taavi's body.

Aarow raised his hands and positioned his feet firmly on the ground. He'd been training for this moment his whole life. He was ready.

The guard flinched at Aarow's stance, not used to anybody defying his instructions or perhaps preparing himself for whatever was coming next.

"Last chance to move," said Aarow.

Instead of stepping aside, the guard reached out to grasp Aarow by the shoulders. Aarow was ready for this and deflected him by snapping out his forearms in a quick, practiced action. The guard recovered quickly and went to grab him again, but again Aarow anticipated his move and took hold of the guard's dominant arm and twisted it behind his back.

Aarow placed his free hand on the guard's shoulder, not because he needed it there to hold him still, but because he wanted the guard to see the bare skin of his hand touching him.

It had the desired effect and the guard yelped, trying to break free of Aarow's hold. The more he struggled, the more pain was inflicted. This guard may be tall, but Aarow was strong. And he knew exactly how to hold him in place.

Standing behind him now, Aarow pulled the guard in close until his torso was pressed up against him, feeling the guard squirm.

"If you don't move, it won't hurt," he hissed in the guard's ear. "We've come here to help you, not to cause you pain. Have you ever wondered who your parents are? If one of the women you walk beside each day is your mother or your sister? Have you ever wanted to meet your son? Surely a big man like you has had a son. I wonder if he looks like you."

The guard groaned. It was the sound of a man in mental anguish more than the sound of a man in physical pain. Aarow had hit a nerve as he thought he might if he appealed to his ego. A big man like this would no doubt want to produce a carbon copy of himself.

"We're here to change all of that," continued Aarow. "You'll be able to find your son. You'll be able to live in peace. No more releasing innocent people into the desert. Surely that's not part of your job that you enjoy?"

The guard grunted. "They were only released if they broke the law!"

"What if the law itself is what's broken?" As Aarow spoke, he saw a woman run dangerously close to Taavi's body, almost tripping over him. The Emperor called something out to her as he threaded his fingers through his hair and knelt on the ground beside his son.

Aarow needed to wrap this up.

"I'm going to give you two choices here," he said. "In a moment, I'm going to let go of you. You can choose to fight me again, and I promise that you'll lose. Or you can join with me and fight by my side. I'm not going to hurt your Emperor."

Without waiting for a reaction, he let go of the guard, and ran toward Taavi and the Emperor. As expected, the guard didn't make chase, choosing instead to stand in his place with his eyes blinking and his mouth agape. He'd join the revolution. Aarow was certain of it. Nobody liked to back the losing side.

THE EMPEROR

THE BATTLE

The Emperor crouched over his dead son, his heart overflowing with sadness for the boy who'd come into his life as quickly as he'd just departed.

Taavi was a confused boy, so different to his older sister, who'd run into the desert with no concern other than escaping the clutches of the Chairman. And now here she was, having not just returned to the Round, but having returned with an army. An army who were quickly seizing power, no matter whether the surprise of their arrival had been ruined or not. How had Rani achieved such a thing?

For there was no doubt that this was what was happening. Power was being seized. And he couldn't be happier about it, especially if Rani was at the helm. Which kingdom had she convinced to help her? Surely it must be Wintergreen.

A woman holding a guard firm in her grasp, bumped into him as she passed, sending the Emperor wobbling as he tried not to topple onto his son's body. He held out his hands to catch his fall, when he felt a firm grasp around his waist as he was hauled to his feet.

"Don't hurt me!" the Emperor cried, recoiling at the feeling of another human's hands upon on.

He twisted his head to see the man who held him was the same one he'd seen standing next to Rani in her window. The man released his grasp and shook his head. "I'm not going to hurt you. Rani won't allow it."

"Who are you?" the Emperor asked, straightening his back, as he tried to lessen the height difference between them. He knew he wasn't the bravest man in the kingdom, but he had some self-respect. He was the Emperor of The Sands of Naar.

"My name's Aarow. I found Rani in the desert and brought her to safety. We've returned to save the rest of you before it's too late."

"Well, it's too late for my son," the Emperor said, trying to decide if he could trust this man who bore the name of a weapon. Was that a good omen or a bad one? He guessed that depended on whether or not he'd actually saved Rani.

"I'm sorry about your son," Aarow said. "I wasn't fast enough to stop him from falling."

There was something in Aarow's eyes that swayed the Emperor into believing him. A sadness tinged with sincerity. He was here to help them.

Now wasn't the time to ask what happened or why Taavi had jumped from the window. Not with all the mayhem surrounding them.

The invaders were dragging the Board members to the steps of the palace and the Emperor wondered if Aarow was going to do the same to him and if so, why he hadn't taken hold of him by now.

"I'm not going to touch you," Aarow said, as if reading his mind. "But I am going to touch your son. We need to move him out of the way."

The Emperor nodded, grateful that someone had come to his aid at last.

"Thank you," he said, watching as Aarow lifted Taavi's body as if it weighed nothing. How must it feel to possess that kind of physical strength? Yet the gentle way Aarow cradled Taavi in his arms convinced the Emperor that this was indeed a kind man.

Aarow carried Taavi to the top of the palace stairs and took him inside, out of harm's way. Not that anything could harm him further now.

A wave of despair for his son washed over the Emperor. He'd never even gotten to know him. It wasn't right. None of this was.

The sun shifted in the sky and the Shining came to a close. Would he live to see another? Would anybody? Please let these new rulers of their kingdom not destroy the Orbs of Time. Although, he knew if Rani had anything to do with it, the orbs would be safe. Nobody appreciated their magnificence more than she did, even if sometimes he wondered if she looked at them more with dread than delight.

The Board members seemed to have accepted their fate and stood with their eyes cast down, having realized things may go more in their favor if they complied. But not the Chairman. He struggled against the captors holding him firmly by his forearms. When he attempted to kick them, they twisted his arms behind his back and held him at a distance while he yelped for mercy.

The Emperor hid a smile, feeling no sympathy for the heartless man who'd caused his daughter such anguish. Let him feel what it was like to have no control over who put their hands on you and how.

The Round was filling with people now, shoulder to shoulder and hip to hip as they pressed themselves into the communal space, eager to see what was to come of this most unusual invasion. Some of the faces the Emperor recognized and he wondered what the invaders had told them in order to bring them on their side. Although, it wouldn't have had to be much. When you handed a prisoner a key to their cell, they didn't usually stop to ask you why, before turning the key in the lock.

A tall man paced the line of Board members, inspecting them one by one, pausing longer at the Chairman to spit on the ground at his feet. This must be their leader.

He turned to face the crowd, fully trusting his soldiers who held his captives still, cleared his throat and held up his hand.

The crowd fell still and silent, including the guards who'd been captured, many of whom had been released and stood side-by-side with the people.

The man spoke. "We come here in peace."

"Doesn't feel too peaceful to me," shouted the Chairman, putting up a new struggle for release, quickly silenced by another twist of his arms.

"For too long the Capital has been ruled by fear. And we're here to tell you that we've had enough!" The man's voice echoed off the walls, bouncing in the same way the light had only moments before.

"Enough!" called out someone in the crowd and the Emperor found himself nodding, along with the rest of his people.

"My name is the Colonel," the man said. "I am your new Board. I am your new Emperor. I am the new leader of this kingdom." A murmur traveled across the Round as people took in this news. The Emperor himself felt no angst at these words, not feeling as if any power had been taken from him. He'd never had any in the first place.

"But I will not rule alone," the Colonel shouted. "Look to the window above and you'll see your Princess."

The Emperor followed the collective gaze of the crowd to Rani's window and she leaned out, so they could see her better. Aarow had returned to her side and was hovering next to her as if he were her private guard. The Emperor was glad. She'd be safe with a strong man like that to protect her.

"You may be surprised to see me," Rani called out, her voice loud and clear. "You were told that I was released."

The Emperor tilted his head, surprised at her confidence. What had happened to her out in the desert? She was like a different person. She'd left the Capital as a shy girl, yet somehow a girl filled with confidence had returned in her place.

"The truth is that I released myself." Rani's words sent a ripple through the crowd. "I released myself rather than have my rights violated by a kingdom that's been violating its people for generations. The Colonel is right. We live in fear. And those days are over. For I join with the Colonel in saying that it is *enough*."

"Enough! Enough! Enough!" the people chanted, the joy in their faces, lighting a fire in the Emperor's core. His beautiful daughter had these people on her side.

"I went to the desert as many of our people have done before, some by choice, although many by force. I was close to death when the man standing beside me came to my rescue. His name's Aarow and he's the Colonel's son."

His son? The Emperor hadn't picked up on the resemblance, although it did explain the confident way Aarow carried himself.

"One day, Aarow will be your leader," said Rani. "He's a good man, just like his father. These people who stand beside you now aren't from another kingdom. These are people of The Sands of Naar, who live a peaceful life in the desert."

A murmur traveled across the crowd and the Emperor drew in a breath, trying to process what Rani had just said. These people had come from the desert? It was hard to fathom that they were able to survive. He'd always been certain the Capital was the only place to house human life in the kingdom. To think that this whole time there'd been another settlement.

"These people follow their leader," continued Rani. "Not from fear, but from deep respect. Many of our people who were released have joined them and stand with you now. I myself have joined them. And I ask you, all of you, to join us now. The sun has risen on a new Shining. Let this be the Shining of peace, dignity, and respect. Let this be the Shining of freedom. Who stands with me?"

The Emperor's eyes stung with tears, as he looked up at the incredible woman who'd blossomed from the young girl he'd helped raise. The young girl who he'd been unable to protect but had just proven she knew how to protect herself.

Rani and Aarow held their hands out the window and pressed their palms together, lacing their fingers together.

The Emperor watched as the most incredible sight formed in front of him. Members of the crowd grasped hands with the person beside them and held them in the air, the chain of flesh they formed, a symbol of the breaking of the chains that'd bound them in place for so long.

He stepped back into the crowd and the two people behind him released their hands to welcome him in, taking one of his hands each and hoisting them into the air.

"Enough!" someone called over the rumble of the crowd and soon they were chanting once more. "Enough! Enough!"

The people had had enough. Rani may never become the Empress of The Sands of Naar, but she was most definitely the Empress of all their hearts.

He looked to her window and she smiled at him, enjoying the sight of him hand in hand with his people, not as their leader, but as one of them.

The Emperor opened his mouth and shouted to his daughter as his chest burst with pride. "Enough!"

RANI

THE AFTER

"We did it," said Rani, still holding Aarow's hand out the window.

"We did," said Aarow.

"Then why does it feel a little like we lost?" she asked, unable to shake the sadness that'd gripped her since Taavi slipped from her fingertips.

"Because one death was one too many." He seemed to understand her grief in an instant. Was that because he was feeling it too?

"Where did you take him?" she asked, dropping his hand and stepping away from the window.

"To a room near the bottom of the stairs," he said. "He's out of harm's way."

She nodded. All the mayhem was outside the palace, not within. "Thank you."

"Does it upset you that you won't be Empress now?" he asked, brushing her hair back from her face in such a natural movement she barely registered she'd been touched.

"Bother me?" She sighed. "I never wanted to be Empress. Not if my opinions don't count. What's the point? At least you know when you're the Colonel one day, you'll be able to shape the Colony—the whole kingdom, now—in the best way you see fit."

"Rani, maybe..." Aarow hesitated in a way that was unusual for someone normally so sure about themselves.

He looked away from her and she touched him gently on the arm. "What is it?"

Before he could answer her, the noise coming from the Round lifted and they returned to the window to see what the commotion was about.

The Colonel was directing his people to bring the Board members inside the palace and as they were led away, the revelers in the Round were hollering suggestions about what they thought should be done with them. None of the suggestions were kind.

"Kill them!"

"Release them!"

"Throw them to the coyotes!"

"Strip them of their clothes!"

Rani felt her stomach drop. This wasn't the kingdom of peace they'd been trying to create. Had they given the people back their dignity only to have them crying for it to be taken from someone else?

As the last of the Board members were led away, the Colonel turned to address the crowd once more, holding up his hand and waiting for quiet.

"Today is a day of celebration. But it's also a day of judgment. These Board members will be given a fair trial. If they cooperate, they'll be shown mercy. If not, they'll be dealt with. We mustn't replace cruelty with more cruelty. Please be kind to each other. A new future awaits."

Rani let out a long breath, pleased the Colonel was thinking along the same lines. She'd been right to align herself with him.

The crowd murmured their agreement as the Colonel turned to follow the Board inside, motioning for the Emperor to come with him.

"Your father's quite the speaker," Rani said to Aarow.

"You're not so bad yourself." He closed one eye quickly and grinned.

"What was that?" she asked. "That thing you just did with your eye?"

"You mean, nobody's ever winked at you?" He closed his eye again and she laughed at the absurdity of it, as she tried to do it back. What a strange thing to do.

"What does it mean?" she asked, giving up as she decided that both her eyes liked to close at the same time.

"It means someone's joking or having fun. It can also mean someone likes you." He winked again, more slowly, with a different kind of smile on his face. One that tugged at the edges of her stomach in all the best ways.

"Do you like me?" she asked, feeling her teeth slide over each other and trying to stop herself. She wasn't frightened of Aarow. Well, not frightened that he'd hurt her. He did make her nervous though, and nerves and fear were closely related.

"I like you a lot," he said, reaching for her, and letting his hands fall before he made contact.

"You're scared to touch me," she said, looking at his hands.

"You're scared of my touch," he replied, his pupils expanding over the dark brown of his irises.

"I held your hand during the Shining." She blinked up at him.

"I don't want to rush you." He bit down on his bottom lip, another gesture she was unfamiliar with, yet one that evoked an entirely different set of emotions in her than his wink had done.

They stood, looking at each other in silence, as if their minds could explain how they were feeling without the need for words.

"I *am* scared of your touch," she said. "But I'm more scared of what will happen if you don't touch me."

He leaned toward her, taking in her every reaction to his movements. She held steady, not wanting to do anything that might cause him to pull away. Sharma had told her that people in generations gone by had pressed their lips together in a kiss, and she'd witnessed such kisses in the Colony. Was she about to experience this strange and complex action herself for the first time?

His lips came closer to hers. So close. Still, he didn't touch her.

She blinked. Waited. Drew in a breath and wondered what it would feel like to kiss the man who'd saved her life. The man she'd come to admire in so many different ways.

His face hovered before hers as if frozen in time and he hesitated, not pulling away, but not coming any closer.

It was then that she stepped onto her toes and lifted her face, pressing her lips to his. She had to be the one to close the gap between them. It was the only way to let him know his touch was welcome. That she wanted him as much as he seemed to want her.

He kissed her so gently it felt like she was being swept into a cloud. His lips were soft, and she could feel the prickle of the dark bristles sprouting from his face. The contrast was intoxicating. It was no wonder people in the Colony had seemed so obsessed with kissing.

She attempted to kiss him back, unsure exactly what to do, following his lead as she let what felt natural take over, and soon she felt her lips parting as her heart pumped hard and her breath caught in her throat. The cramp in her stomach tightened and she pulled back, worried she was having some kind of problem with her health. Was this a normal response?

"I'm sorry," Aarow said, stepping away and putting his fingers to his lips. "Was that too much?"

She nodded, taking comfort from the soulful depths of his eyes. "Too much. And not enough."

"Oh, Rani," he said, breathing a sigh. "What have you done to me?"

"To you?" Her eyes widened as she clutched her chest. "That kiss almost killed me."

"I'm sorry."

"Will you do it again?" she asked.

His laugh was as loud as his kiss had been gentle. "Let's not rush this. We have a lot to do right now. We need to find my father. We have a Board meeting to attend."

"Oh. Of course, we do." Rani pushed down the disappointment at having to wait to experience another one of Aarow's kisses and turned her attention to what she was about to face.

The Chairman.

Only this time she was going to be the one to decide his fate. The Colonel had promised her that. He may have used the word 'mercy' in his speech to the people, but Rani had another word in mind.

Justice.

AAROW

THE AFTER

*A*arow followed Rani through the palace, trying to sort out the racing of his mind before they found his father.

The Colony had successfully overthrown the Capital and set the people free from its vicious laws, and all he could think about was how Rani's lips had felt underneath his own. Did that make him a terrible future leader? Or just an excellent future husband? Because if he got his way, that was exactly what he'd be to Rani one day. He'd almost said as much, just before the commotion outside the window had distracted them. He'd wanted to tell her that although she'd never be Empress of The Sands of Naar, that perhaps one day she'd still rule the kingdom. For when he took on the Colonel's role, he didn't intend to do it alone. He wanted a strong woman by his side who could balance out all the sides of him that he knew left him lacking.

He'd become certain Rani was that woman and together they could rule the kingdom, far better than either of them could do alone. Perhaps they could still call her Empress. After all, the Colonel was a made-up title. What did it matter what names they gave themselves?

It was for the best he'd kept these thoughts to himself for now.

Because one of the sides of Rani that was a contrast to himself was that although she was wise, she lacked confidence. She didn't really know who she was, let alone who he was and whether she could trust him. He didn't want to scare her away, having seen what happened the last time someone tried to force themselves upon her.

If they were meant to be together, then she had to come to him, just like she had with that incredible kiss. It'd taken all his self-control not to deepen that kiss. But just like his father had to go slowly with his mother when he'd found her in the desert, he too had to move slowly with Rani. If he moved too fast, he'd send her running in the opposite direction. Although, at least with Rani she hadn't been violated in the same way as his mother. Hopefully, her wounds were easier to heal.

"We're almost at the Boardroom," said Rani, coming to a stop. "I'm certain that's where my father will have taken them."

"Are you ready for this?" Aarow asked. "You don't have to come inside. I'll make sure the Chairman gets his dues."

"Aarow, you've been my savior and my protector, and I appreciate that. But now I need to step up and do this for myself. I'm not as weak as people think I am."

His heart almost beat to a stop. "Rani! People don't think you're weak. I've never thought that. Even when I found you underneath that tree, I knew you were strong. You've proven that ever since."

"Thank you." She lifted her lips into a smile, yet her eyes remained distant. Clearly, she was focused on the Chairman now and what she needed to do. He liked that. Part of being a good leader was being able to compartmentalize your feelings when needed.

They descended a set of curved stairs and reached a set of double doors, made from solid wood.

Rani drew in a deep breath and opened them.

Ten men and one woman were seated at a large round table with members of the Colony standing behind them, ready to remind them who was really in charge here.

Aarow's father was pacing the room as he spoke, stopping mid-sentence when he noticed their arrival. He nodded at Aarow with just the hint of a smile on his lips. There'd be time for celebrating their victory later. Right now, it was time for business.

"Excellent timing," he said. "I was just asking the members of this Board for their honest opinion on the laws they've been enforcing here."

Aarow nodded, watching as Rani went to her father's side.

"My daughter," he heard her father say.

Those two had so much to talk about. But Aarow's father had kept his promise and no harm had come to Rani's father, who did seem to be genuinely pleased the revolution had succeeded. Rani had been right to put her faith in him.

Rani reached for the Emperor's hand and held it in her own in the most loving and awkward handshake Aarow had ever witnessed. It was strange seeing them together like this. The similarities between them were striking. Although, there was something around Rani's eyes that wasn't quite like her father, yet familiar nonetheless. Aarow's jaw fell open when he realized whose face made up the missing parts to Rani's features.

Before he had a chance to process this, his father spoke again, in a tone that was not to be ignored.

"This here is the Jobs Master," said the Colonel, looking from Aarow to a rotund man, quivering in his seat. "I'm told he assigns all the jobs in the kingdom, whether people wish to do them or not. He's also released many who haven't been happy with their assignments, despite their willingness to contribute elsewhere."

Aarow nodded, remembering the story Azrael had told him back at the Colony about the assignment she was given that she chose never to take up.

"I'm sorry!" the man said, putting his head in his hands.

"Please look at us while you speak," boomed Aarow's father, having heard the same story from Azrael and finding sympathy hard to come by right now.

"I've done wrong! The laws are wrong! I'll do anything you say. Anything! Just please don't release me. It's dark in the desert. I'm afraid of the dark."

Aarow saw his father stifle a smile.

"May I make a suggestion?" asked Aarow, coming forward to stand beside his father.

"Of course." His father pulled his face into a serious expression, aware that someone's fate was in his hands.

"Perhaps we can ask this master of jobs to assign himself a new job, now that his role's no longer required? One he feels is appropriate for someone who's done wrong, as he's said so himself."

"Excellent. Yes." The Colonel clapped his hands. "Please assign yourself a job. What will it be?"

The Jobs Master lifted his head, glancing around the room as if to confirm he really was going to be allowed to live.

"I'd make an excellent weaver," he said.

"Try again," said Aarow, aware this was the job Azrael had requested for herself and been refused.

"Hunter?" he suggested, raising his eyebrows in hope.

"Not a chance we're putting a weapon in your hands," Aarow said.

"Guard?"

Aarow sighed, not seeing the need to give this a response.

"Supply worker?"

"I was thinking something a little more...hands on," said Aarow, waiting for him to come to the realization he wasn't going to get off this lightly.

"The Growing Center? I do love children."

"Perhaps we should release this one?" Aarow said to his father, enjoying the man's resulting yelp. "He doesn't seem to know his place."

"Where's your book of jobs?" said Rani, stepping forward.

The man held out a shaking finger, pointing to a cupboard next to the window. "Kept in there."

"Well, hurry up then. Get it," she said.

The man leaped from his chair and went to the cupboard for his book, opening it up on the table and slinking back to his chair.

"You recently assigned a job to a girl named Azrael," said Rani. "Find it and tell us why you assigned it to her."

Aarow glanced at his father to see if he was fine with letting Rani take over like this. He'd stepped back and was nodding each time Rani spoke, clearly happy with the direction this had taken.

"Yes, I'd like to know the answer to that, too," the Colonel said.

The Jobs Master flicked through some pages, his shaking finger landing on a line a few pages from the back.

"Read it out loud," said Aarow.

"Waste management." His voice was low, almost a whisper. But the room had no trouble hearing him and a murmur of amusement rippled from person to person.

"The Princess would like to know why you assigned this job to Azrael," said Aarow.

"There was a vacancy," the Jobs Master said. "It's an important job. Someone has to do it."

"Even a girl, barely strong enough to lift a bucket?" asked Rani. "A girl who was recovering from a violation at the hands of your colleagues and was possibly with child?"

The man swallowed, able to see where this was heading.

"I believe there's a vacancy for this job now," said Aarow, saving Rani the pain. "Do you have any suggestions as to who can fill it?"

"Me," whispered the man, with his head down.

"Excellent!" said Aarow's father, taking charge once more. "We have a volunteer. Congratulations on your new job. Give our new waste worker an applause."

The room broke into a series of claps and cheers, none louder than Rani and Aarow. This seemed a fair punishment.

"Next up is the Registrar," said his father.

The Emperor rose from his chair and cleared his throat. "Please Colonel, would you let me deal with the Registrar?"

"I don't see why not," said the Colonel. "What did you have in mind?"

"I was thinking he could set out his books in the Conception Center and work with the people to unite them with their families. It's a long and tedious job, and nobody knows how to read the books like he does. That will be punishment enough for now."

Aarow watched his father scratch his chin while he considered this request. Clearly there was more behind this. It seemed extremely lenient. What was it? Had some kind of deal been struck between these two men?

"Very well," said Aarow's father. "As you wish. He can get started immediately."

The Registrar stood.

"Thank you," he said, scuttling from the room before anybody changed their mind.

"We might have a chat about this later," the Colonel said, smiling at the Emperor.

"Of course." The Emperor dropped his head in a bow. "Thank you for trusting me."

"Now, Princess," said his father, directing his gaze at Rani. "You did so well with the Jobs Master, how about you try again? Next up is our Chairman. I believe you've already had some ideas about what we can do with him."

"That's right," said Rani, seeming far less confident than she had only moments ago. This vile man may not have laid a hand on her, but clearly the threat of it had been enough to leave her feeling a certain level of trauma.

Aarow looked at the Chairman, studying him up close for the first time. He was an awful looking man, with narrow eyes, a hooked nose and long fingers that he seemed to like rubbing together. But it wasn't so much how he looked. It was the vile aura that swam around him. The Healers back in the Colony would have a hard time balancing the sort of energy he threw out. He doubted they'd even bother trying.

Aarow took in a breath and let it go, trying to expel some of his anger with it. But there was far too much of it trapped inside.

"Let the Chairman speak first," said Rani, refusing to look at the man who'd caused her such pain. "I want to hear where he stands now."

The Chairman stood with a straight back and clasped his hands in front of him as he composed himself. "I'm not going to grovel like the rest of the spineless fools here at the table."

"Sit down," said Aarow's father.

"Don't tell me what to do." The Chairman's eyes burned with defiance.

Aarow and his father went to the Chairman and stood either side of him, towering over this pathetic excuse of a man.

"Sit down!" the Colonel said, more loudly this time.

"I will not." The Chairman lifted his chin, as if that could make him taller.

"Sit. Down." This time it wasn't the volume of the Colonel's voice that made him a force not to mess with, it was his tone.

The Chairman sat, looking between them both like he could strike them down with the poison in his eyes.

"What do you have to say?" Aarow's father asked.

"She wanted me," the Chairman said, nodding in Rani's direction. "I could see it in her eyes whenever she came near. The bitch was practically in heat, panting for me like one of those coyotes on the dunes. I was only doing her a favor by volunteering to sire her child. Give her what she was so desperate for."

Aarow left the Chairman and went to Rani, putting his arm around her shoulders and pinning her to his side.

"But..." said Rani. "It's not—"

"Don't!" Aarow said, cutting off her words. "Don't say it's not true. We all know it's not. You don't have to defend yourself here. You're not the one on trial."

"He must be released," said Aarow, letting go of Rani and moving toward the human who redefined the feeling of hate.

His father motioned for Aarow to stay back. "You look after Rani. We'll sentence the rest of the Board later. I'm going to release this piece of shit myself."

THE CHAIRMAN

THE AFTER

The Chairman struggled against the Coward who was leading him into the desert. It was the tall man, the one who called himself the Colonel. But the Chairman refused to give him such a title. He was the Coward to him.

"Quit your struggling," the Coward said, pushing him forward.

The Chairman felt his ankle twist and he stumbled, lifted back to his feet by his hands that were bound behind his back. Pain shot up his arms to mingle with the throbbing in his ankle.

"This is far enough," said the Chairman. "We never release people further out than this."

"You had no fear of them returning, did you?" The Coward pushed him forward again. "How do we know you won't try to find your way back? Rats always remember where they found their last crumb."

How dare this man compare him to a rodent! He had no idea who he was dealing with. He didn't voice his complaint, concentrating instead on taking the steps being forced upon him without inflicting further pain. His ankle burned with every step.

Despite the pain, he still couldn't bring himself to feel sorry for what he'd said. He'd spoken the truth. The Princess *had* wanted him. The only thing he was sorry for was that he hadn't seen this invasion coming in time to stop it. Taavi had tried to warn them, although sadly his shouts had come too late.

The Coward walked him further still, his twisted ankle buckling under his weight.

"Enough!" cried the Chairman, borrowing the word the people in the Round had used to cry for freedom and hoping this would hit home with the Coward. Did he have no mercy?

The Coward tensed at the word and threw him to the ground. The Chairman felt a snap in his other ankle as the pain intensified beyond anything he'd felt before.

"You broke my ankle!" he screamed. "What hope do I have out here now?"

Although, he already knew he had no hope. He was never going to survive the desert. All those times he'd had people released, he'd never imagined the reality of it would be quite so hot, so painful, so... frightening.

"Well, you did say enough," said the Coward, scratching his beard.

The Chairman pulled his ankle toward him and rubbed it as he watched the Coward take a long swig of water from the skin he carried around his neck. The pain in his broken ankle made his twisted one feel like nothing. He was unable to take another step.

"Water," the Chairman said, the thirst burning his throat far worse than the humiliation of having to ask for such a basic need.

"I don't think so," the Coward said. "Did you send the people you released out here with water? I'd like this to be an authentic experience for you."

"What will happen to the other Board members?" the Chairman asked, wondering if maybe he could find one of them out here and they could carry him to the river.

"We'll figure that out when I return," said the Coward. "Princess Rani will continue to assist me. You do know it's because of you that she ran into the desert in the first place, don't you?"

The Chairman groaned, trying to block out the relentless

onslaught of words from the Coward. The Princess would've been lucky to have had her heir sired by him. She'd run away because she'd been foolish, not because of him.

"I know you're listening to me," said the Coward, taking another sip of his water, letting a few drops spill carelessly down his chin. "The Princess was so repulsed by the idea of you going anywhere near her, that she decided she'd rather take her chances out here. Do you think that was fair?"

The Chairman tucked his face into his knees, refusing to answer.

"Sharma ran too," said the Coward. "All she wanted was the right to love her own children. Not too much of a request, don't you think?"

He waited for what he knew would surely be another question.

"And Azrael. I don't think you knew her, though. She was just one of the many faceless women whose dignity your cruel laws stole. And to make it worse, she was given a job that no young girl should have to do, carrying buckets of your waste out here to rot. She took her chances, too. What chance do you think you have out here?"

"You won't leave me out here," the Chairman sneered. "You're all about peace and safety or whatever rubbish you told the people in the Round. How will they trust you if they see you inflicting the same punishments that you claim to be opposed to? You said it yourself. Cruelty can't replace cruelty."

"That's an excellent point," said the Coward, adjusting his scarf to cover the lower half of his face. "Which is why I don't think I'll tell the people about this."

He turned his back and walked away, calling the Chairman's bluff.

"Get back here!" the Chairman cried, rising to his knees.

Each step the Coward took away from him created just a little more doubt in his mind. The Coward didn't slow his pace or turn to see if he was following. He knew he couldn't with one ankle broken, the other twisted and a thirst the size of the desert itself.

"Okay!" he shouted, trying to project his voice across the sand to reach the Coward's ears. "I'm sorry! I made a mistake. Don't leave me out here! Please! I beg for mercy."

But the Coward continued on and soon he was a small dot on the horizon, the Chairman's hope diminishing the smaller the dot became. Then the dot dipped below the crest of a dune and vanished.

That was when he knew for certain that he'd soon be dead. He'd dedicated his life to serving his kingdom and this was the thanks he got.

The wind picked up its pace, as if keen to hurry him to his demise. Sand found its way between the folds of his scarf and scratched at his skin.

"You coward!" he called, collapsing back on the harsh red sand, his voice weakening as the beat of his heart picked up.

He looked to the sky and felt himself falling toward it, hurtling to the clouds and spinning back to earth with a crash.

He was just dizzy. That was all. Not dying. Just dizzy.

A great injustice had been inflicted upon him today, but someone would come and save him. Soon. The Coward wouldn't leave him out here.

The Chairman closed his eyes and time passed. So much time. When he finally found the strength to open his eyes again, he felt himself fly to the clouds once more. Only this time when he crashed back, he sank beneath the sand and down, down, down into a place so hot it made the desert feel like ice.

THE COLONEL

THE AFTER

The Colonel had thought leaving the Chairman in the desert would be a pleasure. The truth was that he took very little joy from it. His job was to rescue people, not abandon them when they begged for mercy.

But it had to be done. Once in the Colony, a lizard had found its way into his quarters. Its back had been broken and it was dragging its hind legs like a weight. He'd had to crush it under his shoe to put an end to its misery.

The Chairman was that rat, only it was his soul that was broken instead of his spine. There was no hope of rehabilitation. His time in The Sands of Naar was over. Perhaps he should've crushed the Chairman's skull like he had with the lizard and gotten it over with quickly? However, this seemed too kind and would rob the Chairman of the chance to repent. He needed to understand the gravity of what he'd done to all those people in the only way possible, which was to live the same pain himself.

This was why the Colonel had continued to push his footsteps forward, leading him back to the Capital when all he wanted to do was go home to the peaceful life his ancestors created in the Colony. To his wife and daughter.

He wrapped his scarf around his face, blinking as a gust of wind sent red grains of sand into his eyes, and he reminded himself why the Capital needed him. The people in there had never had a wife or daughter, forced to live a solitary life. It was no wonder they all died so young. What did they have to live for?

But he had more than just a wife and daughter. He had his people. And he had his son.

All Aarow had to do to earn his love was be born. Respect was harder won than love, and over the years Aarow had managed to earn that, too. He had so many good qualities, but the one the Colonel admired most of all was how sure of himself Aarow was. He never doubted himself when heading into the desert to rescue a reborn. He never doubted the Colony's success invading the Capital. And he could see the gleam in his son's eyes when he looked at the Princess, never doubting that she'd be a part of his future, even if he didn't quite know how to go about that.

And this was why he hadn't wanted Aarow to release the Chairman himself. Because there was no task that would make someone question themselves more than leading a man to his death.

There was so much he hadn't been able to protect Aarow from in life, including having his own mother taken from him at birth. He wanted to protect him from this one thing. He'd been able to repair some of the damage of his mother's loss by bringing Freya into his life, but once his surety about himself was lost, there was no getting that back. He wanted Aarow to hold onto that for as long as possible.

The Capital came into sight. The ugly stone wall that would maybe be beautiful if it weren't a symbol of such misery. Perhaps they could make it beautiful again one day.

This was going to be a challenge. The Sands of Naar had always been a kingdom of one city in the middle of a desert. Now it was two. One thriving and one damaged. How were they going to merge these into a coherent whole?

He wasn't sure yet if the Emperor was a man he could work with to make this happen. There was going to need to be some teamwork here. Not the sort of Board that pretended to work as a team only to serve the evil desires of one man, but the sort where everyone had their say and the true needs of the people were met. So far, the Emperor had shown himself to lack confidence, but his heart seemed pure enough.

He walked through the archway to the Capital, smiling to see people holding hands and bumping shoulders as they walked, free from the threat of death. The Registrar's books had been made publicly available and citizens were pouring over them as they mapped out their family trees, figuring out who their parents, children, and siblings were. The atmosphere was one of both happy reunion and sadness of lost time.

The Colonel was pleased to let the people revel in their new freedom for a time, but soon some kind of order would need to be established before things got chaotic. Tasks still needed to be done. Blankets still needed to be woven, livestock needed to be fed and waste still needed to be collected. These jobs didn't go away. But there were better systems to put in place than ones reliant on force and fear. In the Colony, each citizen was rewarded fairly for the work they did. The jobs nobody wanted were rewarded with more rations until the unwanted became the wanted.

But before the Colonel returned to the Boardroom, he had somewhere else he needed to go first. He needed to see the Registrar's books for himself. There was one book in particular he needed to look at, dating back many years now.

It was crowded in the Reception Center, with groups of people studying the volumes the Registrar had kept so meticulously. They were laid out in the order they were kept. As people noticed who'd stepped into the room, they moved aside to let him pass.

"I can wait my turn," he said, not thinking for a moment that his needs were any more important than those who stood before him.

"You have important work to do," one woman said. "Please go ahead."

The surrounding people nodded their agreement.

It was true, he supposed. Aarow and the Emperor were waiting for him in the Boardroom.

"I'll be quick," he said. "I'm looking for the records from seventeen years ago. Shinings, I mean. Seventeen Shinings."

A man pointed to a table and a path cleared as he went toward it.

"Please, as you were," the Colonel said, not wanting the attention being cast upon him. This was a private moment.

A gentle chatter picked up in the room as people continued to flick through the other books. Although most of them were taught basic reading and writing skills in the Growing Center, it seemed these weren't skills that were practiced and finding the names was difficult for them. The Registrar was indeed working hard to assist them all, as the Emperor had said he'd have to.

"Do you need assistance?" the Registrar asked, approaching him with caution.

The Colonel waved his hand. "No, please help the others. I know what I'm looking for."

The Registrar stepped away, his brow wrinkled in curiosity.

The Colonel scanned the pages of the book in front of him, looking for one name and one name only.

Freya.

He'd promised to bring back the daughter she pined for. How could he do that if he didn't know who she was?

He ran his finger over the names in the book, each line tearing at the cracks in his heart, for each line in this book represented a mother being taken from her child.

After many lines on many pages, eventually he saw it.

Her name was right. The timing was right. The gender of her child was right.

He ran his finger across the page to find the name of the child, added in a different color ink, and felt his legs weaken when he recognized her name.

AZRAEL

THE AFTER

*A*zrael watched the sun dip below the horizon and decided it was safe to go and look for Rani. It felt like such a long time since she'd let go of her friend's hand in the dunes that morning.

Azrael's job during the battle had been important. Not one person she'd spoken to outside the Round had wanted to defend their kingdom. Not even the guards. Everyone had had enough. They were all ready to take their chances under a new ruler. It couldn't be any worse than the life they were already subjected to.

The revolution had been the biggest thrill of Azrael's life. Even bigger than running into the desert with Rani and Sharma by her side. Because when she'd left the Capital, she'd been a victim. When she'd returned, she'd been a victor. A reborn, rebirthing citizens of her own.

During the Shining, she'd stood outside the archway with the other reborns, listening to what was happening inside, ready to run in and help if needed. But they hadn't been needed. The battle had morphed into a celebration. It was hard to fight someone who was already on your side.

When the Board had been captured, Azrael had fought her way

through the crowd, looking to Rani's window to see how her friend had fared. She'd arrived just in time to hear Rani speak to the people and her heart had swollen with pride, filling her chest until it felt like it might burst. Rani had come so far from being the quiet girl who'd ground her teeth as she'd prepared to leap from her window.

Aarow had been right to insist that Rani remain in her bedchamber during the Battle. It was crucial to keep her safe, so the people could see she was firmly on the Colonel's side. This wasn't so much a takeover but a merger of the cities in the kingdom and having the Princess so visible to everyone in the Round, standing in her window offering words of support for the Colonel, was a very clear message.

Azrael walked through the Round and went to go into the palace, distracted by the crowds of people lining up to get into the Conception Center to review their birth records. She'd do this in time. It would be nice to know who her parents were and find out if they were still alive. Maybe she'd go later with Rani, who'd surely also be curious to know her mother's name. She'd waited this long for the information. Waiting a bit longer wouldn't hurt.

It was dark in the Round now, although Azrael doubted anyone here would be getting much sleep.

Two guards stopped her at the entrance to the palace. Not guards from the Capital, but guards appointed by the Colony. She quickly recognized one as Jinn, the friend of Aarow's who'd paid her far too much attention in the Colony. He smiled to see her now.

"What business do you have in the palace?" the other guard asked.

"It's okay," Jinn said. "She's Rani's friend. Remember?"

"Oh." The other guard quickly lost interest now that she posed no threat.

"How are you?" Jinn asked, seeming genuinely concerned.

"Good, thank you." She looked away, not comfortable meeting his eye for too long. "You?"

"Good thanks."

"Oh, for goodness sake!" said the other guard, shaking his head and laughing. "Ask the girl out on the date and be done with it! I can't stand this another moment. It's painful to watch."

Azrael took a step back. "What's a date?"

"Forget about it," the guard said. "Let me check if the Princess is happy to see you. We were asked to check first before allowing anyone in."

He walked away, still shaking his head, leaving Azrael more confused than ever.

"Ignore him," said Jinn.

"What did he mean? He wants us to eat dates together?"

Jinn smiled, not mocking her like his friend had done, but seeming to find her endearing. "A date is when two people go out and do something together."

"Like when you and Aarow rescue people in the desert?"

"No." His face was serious now. "Two people who like each other… as more than friends."

"Oh." She knew people in the Colony had romantic relationships, although she hadn't given any thought to how they got started. It wasn't something she'd thought would ever apply to her.

"So, would you like to? Go on a date, I mean." He gave her a shy smile.

She shook her head, wiping the smile from his face.

"I'm sorry. I'm just not…I don't…I mean." She gave up trying to find any words to explain how she felt. Jinn was a nice guy. But she wasn't interested in any dates.

"Is it because of Rani?" he asked.

"Rani?" Just when she thought things were starting to make sense, he had to confuse her again.

"You know. Are you and her…ummm….Well, you know. Do you go on dates with her?"

"You mean…two girls can go on dates?" The thought had never occurred to her and the way the idea of it pulled at her stomach caused her yet more confusion still.

But before Jinn could answer, the other guard returned.

"In you go," he said. "The Princess is keen to see you."

"Thank you." Azrael scurried away, trying to push away the conversation she'd just had with Jinn to digest later.

She entered the Boardroom, unsure what to expect, not having ever been in there before.

Rani and Aarow were seated at a round table with the Emperor. They looked up expectantly at her.

"Azrael!" said Rani, leaping from her chair and standing before her.

They didn't embrace, for that was a gesture that still didn't come naturally to either of them. Instead, they took each other's hands and squeezed them tightly.

"Are you okay?" Rani asked. "I was starting to get worried about you."

"I'm fine," Azrael said, letting go of her hands, now that the innocence of this simple touch had been shattered by Jinn's words. With this new knowledge and Rani standing before her, she wondered if perhaps Jinn had seen something she'd been blind to. "It couldn't have gone any better out there. Your speech was incredible."

Rani waved her hand as if to wipe away her words and took her seat back at the table, gesturing for Azrael to do the same.

But Azrael hesitated, the presence of the Emperor making her nervous.

"Azrael, this is my father," said Rani, realizing what the problem was.

The Emperor smiled warmly at her. "It's a pleasure to meet you. Thank you for looking after my daughter out there in the desert."

"I assure you that it was the other way around," said Azrael.

"Please, sit down," he said. "We're just waiting for the Colonel to return. He had some urgent business to attend to. It couldn't wait."

Azrael took her seat, noticing the way Rani was sneaking glances at Aarow and knew without a doubt that whatever confusing feelings had been running through her own mind, they were only flowing in one direction. Something had passed between Rani and Aarow. There was an obvious shift in the way they related to each other, like an ease or a closeness that puts up walls for everyone else.

"Thanks so much for everything you did," said Aarow, his handsome face smiling warmly at her. "I'm told the reborns were incredible out there, the way you recruited so many people so quickly."

Azrael smiled. "They recruited themselves. It was easy."

"Well, you're appreciated," said Aarow. "And we'll never forget that the idea of doing this on a Shining was yours either. That was inspired."

"Thank you." She took the credit, although didn't feel as if she deserved it. The idea had come to her in a dream and she'd somehow known this was what they were meant to do. It'd come to her with the same force as when she'd known she had to stop Rani jumping from her window.

These visions and dreams had been getting sharper since she left the Capital, as though once control over her body had been returned to her, so had her mind. But she wasn't sure what any of it meant and if this was some kind of gift or a sign that she was going insane. She was hoping to talk to Freya about it when she returned to the Colony, having had a sense that she was the only one who could possibly help her understand.

The Colonel burst through the door, his face pale and his eyes darting around the room, taking in who was here.

"Good," he said. "You're all here."

Azrael stood. "I'll leave you all. I know you have a lot to discuss."

"Stay," said Rani and the Colonel at the same time.

"Please," said the Colonel. "You were an important part of what happened today."

Azrael sat back in her chair, still unsure that a few dreams were enough to earn her place at this table.

"How did you go?" asked Aarow. "Is it done?"

The Colonel nodded, his face solemn. "He's been released."

Rani let out a loud breath that told Azrael exactly who *he* was. Good! Let the Chairman suffer the same fate he'd inflicted on so many others. She couldn't find any sympathy in her heart for him.

"Thank you," Rani said to the Colonel, her eyes filling with tears.

The Colonel nodded and folded his hands on the table as he sat down.

"It's been a long day," he said. "This meeting can wait until morning. We all need some sleep."

"We have enough beds in the palace for all of you," said the Emperor. "But something will need to be figured out for the rest of your people."

"They're content to revel through the night," said the Colonel. "Tomorrow we'll figure out who we need here and who can return to their families at the Colony."

The Emperor nodded and Azrael realized for the first time just what this invasion meant. It wasn't just a case of seizing power, it was what you did with it afterward that decided if you'd failed or succeeded. Many decisions were going to need to be made. She'd do what she could to help but was glad she wasn't the ruler of this kingdom. She wouldn't know where to start.

"I looked at the Registrar's books just now," the Colonel said.

Azrael furrowed her brow, wondering what he could possibly have found of use in there. He was born in the Colony as were his two children. She remained, quiet, waiting to hear what he had to say.

"My wife, Freya, was born here in the Capital," he said, looking around the table.

"I didn't realize," said Rani. "I just assumed..."

"I rescued her in the desert, in the same way Aarow rescued you," said the Colonel. "She was released after refusing to give up her baby without holding her first."

Azrael shook her head, unable to imagine the pain Freya had been through. It was no wonder she carried Aarow's baby sister around with her everywhere she went.

"I brought Freya back to the Colony and she bonded immediately with Aarow who was a small child at the time, having lost his mother not long before."

"I didn't know," said Rani, looking at Aarow with tears spilling from her eyes.

Aarow patted her on the hand. "I couldn't tell you that she's not my mother, because she is. I was blessed with two mothers."

"She never gave up on the daughter taken from her," said the

Colonel, shaking his head as he looked toward the darkness spilling in from the window, the lanterns on the table casting shadows across his face. "I promised her that I'd find her one day. And although this revolution happened for many reasons that had nothing to do with that child, I confess that for me, today was also personal. I had to get Freya's daughter back."

"Did you find her name on the registry?" asked Aarow, sitting forward.

"My mother was released after giving birth to me," said Rani, her words neutral, almost as if she'd disconnected her heart from her mouth as she prepared herself for a shock. "And I'm three Shinings younger than Aarow."

Azrael's hand flew to her mouth as she realized what Rani was thinking. Was Freya the mother Rani had been missing all her life? It made sense. Rani's mother had been released shortly after giving birth to her and the Colonel just said the same applied to Freya. What relation would that make her to Aarow? No blood passed between them but sharing a mother with the man you loved didn't seem right.

The Colonel shook his head. "No, Rani. I'm sorry, but it wasn't you."

Rani's mouth fell open. "Then...who is it?"

"Azrael," said the Colonel, causing her to leap at the sound of her name. "It is you. You are the daughter of my wife."

It took Azrael a few moments to process what he'd just said. When the words unscrambled themselves, all she was able to do was let out a gasp.

FREYA

THE EVERNOW

Freya paced the entryway to the Colony, pretending she was waiting for Miro and Aarow. She knew they wouldn't be back so soon, but it helped if she fooled her brain into thinking their return was close.

She could go to the Capital to see them, except...no, she couldn't return there. The memories were still too sharp. She didn't want to ever go back there again.

Spector had returned to the Colony faster than anybody could've imagined. The Colonel had sent him home to tell them the revolution had been a success. He'd run into the Colony calling like an eagle until everyone had gathered to hear his good news.

Spector's mother had fallen to her knees and wept at the sight of her son's safe return and Freya realized she'd thought she was never going to see him again. It was a feeling she could relate to. Aarow's absence was like a sharp pain in her heart. Hearing from Spector that there'd been only one death in the battle had restored the oxygen to her lungs. Especially when she found out it wasn't one of their own. The battle had apparently been swift and Spector said the people in the Capital had welcomed them with open arms, treating them more as rescuers than revolutionaries.

Aarow was safe. Miro was safe. And her daughter must be too. If indeed she was still alive in the first place. Of course she was, Freya told herself. She'd know if her daughter was dead. She'd be able to feel the loss in her soul.

Spector had returned to the Capital almost immediately, insisting the Colonel needed him. Freya had smiled, wishing things were different and she could go with him, not because the Colonel needed her, but because she needed him. He'd crept his way into her heart so slowly that she'd barely noticed, and now his absence left her feeling empty.

It was early morning and Freya decided to step outside the Colony entrance to watch the sun rise over the dunes. Bindi was still asleep in her bed, not due to wake for some time yet and Freya had asked one of the healers to watch over her. The walls of her family's quarters had been closing in on her, which was strange because she'd thought with fewer people to share the space with it would feel larger, not smaller. For the first time since arriving at the Colony, she'd wished to sleep above the ground, instead of entombed underneath countless grains of red sand.

She walked out on the sand now and went to the spot that she and Miro favored when they woke early and came outside to see what marvelous performance Mother Nature would put on for them.

Sitting down, she smoothed out the fabric of her skirt and tilted her face to the sky. It was the most spectacular pink color with wispy blue clouds crisscrossing in lines and contrasting with the dunes that looked more black than red in the budding light. A brilliant orange ball burst over the dunes sending sparkling rays across the sand.

It was breathtaking, but today it failed to steal Freya's breath. It wasn't the sun she wanted to rise over the dunes. It was her family.

A shadow appeared in the distance and Freya scrambled to her feet. She squinted into the morning sun, trying to get a better look.

Two people. Definitely two people. And the way one of them was darting about, she was certain it was Spector.

She focused on the other figure, wondering if it could possibly be Aarow or Miro, disappointed to realize the figure was shorter than Spector. It couldn't be either of them.

As they came closer, it was clear it was a female.

She waited, figuring she may as well greet whoever it was in case they needed healing. Perhaps Spector had started to bring the injured home.

As the sun climbed higher in the sky and the figures came closer, she soon realized it was Azrael with Spector. How odd they'd traveled through the night to get here. What could possibly be so urgent it couldn't have waited? They could've gotten lost, walking at night like that. Although, not Spector. He could walk through the desert blindfolded and he'd still know his way.

Freya had liked Azrael immediately upon meeting her. She was the opposite of how she herself had been when she'd arrived at the Colony. Talkative. Inquisitive. Excited. But there was more to her than that. She'd admitted to having dreams she didn't understand and some of those dreams had led to ideas for the revolution that'd helped them enormously. Freya had dreams sometimes too and hoped one day to speak to Azrael about this. It was through her dreams that she'd learned to be a healer.

She'd also noticed how Azrael looked at Rani and wondered if she was aware of how deeply her feelings ran. But Rani seemed to only have eyes for Aarow. Relationships were so complex. That was perhaps one advantage of living in the Capital—you didn't have to put any energy into thinking about these things. Nobody could break your heart when you weren't allowed to give it to them.

That wasn't really an advantage, was it? Relationships were what made life worth living. The family Freya had created inside the Colony was what sustained her. There was nothing she loved more than Miro, Aarow, and Bindi. Except perhaps her missing daughter.

Spector streaked off ahead of Azrael, bending over when he reached Freya, with his hands on his knees as he panted for breath.

"Colonel's wife!" This was the name he insisted on using for her, no matter how many times she'd asked him to call her Freya. It'd grown on her and she'd long ago given up asking. It was an honor to be known as such a great man's wife.

"Spector, take your time. Catch your breath."

"Azrael," he said pointing. She was still several yards away, unable to move as quickly as Spector. "She's here."

"I can see that. Is she okay? Why's she back so soon?"

"You," he said, sucking in a few deep breaths and attempting to stand up straight.

"Me?"

"Yes, Colonel's wife. She had to see you. She couldn't wait until morning. She ran out into the desert and the Colonel asked me to go with her to keep her safe."

Freya tilted her head, trying to make sense of what he was saying. Azrael was certainly lovely, but she hadn't thought she'd made that much of an impression on her that the girl had missed her so much she had to return. Although, she supposed Azrael had grown up without a mother. She knew how that felt. Perhaps she'd started to see her as a mother in the time they'd been in the Colony. Or perhaps being in the Capital had triggered some memories and she needed a healing.

"Come on!" said Spector, waving his hands madly at Azrael, who already seemed to be walking as quickly as she could.

"Leave her be," said Freya. "She'll be here in a moment."

"How did you know she was coming to see you?" Spector asked.

"I didn't," she said. "I just felt the urge to see the sunrise."

"You knew. Mothers always know when their children need them. My mother knows everything."

"I'm not Azrael's mother." Freya smiled.

"Yes, you are! You are!" Spector was jumping up and down now, clapping his hands. "The Colonel told her. He read it in the book in the Capital. You're Azrael's mother."

Freya's breath caught in her throat and her hands fluttered to her mouth as she took in Spector's words.

She looked to Azrael, still plowing through the sand toward her and soon Freya was running too. Toward the dunes. Toward the sunrise. Toward the girl who owned a piece of her heart. Her beautiful daughter.

"Azrael!" she cried, choking on her name, for her tears were flowing now and her breath coming in gasps. "Azrael!"

Azrael stumbled to her and Freya threw open her arms, her daughter landing in them and pressing her body to her own. This small girl who was once the child she grew inside her belly. The child who was torn from her, breaking her heart in ways she thought she'd never be able to repair.

"My daughter," she said, smoothing down Azrael's hair with her fingertips. "I'm so sorry. I'm so sorry."

Azrael pulled back from her, tears of her own streaking their way down her face.

"It wasn't your fault," she said.

"I should've gone back for you."

"You did," said Azrael. "You sent a whole army for me."

Freya lifted her hands to Azrael's face, wiping her tears away with her thumbs.

"You're perfect," she said. "Beautiful when you were born and even more beautiful now. I should've recognized you immediately. We wasted so much time."

Once again, Azrael shook her head. "We still have time. Let's not waste any of it wishing things had been different or worrying about how much of it we have left. Let's just enjoy every moment."

"Evernow," said Freya. "It's here. Evernow is here."

Azrael nodded, and Freya embraced her once again. Her daughter was in her arms for the first time in her life. The final piece of her heart had slotted into place and finally—finally—she felt like she could breathe.

RANI

THE EVERNOW

*R*ani was aware of every nerve ending in her body tingling as Aarow pressed his lips to hers once more. This was different to the last kiss. It had less surprise and more desperation. She'd never imagined that kissing someone could make you feel like this. Like she wanted to release the soul from her body and merge it with Aarow's. How had her kingdom been denying its people this basic human right?

She tightened her grip around Aarow's neck and pulled him closer, her heart rate beating wildly now, as a feeling of warmth flooded her core.

"Rani," he said, pulling away. "We have to stop."

"I don't want to," she said, standing on tiptoes and kissing him again.

"No, we really have to stop." He pulled away again.

"You weren't enjoying that?" She tried not to pout.

"I was." He pressed his forehead to hers. "Too much."

Rani didn't fully understand what that meant but let it go for now. There was still so much she had to learn about Aarow. About relationships. About what happened when kissing became too much and not enough at the same time.

The Boardroom door opened and Rani and Aarow sprang away from each other.

"Father," Rani said, wiping at her mouth, unsure if she was wiping away the kiss or trying to catch it in her hand.

"I hope you know what you're doing, my daughter." Her father walked in and took a seat, not meeting Rani's eye.

The truth was she had no idea what she was doing. She also didn't know how to stop.

The Colonel walked in before she could mumble an answer.

"It's been a long few days," he said, taking a seat. "I think we're maintaining some kind of order."

"The people are still rejoicing," said the Emperor.

"The problem is when the rejoicing stops," said Aarow. "What then? The celebrations can't last forever."

"Let's worry about that then, not now." Rani's father waved his hands in front of him. "These people have suffered long enough. They deserve some days of happiness."

"I wonder if Azrael made it back," said Rani, letting her eyes drift to the window.

"Oh, she did," said the Colonel. "Spector came back not long ago. I didn't get a chance to let you know."

"What did he say?"

"That Freya and Azrael have barely left each other's arms." The Colonel's eyes misted over, and Rani smiled to see this sensitive side of him.

"What happened to her f…" Rani let her question trail off as she realized the inappropriateness of asking Freya's husband about Azrael's father.

"Her father?" asked the Colonel.

Rani nodded. "I'm sorry."

"It's okay. He's no longer with us. He was released long ago, and his name isn't familiar in the Colony."

Rani nodded, realizing that perhaps this was just as well. The

Colonel wouldn't be at all pleased to meet the man who'd violated his wife.

"Not everyone's like you," the Colonel said. "To have had both your parents with you your whole life."

"Oh no," she corrected. "I never met my mother. She was released not long after my birth. I'd wondered if maybe she's at the Colony, just like Freya."

"But…" Now it was the Colonel's turn to let his question fade away.

"What?" asked Rani, too curious to let this go.

"It's nothing." He shook his head.

"You see it too?" Aarow asked his father. "The resemblance?"

The Colonel nodded.

"What are you two talking about?" Rani looked between Aarow and his father, waiting to be let in on their thoughts. Surely Aarow wouldn't keep a secret like this from her.

"Please would you leave us a moment?" asked the Emperor, his face full of distress. "It's time I talked to my daughter. Properly."

Aarow put a gentle hand on Rani's back and she gave him a confused smile. Was she the only one here who didn't know what was going on?

He left the room with the Colonel, leaving her alone with her father.

"What's going on, Father? Please, tell me. Who do I resemble? Do they know who my mother is?"

Her father nodded slowly.

"Which means you know who she is too. Did she make it to the Colony after she was released?"

Her father's head paused in its nodding as he changed directions and shook it from left to right.

"Rani, I'm so sorry. Your mother was never released."

Rani's spine slid to the back of her chair. "What do you mean? You said… Father, what's happening here? Who is she? Who's my mother?"

"You can't guess? I honestly thought you knew. Or at least suspected. You were always so close."

"Sharma." The word tumbled from Rani's lips before she had a chance to process it. "Sharma's my mother? Why would you lie about this? And Sharma. I trusted you both!"

"Don't blame Sharma for this." He sat beside her, trying to reach her with his eyes instead of his hands. "She had no choice. She was forbidden to tell you. Nobody here was allowed to know who their mother was, and that included you."

None of this made sense. Did Sharma and her father not trust her with such a secret? She'd barely talked as a child. She would never have said a word.

"I'm sorry, my daughter." His eyes were locked on hers. "We had to keep it from you for your own safety."

"I don't understand."

"Rani, there's so much you don't understand."

"Then talk to me!" She raked her fingers through her hair. "Tell me. Help me understand."

He sighed, seeming to find these words difficult. "You know that I was only a boy when I was taken to the Conception Center to sire an heir. Only thirteen Shinings. The process for the girls of the kingdom is a horrific violation, but please believe me when I say it was just as bad when it happened to me. It wasn't something I was ready for. Or wanted. It was a humiliation beyond what I'm able to describe."

Rani lifted her head, not having ever thought about what happened to him like this. She'd just assumed he'd been pleased to be made a man before his time. Shame washed over her as she studied her father's broken face.

"Sharma's number was assigned to me in the Conception Center, although I didn't know her name at the time. She was just as distressed as I was. Only a few years older than me, it was her first time too. We were both shaking throughout the ordeal but somehow the duty was performed to the Chairman's satisfaction...please forgive me if I leave out those details."

Rani nodded. These weren't details she needed or wanted. She knew Sharma still carried the emotional scars.

"Sharma was brought to live in the palace, so a close eye could be kept on her and any potential pregnancy. And when the previous female Board member was released, the Chairman decided she may as well earn her keep and join the Board."

"Was she pregnant with me at that time?"

Her father shook his head. "No, not that time. We had to attend the Conception Center three more times before Sharma fell pregnant. With you, of course. And I'd sit in the Board meetings and stare at her, knowing she carried my child in her belly and...I confess that I fell in love with her. Wildly in love. Like a man whose soul was possessed. I still feel that way about her."

Rani's jaw fell open, unable to process that her father had the capacity to feel that way. Although she'd fallen for Aarow. Why should her father be any different?

"You were born, and the Chairman was making noises about releasing Sharma. Which was when the deal was struck."

"The deal?" This sounded a little like making a deal with the devil. Only worse. Because surely the devil was preferable to the Chairman and the evil he'd wreaked.

"The Chairman had been having problems with the female Board members before Sharma and had dismissed several of them in the past Shining alone. They refused to vote in line with what he wanted, preferring to be released than play a part in his evil ideas. People were starting to ask questions. So, I suggested that if Sharma agreed to vote in line with the Chairman on each and every one of his decisions, that he'd keep her alive."

"Some deal," said Rani, not even able to imagine what kind of atrocities Sharma would have had to vote for in order to stay alive.

"Sharma wouldn't agree to it. Just like the female board members who came before her, she said she'd rather die. But the Chairman had decided by then that he liked the sound of this deal, so he threatened Sharma with something she valued more than her life."

Rani swallowed, guessing what was to come, and waiting for her father to say it.

"You," he said. "The Chairman threatened to have you released if she didn't agree to the deal."

Rani shook her head. All her life, Sharma had been protecting her and she hadn't had a clue what was happening.

"Sharma had no choice but to agree. She didn't want any harm to come to you. So, she agreed and the Chairman told her that you were never to know she's your mother, claiming that was against the laws of the kingdom, but we all knew it was just to torture her further for his own amusement. If he got even one hint you'd found out about this, he swore to release both you and Sharma at once."

Rani drew in a breath. So, the secret had been kept for her own protection. How hard it must've been for Sharma to keep this secret while living right beside her.

"It seemed to me that our problems had been solved. Both you and Sharma were safe. Then the Chairman questioned why Sharma hadn't been placed back on his registry for further conceptions. The idea of another man siring a child with her, tore me apart. It tore her apart too. She didn't love me in the same way I loved her, but she confessed to me that if it had to be anyone, then she'd rather it was me, for as traumatic as she still found the experience, at least there was trust that existed between us."

"But conceptions can't happen between the same two people twice," said Rani.

"I figured if a deal could be struck with the Chairman, then certainly a deal with the Registrar was possible, too. I asked him if I attended the Conception Center on the days Sharma was required, if he'd be sure to assign me to her. The problem was that I had nothing to offer him in return other than the promise I'd one day find a way to make it up to him. He agreed, liking the idea of me being in his debt and would remind me of it from time to time to ensure I never forgot."

"This is why you were lenient on him with his punishment after the revolution." At least one thing made sense now.

Her father nodded. "The favor was finally repaid."

"So, are you telling me you're the father of all Sharma's children?"

He nodded once more.

"You mean, Horrie is...my full blood brother?"

"Yes. And you saved his life out there in the desert. I'm so proud of you."

Rani leaned forward and rested her head in her hands to try to stop the room spinning. How was this possible? Sharma her mother? Horrie her brother?"

"What about Taavi?" she asked. "Was he Sharma's too?

Her father nodded and Rani felt the loss of her brother even more acutely now that she knew they shared two parents.

"Do you have children with women other than Sharma?" she asked, wondering just how many siblings she had.

He nodded. "I'm afraid, I do. Although Sharma trusts me, she's never loved me the way I loved her. I confess I visited the Conception Center on occasions when I knew Sharma wasn't there to convince myself she meant nothing to me. This resulted in other children. There's nothing more painful than loving someone who doesn't love you in return. As time passed, my visits were for far more selfish reasons. My own need to connect with another person outweighed my concern for the impact it may have. I'm ashamed of myself."

This came as a shock. She knew her father had gone to the Conception Center, however, hearing him talk about it like this was so primal. She hated it. And part of her hated him for it, too. Just when she'd started to think he was different. She'd been certain his visits to the Conception Center had been forced upon him. An expectation by the Board to ensure enough potential heirs were sired. To think he'd been going there by choice!

"Thank you for the truth," she said, standing and smoothing down the creases of her dress.

"Are you leaving?" he asked. "I hope I haven't upset you too much."

"It's a lot to take in. Please, I need some time."

Without saying another word, she left the room. She'd heard enough words for now and had none of her own to offer in return, until she'd had time to process it all.

She held up her hand as Aarow and the Colonel approached her, indicating that she didn't wish to speak to them either.

Ignoring the hurt look on Aarow's face, she took the stairs to her bedchamber, wanting the familiarity of the four walls that'd cocooned her for most of her life.

Nothing was as she'd thought it'd been. Life was infinitely more complicated than she'd believed possible.

Was her father good? Or was he just as bad as the Chairman? And how could Sharma have kept this from her, no matter what the threat? It felt like such a betrayal from the two people she'd thought she'd known best. Who else had been lying to her? Aarow? After all, he was a man and men seemed to be wired in a different way to women. She had no idea what he was thinking at all. Her own father claimed to love Sharma, yet that wasn't enough to keep him away from other women.

During the revolution, she'd thought she'd finally discovered who she really was. She'd thought maybe it was possible she was brave and able to lead a kingdom. The truth was that she was a gullible fool.

She threw herself on her bed and ground her teeth down hard, her eyes drawn to the window that'd once offered her a way out of her problems. Was it still the way out?

Putting her hands over her ears and squeezing her eyes shut, she blocked out the world and all the misery it insisted on throwing her way. The Chairman may no longer be threatening to tear her world apart. But the truth had done a good enough job of that instead.

SHARMA

THE EVERNOW

*S*harma took a long drink from her waterskin and walked on. Horrie was in the scarf around her neck, wide awake, with no intention of sleeping any time soon, a sign he was getting older and more curious about the world around him. How different his life would've been had he been born in the Capital and sent to the Growing Center to cry alone in a crib. Had that been what'd gone wrong with her second born child, who Spector had informed her had jumped from a window during the revolution?

Spector had given her this information in the same way he'd tell someone the weather was warmer than usual today. As if it meant nothing. He had no way of knowing the Emperor's second born child was also her own and his words had been like a dagger to her heart. Spector had gone on to say that her son had double-crossed Rani and Aarow and called out the window, trying to ruin the Battle game before it even started.

These words were a blur to Sharma's ears. Her son hadn't known any better. Raised by people who touched him only when necessary and then only with gloved hands, how could anyone expect him to understand things like loyalty and love? It wasn't her poor son's fault. If she'd had the chance to influence him in the same way she'd been able to with Rani, he'd have grown into a different young man. His actions were the Capital's fault, not his own.

This was why she'd made the decision to return with Spector to the Capital. She wanted to make sure her son had a proper burial. He needed to be treated with respect.

Watching Azrael and Freya bonding as mother and daughter had also sealed the decision for her. This reunion was something she craved for herself. Not finding her own mother, as she'd surely have been released long ago, but finding her children. Starting with Rani. The daughter she'd been allowed to see grow, yet never able to lay a hand on her or tell her just how much she loved her. It'd been torture and many times she wondered if life would've been easier if they'd been kept apart, like with her other children. Having Rani right there had been like putting a plate of hot food in front of a starving man and telling him not to eat.

Spector led her to the Round, relishing his job as the guide between the kingdom's two cities. Sharma had thought she'd never return to the Capital, but now she couldn't wait.

"Shhh," she said to Horrie, wishing he'd go back to sleep. He was getting heavier now and more difficult to carry. Although, the ache around her neck from the tugging of the scarf that held him seemed a small price to pay to be reunited with her other children.

She could hear the Round, before she saw it, the sound of freedom floating across the dunes. As she got closer she could pick out individual voices and realized not all the noise was of happiness. Freedom came with sadness as well, as people mourned the time and loves they'd lost, as well as celebrating the ones they'd found.

The biggest difference as she got closer still, was the way people were holding each other, dancing, hugging, kissing and walking with their hands locked together. Time was being made up for and she had no doubt that many of the tents in the village were filled with far more contact than she could see out here.

Sharma thanked Spector and he darted away as she went directly through the archway, ignoring the blisters on her feet as she walked past the Orbs of Time, the sand still flowing through them at a steady rate. She wasn't surprised the timekeepers had continued to turn them. Their dedication to their job was like a calling. Nothing would get in the way of it, not even a revolution.

The two guards at the entrance to the palace were from the Colony, not the Capital. Recognizing her as Rani's friend, they stepped aside to let her through.

"The Princess is up those stairs," one of the guards said.

Sharma took the stairs faster than she'd ever done in all her Shinings in the palace. Winding through the corridors, she reached Rani's door and pushed it open to see her lying on her bed with her hands over her ears and her eyes scrunched up as if a speck of light would destroy her.

"Rani," she said, breathless.

Her daughter couldn't hear her through her clamped down hands.

Now that Horrie was finally asleep, she settled him onto a rug on the floor and lay down on the bed next to Rani, startling her.

Her daughter's eyes sprang open and her hands fell away from her ears.

"Sharma," she said, turning her face but not sitting up. Her eyes filled with tears and the way she took in Sharma, she knew immediately that someone had told her the truth after all these years.

"Rani. You know?"

Rani nodded, the tears making their way out of the corners of her eyes now and spilling down her face. "Father told me. Just now. And here you are."

Sharma propped herself up on one elbow and reached across with her free hand, drawing a line down Rani's nose in the same way she did to Horrie when he fed. But this wasn't enough and soon she cupped Rani's soft cheek in the palm of her hand and leaned forward to kiss her other cheek.

"I'm sorry," she said. "I wanted to tell you, but..."

"You were protecting me," said Rani.

Sharma nodded. "I was scared."

Rani swallowed and hauled herself to a seated position. Sharma sat up beside her, wrapping a tentative arm around her daughter's shoulders. Rani didn't move closer, but she didn't move away.

"You could have told me in the desert," Rani said, her voice a whisper.

"I was afraid of how you'd react." Sharma didn't want to point out that she was afraid Rani would react in the exact way she was reacting now. They hadn't had the energy for that in the desert.

"Do I call you Mother now?" Rani asked.

"If you like. But Sharma's fine, too."

Rani nodded. "Father loves you."

"I know. He's been good to me. I'd have died long ago without him."

"But you don't love him?"

Sharma let out a long sigh, wondering how to explain her feelings when she didn't understand them herself. "Not in the way he wants me to. But I do love him."

"Father told me about his visits to the Conception Center." She paused. "The ones when you weren't there."

Sharma nodded. She knew about these visits too, although she'd tried not to give them too much space in her mind. Clearly, they were occupying a fair amount of space in Rani's mind right now.

"You're okay about it?" Rani asked. "It seems an awful thing to do."

"I don't know how I feel about it," she said, offering her the truth. Never again would she lie to this sweet girl.

"Where's Horrie?" Rani asked, not seeming to want to think about this too much either.

Sharma got up from the bed and scooped her youngest child from the floor, placing him in the arms of her eldest.

"He's my brother," said Rani, feathering a kiss on his forehead.

"He is."

"And now I know why you called him Horus. He's named for his father."

"Your father's a good man," she said. "Not perfect. None of us are.

He's made mistakes, just like we all have. But he has a good heart. He loves us."

"How many more brothers do I have? And sisters? On just your side, I mean."

"Two more brothers. Three sisters. And your brother who Spector said fell..."

Rani looked away. "It was an accident. He didn't suffer. It was quick."

Sharma nodded, not daring to look at the very window he'd fallen from. Her poor, sweet son. "Where is he? I want to bury him."

"Father's ensured he's been kept safe."

Sharma nodded, trying to sweep away the cloud of sadness as she came to grips with the realization that the only time she'd be able to see her son would be with his skin cold and his eyes closed.

"Lie back down," said Rani. "You're exhausted. It's been a long walk. Sleep for a while, then we'll search for your children."

Sharma didn't have the energy to complain. Her bones were tired.

She closed her eyes, listening to the soft breathing of two of her children beside her. Please let the others still be breathing, too.

AAROW

THE EVERNOW

Giving Rani the space she clearly needed wasn't easy for Aarow. When she'd left the Boardroom to head upstairs, his father had to put a hand on his arm to stop him running after her.

"Leave her for a little bit," he'd said. "Trust me."

Aarow had listened, knowing his mother had been the same when she'd first arrived at the Colony. His father had played the long game, giving her all the time she needed and ultimately, he'd won her over. If he'd pushed too hard, things may not have turned out so well. He must do the same with Rani. She was too special to lose. Finding out Sharma was her mother had clearly come as a shock. Something that was obvious to everyone else, yet Rani hadn't had any idea. Perhaps Aarow should've told her about his suspicions earlier.

The Emperor emerged from the Boardroom some time later and beckoned Aarow and his father back inside.

"Rani seemed upset," said Aarow.

The Emperor nodded. "She knows the full truth now. About her mother. And about me."

Aarow wondered what secrets the Emperor had revealed about himself to Rani, but kept his mouth closed. If Rani wanted to talk to him about it, he'd listen. However, it really wasn't any of his business. Unless those secrets affected the future of the kingdom, although he doubted that. It seemed far more personal.

"My daughter will be fine," said the Emperor, as Aarow and his father took their seats. "She just needs a little time to think about what I told her. She's a deep thinker."

"Sharma's here," said the Colonel. "We saw her come in, although she didn't see us. She was too focused on finding Rani. The guards sent her straight upstairs."

"She's here? Did she look...well?"

"Yes," said Aarow, wondering how deeply the Emperor's feelings for the mother of his daughter ran. "Just in a hurry to see Rani. She had her baby with her, too."

The Emperor nodded. "Let's keep this quick then. I'd like to see Sharma for myself. We have a son to bury."

"Sharma was Taavi's mother?" asked Aarow, having already suspected this may be the case.

"Yes. I'm the father of all her children," the Emperor said.

"Even baby Horrie?" asked the Colonel.

"She called him Horrie?" The Emperor's eyebrows shot up.

"It's short for Horus, I believe," said Aarow.

The Emperor beamed. "My name is Horus."

"Oh," Aarow and his father said in unison, the baby's strange name making sense now.

"I really am sorry about what happened to Taavi," said Aarow, not feeling like enough apologies would ever make up for not being able to grab hold of his son in time before he fell.

"Please, it wasn't your fault," the Emperor said, as the smile slid from his face.

"You're far too kind." Aarow bowed his head.

"I wanted to talk to you about something that was delivered to me by a raven, just before Rani ran away," said the Emperor, pushing a piece of parchment across the table. "Before your arrival, obviously."

Aarow reached out for the parchment, appreciating the Emperor's diplomatic choice of words. Arrival sounded far better than invasion.

"It's an invitation," said Aarow's father, leaning in to read it.

"It's from the King of Wintergreen," said the Emperor. "Inviting me to his son's wedding. He's formed an alliance with Forte Cadence and has reached out to us. This was the reason I helped Rani leave the Capital and head for the river. I knew if she could make it safely across that she'd be greeted by friends. I thought I provided her with enough equipment to get there safely, although it seems the desert is even more brutal than I realized. I had no idea of what risk I was putting her at or I'd never have let her leave."

This made sense to Aarow, filling in yet another gap. He'd never quite been able to grasp why the Emperor would allow Rani to leave, no matter how bad her life had become in the Capital. The Emperor had thought she had a chance to have a happy life in Wintergreen.

"Attendance at the wedding would be seen as a symbol of The Sands of Naar's willingness to work with our neighbors," said the Emperor.

Aarow sat back and tried to gauge his father's reaction to this development. It was a delicate matter. Not so much whether peace with the other kingdoms was desirable—that was a given—but who would be appropriate to attend such a wedding. The Emperor? Or the Colonel?

The Colonel cleared his throat. "What are your thoughts on this matter, Emperor?"

"I'm Emperor in name only. That's no different now to how it's always been, only now you're in power instead of the Board. I hid this invitation from the Chairman as he'd never have agreed to it. Peace wasn't in his heart. But I suspect this is something you may be interested in."

"It is," the Colonel said. "However, I'm asking what you think."

The Emperor sat up straight in his chair, clearly not used to anyone asking for his thoughts. "I think...I think we could use the assistance of our two neighbors to find better ways to run this kingdom. I'm sure you'll agree that it's fair to say since your arrival, we've struggled to decide how to best do things. Currency, for example. We have none. I understand the other kingdoms use coins to entice their people to do necessary jobs. Jobs that people may not wish to do otherwise. This is just one thing I feel we could understand better."

"He's right," said Aarow, surprised the Emperor had such insight. "The ways of the Colony will be difficult to implement here. It'd be useful to see how other kingdoms run their affairs."

His father nodded and turned to the Emperor. "There's too much for the both of us to do right now to be able to leave for this wedding. It'll send the wrong message to the people. I can't possibly leave and I've come to depend on your help."

The Emperor nodded and Aarow opened his mouth to question this decision, when his father continued.

"Aarow and Rani should go as our representatives, instead," he said. "They're the future of this kingdom."

Aarow's mouth remained open, only this time in shock. The idea of traveling with Rani to a wedding in another kingdom was more than a little appealing. The journey would take a long time. And that was a long time he'd get to spend with her. He waited to see the Emperor's response to this. Would he trust him with his daughter?

"Is it appropriate to send Aarow and Rani together?" asked the Emperor.

"What's inappropriate about it?" asked Aarow, working his way back into the discussion. "We wouldn't travel alone and I care for your daughter greatly. And I respect her."

"This is my concern," said the Emperor. "Because I can see the feeling's mutual. I'm worried for her heart. Do you wish to marry her one day? This isn't something we're used to in the Capital. Nobody has been married here for generations."

Aarow shifted in his seat, not having expected such a direct question. But the truth was undeniable. He'd marry Rani right now if it were possible.

"I do wish for that."

"Then you shall marry before your departure," the Emperor said.

"Just a moment," said Aarow's father, stepping in. "There's no rush for marriage. Rani has only just gained her freedom. She may not want to feel like she's being tied to someone so soon. It'd be best to give her time. Trust me, I've been through this with my own wife. If Rani's rushed, Aarow may lose her altogether."

"Let me take her to the wedding," said Aarow. "If the trip's a success, I'll ask for her hand upon our return. I give you my word on that."

"Your marriage in the future would solve a lot of problems," the Colonel said.

Aarow raised his eyebrows, not having expected this from his father. "How so?"

"Well, currently we have two rulers of this kingdom."

"I am no ruler," said the Emperor. "I never have been. You said it yourself when you made your speech in the Round. You're the ruler of this kingdom now."

"I did say that," said Aarow's father. "But I've learned a lot in the past few days and have come to think quite differently now. The way I see it is like this. The Colony and the Capital both need leaders who understand their unique needs. You're best placed to rule the Capital and I'm best placed to return to the Colony. When our children marry, I suggest we hand the kingdom to them to rule as a united front. Their union is ideal for the good of the kingdom."

Aarow sighed. He didn't want his relationship with Rani treated like a business arrangement. He'd said he wanted to marry her because he loved her, not because it was for the benefit of the kingdom.

There was no denying that both he and Rani had been raised to believe they'd be leading their kingdom one day, even if Rani had thought it would be in name only. If they were to marry, then they could rule the kingdom together. A lot would ride on this trip to Wintergreen. Not just Aarow's heart, but the future direction of the kingdom.

"I'm not sure I can rule the Capital," said the Emperor.

"Nonsense," the Colonel said. "You're more than capable. And I'll be here to guide you. We're a team. I'm not in competition with you."

"But you invaded us." The Emperor said this plainly, without malice.

"We were setting the Capital free from the Board, not from you."

The Emperor smiled at this. "So, my daughter will still be Empress one day?"

Aarow watched his father break into a smile. "The Empress and the Colonel. I like the sound of that. Equal rulers."

The Emperor stood up as if unable to contain his excitement while seated in a chair. "If we join the alliance with Forte Cadence and Wintergreen, together we can work toward strengthening our kingdom and bringing true peace to our people."

"Spoken like a true leader," said Aarow, smiling at the change in this man since he'd first laid eyes on him. "But do you mind if I talk to Rani about the wedding? I'd like to be the one to raise it with her. And perhaps we could keep the details of our meeting here today private?"

"Private from Rani?" the Emperor asked. "I think enough secrets have been kept from her already."

Aarow nodded. "Just about our marriage. I'll tell her in time, but I'd hate for her to think the only reason I'm interested in her is because of her title, and not because of who she is. She's had a lot of surprises recently and I think speaking to her so candidly could be detrimental to her health. I need to make certain she trusts me first."

"Very well," the Emperor said.

His father nodded in agreement. "It looks like we have a plan."

RANI

THE EVERNOW

*R*ani watched Sharma—her mother—sleep. She wondered if she'd ever get used to thinking of her as her mother. It was strange to think that the beating of Sharma's heart was the first sound she'd ever heard.

She couldn't be upset with her for keeping the secret. She'd done it to protect her, not to hurt her. If Rani had known who Sharma really was, then she'd have had to carry the burden of secrecy, too.

She looked down at Horrie, sleeping peacefully on the bed next to her. Her baby brother, who'd already wormed his way into her heart but now that she knew their blood connection, he occupied an even more generous space in there. She'd lie to him too if it meant protecting him. Especially if the lie was more leaving information out, rather than inventing stories.

So, if she wasn't upset with Sharma, then why did she still have a feeling of unease bubbling inside her? Was it her father? What he'd told her had both warmed her to him and repelled her. He loved her. That was clear. And he loved Sharma. But how could he have gone willingly to the Conception Center and performed those acts despite knowing exactly how distressing it was to the women?

Was it because of the way he'd been raised to think that was normal? Perhaps that was part of it. Or was it revenge, punishing Sharma for not loving him in the way he craved to be loved by her? Once again, perhaps this was part of it. She had to accept that sometimes there were no clear reasons about why someone did something. Decisions were often made up of many complicated parts.

Her father certainly seemed to have come to the realization that what he'd done was wrong. There was no doubt he was sorry.

Rani drew in a breath and decided to give him the benefit of the doubt for now. Let him prove just how sorry he was with his next actions moving forward. He was being reborn as well, only in the Capital, not in the Colony. Let him help the Colonel build a kingdom that was a safe place to live. A place where happiness could thrive.

Happiness. Was she happy? She wasn't sure. She certainly had hopes of being happy. And that was thanks to Aarow.

She remembered the look on his face as she'd left the Boardroom earlier. He'd wanted to follow her, but his father had put his hand on his arm and urged him to leave her alone. The Colonel had been right.

She crawled off the bed, careful not to wake Horrie or Sharma, and left the room to go in search of Aarow. It was getting dark now and she didn't want him to spend a restless night worrying about her. Not if she could set his mind at ease.

Closing the door quietly behind her, she went down the stairs to the Boardroom.

Seeing the Orbs of Time looming from the window, she went outside intending to sit on the grass for a while, but soon saw there was barely a blade visible underneath the sleeping bodies. Many of the Colonists had gone home now, some taking new friends with them. And the occupants of the tents in the villages were being swapped around as people chose who'd they'd like to share with, rather than who they'd been assigned. Those with no place to go, must be coming here to the Round.

Rani had heard her father talking about turning the Conception

Center into temporary accommodation. It wasn't right to have so many people sleeping under the stars.

She made her way to the archway, her face bare to the night air. She saw no need to disguise herself anymore. People smiled at her as they passed, nodding their heads in recognition. Nobody stopped to talk, either assuming she was busy, or they were too busy themselves.

She walked through the archway and took a few paces toward the desert, scanning her eyes across the dunes in the fading light. All her life she'd thought the life of her kingdom was contained within the Round, when there was so much more of it happening across the dunes. Were there other colonies out there? It was possible, albeit unlikely.

A familiar shape stood on the horizon and she smiled to realize why she'd felt drawn to this spot. It was like her connection to Aarow had led her here with an invisible thread.

As she walked toward him, he turned, as if sensing her presence, and he took hurried steps to close the gap between them.

"Rani," he said, wrapping his arms around her. "How did you know I was out here?"

"I didn't." She slid her arms around his waist, marveling at how quickly this had begun to feel normal.

"Are you okay?" he asked. "You were so upset earlier. I wanted to follow you, but—"

"Your father advised against it," she finished.

"That's right. He said you needed space."

"I did." She let her arms slide from his waist, wanting to see his face. "I've been doing a lot of thinking. Then Sharma returned, and we had a talk. Why didn't you tell me you suspected she was my mother?"

He shrugged. "I wasn't really sure. You had enough going on and I didn't want to stir up anything that wasn't necessary."

"Do you really think I look like her?" she asked, not seeing the resemblance so much herself.

"You do. Around the eyes. But it was also the way she looks at you."

"Like a mother?"

He nodded. "Come with me. I was looking across the desert just now. It's so pretty at this time of night. And the winds have died down."

He took her hand and led her up to the top of the dune, where they sat side by side surveying the harsh landscape.

"Was I wrong to send the Chairman out there?" she asked, wondering about his death and whether forgiveness would've been a better option.

"Technically I sent him," said Aarow. "So, if you think you're guilty, then I am, too."

She shook her head. "You did it for me. You knew that's what I wanted."

"He caused a lot of pain," said Aarow, placing an arm around her shoulders. "It was his time. Father said he wasn't the least bit repentant, not even when he knew his death was certain. You offered forgiveness to the other Board members when you didn't have to."

She nodded. This was true. All remaining Board members had been allowed to walk free. They'd seemed as relieved as Rani that the Chairman was no longer around to torment them. The Chairman was the only one sentenced to death in the revolution. Unless Taavi was counted in that.

"I should've tried harder to hold onto Taavi," she said. "But he was so heavy, and it happened so fast."

"You did your best," Aarow said. "I did too. It was an accident. Nothing more."

"He was Sharma's child, too. And Horrie is my father's child."

Aarow nodded. "Your father told me that. Do you think there are more full siblings?

"I know there are. Many of them. Assuming they survived, of course. I promised Sharma I'd find them for her. I'll start looking at sun-up."

"Rani, I need to talk to you about something." He dropped his arm from her shoulder and she shuddered, making her wonder if this was good news or bad.

"Go on," she urged.

"There's a wedding," he said. "You know what a wedding is, right?"

"Of course I do. Whose is it?"

"The King of Wintergreen's son is getting married. Prince Ari. He's invited representatives from all the kingdoms as a peace offering. Our fathers agreed it'd be wise for us to attend."

"Why?" Of all the things Aarow may have said, Rani hadn't expected that.

"Wintergreen has made an alliance with Forte Cadence. Together they're far more powerful than either of them were alone. Our fathers think this is a perfect opportunity to strengthen The Sands of Naar. And perhaps get some advice from them as to how to best rule this kingdom."

"Advice from our enemies?" She'd been raised to believe the other kingdoms were evil, ruled by power-hungry monsters. Had this been a lie too?

"They aren't our enemies," said Aarow. "Unless we insist on keeping them that way, of course. It's in our hands."

"And why wouldn't the Colonel go? Or my father? Surely that's more appropriate. Why us?"

Aarow fidgeted with his scarf, not seeming to know how to answer this question. "There's too much for them to do here. It wouldn't send the right message to our people."

"But my father's no longer Emperor. What work does he really have to do?"

"He's still the Emperor. My father insists they rule together. Just like Forte Cadence and Wintergreen are working as an alliance, so are our fathers. It's time to put the needs of the people before the needs of any one ruler."

Rani smiled in the darkness. Not that Aarow could see it, but the smile wasn't for him. It was for the future of her kingdom. There was so much hope.

"Our fathers see both of us playing an important part in the future here. We're the heirs. They want to see us go to the wedding in their place."

"Then we shall go," she said, wondering how a kingdom could have two heirs. Surely Aarow was the true heir and her role would be one in name only, just as it'd always been.

"Are you sure?" he asked. "The journey won't be easy. We'll be traveling on foot."

She gave him one short nod. "When do we leave?"

"At sunrise."

Her jaw fell. "That early?"

"I'm afraid so." He bit down on his bottom lip as he tried to gauge her reaction. "It's the only way we'll make it in time."

"But I promised Sharma I'd help her find her children." She couldn't abandon her now, not when they'd only just found each other.

"She doesn't need you for that." Aarow's voice was gentle and reassuring. "She's proven she's more than capable all on her own. If you explain it to her, then she'll understand. Your father can have a word to the Registrar. I'm certain he'll be happy to help her."

"Yes, I'm certain of that too." She wondered how much Aarow knew of her father's dealings with the Registrar, or his feelings for Sharma, but she held her tongue for now.

"It seems a long way to walk," she said.

"It is. But we'll be well equipped. I won't let anything happen to you. We'll make our way to the river, then it's only a few days from there. If we leave tomorrow, then we can take our time."

"But, last time…"

"Last time you didn't have me with you," he said, allaying her fears.

"Will we travel alone?" She wasn't sure her father would be comfortable with them traveling without a chaperone.

"We'll take Toran and Jinn with us. For safety. And to help carry the equipment."

It seemed he'd thought of everything.

"What about Spector?" she asked.

"That eagle prefers to fly alone. We'll be all right without him. Besides, I think he's enjoying his new role of leading groups between the Colony and the Capital. He came up with a brilliant idea of digging a tunnel between the two settlements. It'd be so much faster to travel underground without the sun and the wind to deal with. Nobody would get lost either."

"Is that even possible?" She had to admit the idea made a lot of sense. Linking the two settlements would be a huge step toward uniting them.

"Anything's possible." He replaced his arm around her shoulders and she shuffled closer to him.

"You've saved my life more times than I can ever thank you for," she said.

"Pretty sure it was only the once." He laughed, squeezing his grip on her.

"No, not once. You may have carried me from the desert, but every day since then, it's been you who's made me decide it's worth keeping on."

She left it at that, not wanting to explain how close she'd once come to taking her own life. He may not understand. Although he'd had his share of problems, his life had been far simpler than hers.

"Happy to help," he said, brushing her cheek with a kiss.

"I've never seen a wedding," she said, wondering what rituals it entailed. Would she and Aarow get married one day? She couldn't imagine being without him, but it was hard to picture herself in a formal union when she'd had such limited exposure to exactly what that involved.

"I hope you like it," he said. And she realized why he'd found his words so difficult to find. He had hopes of a wedding one day. She was glad he hadn't said so, though. It was difficult enough trying to get her head around what it would be like attending a wedding, let along being the bride in one.

"I need to get back to Sharma," she said. "It's late."

"May I kiss you goodnight?" he asked.

Now that was something she was very willing to agree to right here and now. No need to get her head around that.

She tilted her face up and parted her lips in expectation.

And Aarow, being Aarow, certainly didn't disappoint.

AZRAEL

THE EVERNOW

"You're an angel," said Spector, studying Azrael closely.

"I'm not." Azrael laughed, still getting used to this man's odd manner.

"No, you are," he said, without a hint of amusement on his face. "I've never met one before. I thought maybe the Colonel's wife was one, but she's not. It's you."

"Maybe you're the angel," said Azrael, wondering where he was getting his information. Did he dream in the same way she did?

He shook his head. "I'm an eagle."

"Then we can fly in the sky together." She took off across the sand with her arms flapping like wings and Spector chased behind her.

The game didn't last long, and the sun beat down on them, sapping Azrael's energy. Spector seemed as if he could run for hours.

"I didn't notice it at first," said Spector, sitting beside her and fidgeting with the fabric of his shirt. "I was too tracted."

"Tracted?"

"You know. Busy noticing other things. Tracted."

"Oh! Distracted." She smiled, not wanting him to think she was making fun of him. He was a man who liked to be taken seriously.

"You saved everyone," he said.

"I really didn't do anything." She stood up, not knowing how to end the conversation otherwise. Nothing Spector was saying made any sense, yet he was so adamant about it all.

"You saved the Princess and Sharma. Then because of you, the Colonel went and saved everyone else. You're the angel of death."

She frowned, not sure if he was still paying her a compliment. Being the angel of death didn't sound too desirable.

Spector stood and waved his hands about. "It's a good thing, Azrael! You're the angel who protects people from death."

"Fly away, eagle," she said, smiling. "This death angel needs to go back inside."

Spector did his eagle cry, lifted his arms and ran away.

Azrael drew in a breath, not wanting to dismiss Spector's ideas but also not certain what to do with them.

"I hope he wasn't bothering you?"

Azrael spun around to find Freya standing behind her.

"Mother," she said, still training herself to call her this. "No, he wasn't bothering me. He thinks I'm an angel."

"Well, you're my angel," Freya said. "Don't ever underestimate Spector. He sees the world a little differently to us."

Azrael nodded. "He told me that Rani and Aarow are going to Wintergreen. To see the Prince get married. Is it true?"

Freya nodded.

So much for friends never leaving each other behind.

"It's important they attend," Freya said.

"Does that mean Rani and Aarow will get married one day?" she asked.

Freya reached out and put an arm around her shoulder. "I hope so. They make each other very happy."

"Do you think I'll make someone very happy one day?" Azrael asked.

"You've already made me happy. Happier than I've ever been in all my life."

Azrael bit down on her bottom lip, wondering if the love of her mother would be enough, and deciding that it was. For now.

"She didn't ask me to go with her."

"It's a long way," said Freya. "She was protecting you. Besides, I think you're better off here. It's time for you to live your own life, not watch her live hers."

Azrael felt the gush of a sigh fly through her lips.

"I'd like to be a healer," said Azrael, having thought about this ever since being nursed back to health on her arrival at the Colony. "I think I'd be good at it."

"I think so, too," said Freya.

"I've been noticing how much longer people live in the Colony, compared to the Capital. Do you think that's because of your healings?"

"Partly," said Freya. "It certainly has made a difference. But it's also because we don't send our people out in the desert. There are lots of reasons we live longer in the Colony."

"I agree," said Azrael. "Because even people at the Capital who don't get released, still don't live for long. I think the Capital highly underestimated how important human contact is. It may have worked to rid the kingdom of the disease—if there was even such a disease in the first place—but ultimately it's what led to the demise of the people."

"You've really thought about this." Freya nodded, seeming to be impressed, giving her the confidence to continue.

"It's the small things as well as the big. You putting your arm around me just now when I was sad about Rani, took away some of my pain. Pain that normally I'd continue to carry. You picking up Bindi when she cries lets her know that she's loved. Rani grasping my hand as we walked into battle gave me strength. It's all these small things that heal us on the inside that make our bodies stronger on the outside. If you have a broken soul, you can't possibly expect your heart to pump until your hair turns gray."

Freya ran a hand through her own gray strands.

"I didn't mean you, of course!"

"No, it's okay. I hope you did mean me. Because the color of my hair is a privilege I didn't expect to have in life. Each wrinkle on my face, each strand of gray that grows, is evidence I'm alive when the Capital wanted me dead. I hope all my children have gray hair one day."

Azrael's hand fluttered to her dark hair. She hoped so, too. She wanted nothing more.

"Do you think we look alike?" Azrael asked.

"A little," said Freya.

"Do I look like my father?" Now she bit down on her tongue, not her lip. This was likely a question too far.

"I never saw his face. I'm sorry."

Azrael put her own arm around Freya now. "Please don't say sorry. I'm sorry I asked. I've found you and that's enough for me."

"You're going to have a wonderful life," said Freya. "I have a feeling you're going to be the most powerful healer this kingdom has ever seen."

"I'll never be as powerful as you," said Azrael, meaning it.

Freya shook her head. "It's true I've been blessed with a gift, although, I suspect it's present even stronger in you."

"How can you think that?" Azrael asked.

"Because of your dreams. I have them too, but they're nothing like yours. Not as vivid, not as certain, not nearly as powerful."

"What does it feel like to heal someone?" Azrael asked. "What are you actually doing with your hands?"

"Feeling for energy so I can rebalance it. It's like a vibration. You just said how important it is to be healthy on the inside in order to be healthy on the outside."

Azrael nodded, keen to learn more.

"Why don't we go to the Healing Room now and I'll show you?" asked Freya. "The sooner I start teaching you, the better. There are a lot of broken souls on their way here from the Capital. We're going to be very busy with our healings."

"Can I join you in just a moment?" asked Azrael, not wanting to return under the ground so soon. It was difficult to get used to a life without the sky above your head.

"Of course. Come and find me when you're ready."

Azrael watched her mother return to the Colony, then scanned for Spector on the horizon, still turning circles in the sand. Perhaps he really was the eagle he insisted he was. And perhaps she was an angel. She did know things that other people didn't seem to, and Freya was right in saying that her dreams were particularly vivid.

Would she be the most powerful healer the kingdom had ever seen? She wasn't sure about that. But if she had even a small amount of Freya's healing power then she could certainly try to repay her debt to the Colony. After all, she owed these people her life.

She looked at her palms in her lap, hoping they'd be able to sense the vibrations Freya talked about. She was certainly going to try. And whatever the case, she had her whole life ahead to figure all this out. And that life would be far longer than the one she'd expected to have back in the Capital, even if Rani was in love with someone else.

Perhaps sometimes friends did need to leave each other behind.

Rani's destiny was to lead. And it seemed that perhaps hers was to heal.

She just hoped she didn't let Freya down.

FREYA

THE EVERNOW

Freya placed her hand on Azrael's bare feet.

"I'm going to work my way up, scanning your energy centers," she said. "You don't need to do anything. Just lie there, close your eyes and relax."

Azrael nodded her consent.

"Now, normally I wouldn't talk through a healing, but I'm going to explain to you what I'm doing, so you can learn."

She lifted her hands from Azrael's feet and scanned her body with the palms of her hands, hovering just over her, trying not to cringe at just how unbalanced this poor girl was. Although, this was totally normal for a reborn. Especially one who'd experienced the horrors of the Conception Center. But she'd healed the other reborns. She'd be able to heal her daughter, too.

"A number of your energy centers have been blocked," she said. "I can feel this through my palms. It's a tingly feeling, like a hot prickle. When it's your turn to try, I'm certain you'll be able to feel it too."

She placed her hands lightly on Azrael's stomach, which was one of her more compromised centers. Unlike her throat, which was one of her areas of strength, a sign of a good communicator, something that Azrael had certainly proven since her arrival in the Colony.

"Now I'm just going to move my hands through your energy pattern, pulling your energy field up and out to reset it."

She worked on rebalancing Azrael's energy, one center at a time until she'd worked her way up to the top of Azrael's head.

"There's energy all around us," she said, continuing to knead her hands through her daughter's energy. "Learning to feel it is a special skill that not everyone has, but once it's mastered, it can be extremely powerful."

"I can feel it already," said Azrael, her eyelids fluttering open. "I feel lighter, like all the knots in my body have unraveled."

"Don't get up just yet," said Freya, scanning Azrael's body with open palms. "I can feel the edges of your energy field pulling back into balance. Give everything a few moments to settle into a new pattern. I think with a few more treatments we can have you feeling as good as new."

Freya rubbed her hands together, enjoying the warm sensation as the tingling subsided. It felt good to be able to help people like this. Especially people she loved.

"You can sit up slowly now," she said.

"That felt amazing," said Azrael, rubbing her eyes. "Did you do this to us when we were first brought here?"

Freya nodded. "Of course."

"That's why we healed so quickly," said Azrael. "I knew it was more than just food, water, and clean clothing. I felt so energized when I first woke up."

"You respond well to this kind of healing," said Freya. "You'll remember how much more energy you had when you woke than Rani or Sharma had, despite you being in the worst state when you arrived."

"That's true." Azrael blinked in agreement.

"Just another reason why I'm certain you have the touch."

"The touch?" Azrael tilted her head.

"One of the special few who are sensitive to energy. Would you like to try it on me and find out?" she asked.

"I don't want to disappoint you, if I don't." Azrael looked away.

"You could never disappoint me," Freya said, taking her hand and stroking her fingers lightly. "I love you no matter what. You must know that."

Azrael seemed to force a smile as she sat up and swung her legs off the bed. "Let's find out if I have this touch then."

They switched places and soon Freya was lying down with Azrael standing beside her.

"Open your hands and hold them above my body," said Freya. "Concentrate on the feeling in your palms. Move them around and tell me what you can feel."

Azrael moved her hands over Freya's body, biting her bottom lip as she concentrated.

"I can't feel anything yet."

"Don't try too hard," said Freya. "You can't force it. Take your time to tune in. When you feel it, you'll know."

Azrael took in a deep breath and moved her hands up and down from her feet right up to her head. Freya wasn't worried just yet. It took some healers a number of sessions before they felt anything.

But when Azrael paused over her stomach, Freya held her breath and waited, certain there'd been a shift.

"I think I can feel something," said Azrael. "It's like little vibrations. I'm not moving my hands. They seem to be moving themselves."

"That's right. Just focus on that feeling and it'll get stronger."

Azrael nodded, her face deep in concentration, as she proceeded to move her hands.

"Trace the outline of what you can feel," instructed Freya, watching as Azrael moved her hands in an even line over her torso then lifted them high in the air when she got to her head.

"Is that right?" said Azrael. "I feel like the energy around your head is right up here."

Freya smiled. Her daughter had the touch. She was anxious over the pending return of her husband and son. This would be manifesting in the energy center in the top of her head. Only someone with the gift of the touch would've been able to detect this so accurately.

"That's right, my daughter," she said, with tears stinging her eyes. "Now I want you to pull your hands through that blockage, drawing the energy up and out."

She watched as Azrael did as she was told, her movements swift and natural, like she'd been born to do this.

Freya breathed a sigh as she felt her anxiety clear. She spent so much time healing others, it was sometimes easy to forget that she too sometimes needed healing herself.

"Am I doing it right?" asked Azrael.

"It's perfect." Freya nodded, closing her eyes and letting her daughter take over. Her arrival at the Colony had healed Freya's heart and it seemed her ongoing presence was going to heal her body too. The other healers she'd trained hadn't learned the skill as quickly as this, nor had their healings been as immediately effective. With Azrael by her side, maybe, at last, she'd be able to let go of all the damage she'd experienced at the hands of the Capital.

"You're crying," said Azrael, stilling her hands.

"I'm happy," said Freya, reaching out her hands.

Azrael pressed her palms to Freya's and she felt her pain slide free.

AAROW

THE EVERNOW

*a*arow stood at the top of the very same dune where he'd first seen Rani sheltering under the Joshua tree. Only this time she was standing beside him, which was most definitely where he preferred her to be.

Toran and Jinn were also with them, taking their animal hides and laying them on the hot sand.

Excitement pulled at Aarow's stomach. He couldn't wait to share some dune sliding fun with Rani. Everything had been so serious since they'd met. It would be great to just let everything go and feel the wind in their hair and the thrill of being totally in the hands of gravity.

"Are you sure you want to do it?" he asked Rani for the third time since arriving at the top of the dune.

"Of course. I told you. I've been locked in my bedchamber for far too long. I want to experience everything." She grinned at him as if to prove it and he smiled at her tenacity. It was new for him to spend so much time with a girl who was so brave and eager to live a full life.

"You go first," he said to Toran and Jinn.

His friends formed a circle with him and they knocked their fists together.

"Boom!" They splayed their hands and Aarow glanced at Rani, laughing to see a bewildered expression on her face.

"Don't ask," he said to her. "It's just something we've done since we were kids."

She shook her head and unleashed one of her heartbreaking smiles.

Toran had been towing the bulk of their supplies on a separate hide and he pushed it off the edge of the dune first, watching it rocket its way down to the bottom.

Rani gasped. "Will we go that fast?"

Before Aarow could answer, Toran and Jinn jumped on their own hides and set off after their supplies, whooping and hollering. He didn't have to be able to see their faces to know they'd be smiling widely, despite the grains of sand that would be flying into their faces. It was impossible not to smile while sliding across the sand.

"We can walk down if you'd prefer," he said, giving her one last chance.

Rani grinned at him. "Scared?"

Aarow laughed. "Okay then. Let's do it."

He sat down on the hide and patted the space in front of him between his legs for Rani to sit. They'd travel faster with their combined weight, although he wasn't prepared to let her go on her own. It'd be too risky if she wasn't able to hold on. Besides, she didn't weigh very much so hopefully the speed wouldn't increase by too much.

She sat down in front of him and he shifted his legs to lock her into place.

"I won't be able to hold onto you," he said. "I'll need to hold onto the hide."

"Should I sit behind you?" she asked.

"No, because if you let go, you'll go flying. If you're in front of me, the speed will push you back into me. And you can hold onto my legs."

She nodded and looped her arms through his bent knees.

The proximity of having her sitting so intimately was almost a little too much to handle. They were going to need to set off soon before he gave in to the temptation and turned her face to kiss her.

"Quickly!" she said. "Before I change my mind."

He leaned forward and gave her a peck on the cheek, before digging his hands into the sand and pushing them off.

The hide began to slip, and he took hold of the edges, hugging Rani firmly between his thighs. It was officially too late to change their minds now. He just had to hold on tight and hope she enjoyed it as much as he did.

Their speed increased and Rani was pushed back into him until her hair worked its way free from her veil and was whipping him in the face. He leaned forward so his cheek was pressed against hers and her hair flew out behind them like a black sail.

He held on tighter as their speed increased, enjoying the sensation of flying at a greater speed than he'd traveled before, with the girl he loved experiencing this moment with him. Their bodies were pressed so close and the experience so intense that it felt like they were two halves of the one being.

Unlike Toran and Jinn and the hollering noises they made all the way down, Rani remained silent, leaving Aarow unable to tell if she was terrified or enraptured by the experience. Either way, her feelings had to be intense. It'd be impossible not to be moved by the sensation of flying over the sand.

"I love you!" he shouted, unsure if the wind swept away his words before they had a chance to land in her ear.

He couldn't help it. He knew he was supposed to be moving slowly with Rani, but right now, in this moment, nothing else in the world mattered other than his love for her.

She remained silent, leaving him certain she hadn't heard him. He didn't mind. They had their whole lives for him to tell her that he loved her. Hopefully, one day she'd even say it back to him.

He held his breath as they slid over a particularly steep part of the dune, racing toward the bottom where Toran and Jinn stood cheering them on, their two figures getting larger and larger with each moment.

Reaching the base of the dune, they scuttled across the flat sand, eventually skidding to a stop.

When he felt safe to let go, Aarow released his grip on the hide and wrapped his arms around Rani's shoulders.

She turned around and he caught the first glimpse of her face, thrilled to see the enraptured glint of joy in her eyes.

"That was incredible!" Her breath was coming in short gasps and she threw her arms around him, tipping him backward so she was lying on top of him.

He lifted his head to catch her kiss and they broke away, laughing at all the sand stuck to their lips. It was like trying to kiss a cactus. He wiped his mouth with his sleeve as she did the same and they tried again, kissing each other through the rough grains of sand.

Toran and Jinn came running to them, roaring with laughter.

Jinn threw himself on top of them and made kissing sounds, having far too much fun at their expense.

Aarow felt Rani freeze and stiffen, her eyes wide. She may have become comfortable with his touch, but she clearly wasn't comfortable with anybody else going near her.

Jinn must have sensed this too, as he leaped to his feet and smoothed down his clothes, seeming unsure if he should apologize or not.

"Sorry, Rani," he said.

She shook her head and smiled. "It's okay."

"Did you love it?" asked Toran, unaware of what'd just taken place.

"It was brilliant," said Rani. "Better than anything I've ever done in my life. Well, almost." Her eyes trailed to Aarow's lips and he hoped she was thinking about kissing him because he knew he was. There was no more exhilarating feeling than that.

"Give me a hand with the supplies," said Toran, punching Jinn playfully on the arm.

The two of them loped over to where the supplies had come to rest at the bottom of the dune.

Aarow stood and held out his hand to help Rani up.

"I'm so glad you enjoyed it," he said.

"I want to do it again." She bit down on her bottom lip, her body jiggling at the thought of it.

"There'll be more opportunities on the way back," he said. "Come on, let's go to the river and get all this sand off us so I can kiss you properly. It's your favorite thing, remember?"

"How did you know that's what I was talking about?" She giggled.

"Lucky guess."

"Aarow," she said, standing on the tips of her toes, seeming to want to tell him something.

He bent forward so she could press her mouth to his ear.

"I love you, too."

RANI

THE EVERNOW

*R*ani had walked so far she was surprised there was any more of the world left to walk. And to think Sharma had told her that The Sands of Naar was the smallest of the five kingdoms. The others must be enormous.

Sharma had taken the news of Rani's journey well, reassuring her that she was perfectly capable of finding her missing children alone. Rani's father would help her. After all, they were his children too. Hopefully when Rani returned, she'd have more members of her family to meet.

It seemed that half the kingdom had come out to wave their small party farewell, wishing them safe travels. And Rani did feel safe with three strong men walking beside her, ready to protect her from whatever trouble came their way.

Attending a wedding wasn't something Rani had ever expected to do in her life. But nor had she expected to fly down a sand dune while seated on an animal hide. Especially pressed up against a man who made her heart skip so many beats she was surprised she hadn't fainted in his arms by now. That'd been the most thrilling experience.

She'd never felt so alive as in those moments. Nothing else in the world mattered. She could see why Aarow and his friends enjoyed it so much. She was very keen to do it again on the return journey.

But there were no sand dunes now. Not long after crossing the river, the sand had gradually become firmer, until they found themselves walking across hard ground. Toran and Jinn now worked together to pull their supplies behind them, rather than taking turns. The extra effort was compensated for by the ease with which they now planted their steps. It was so much easier to move forward when your feet didn't disappear into the sand.

Aarow had a large pack of additional supplies strapped to his back and all three men insisted that Rani walk unencumbered. They'd said they were stronger than her and used to walking, anticipating she'd find the journey difficult enough. She'd protested but was soon glad they hadn't let her. They seemed to travel with far more ease than she was, carrying her clothes on her back alone. If she had to carry supplies, she'd only slow them down.

Aarow held the map and had said they were getting closer. They weren't headed to the palace, but to something called an apothecary. Apparently, it had a garden filled with thousands of different plants and the people of Wintergreen extracted oils to make elixirs that cured people of all kinds of ailments. It was all a little hard to imagine.

The Prince of Wintergreen was marrying a commoner, who lived in the apothecary with her brother, a man known as the Alchemist. Thankfully the bride didn't have any such strange sounding title and was simply called Jasmine. She and the Prince had fallen in love a long time ago when a plague had been spreading across the kingdom, taking the lives of the male inhabitants. Somehow the women had been immune.

Rani didn't quite understand how the Prince and Jasmine had managed to cure the plague, but apparently they had, and the kingdom now thrived, living in peace alongside its neighbor, Forte Cadence.

She liked the idea of being friendly with the neighboring kingdoms. There was so much more to be gained by that than fighting them for land they didn't need.

As she continued walking, too exhausted to air any of these concerns with Aarow, she mulled over the possibility of her future, ruling the kingdom with Aarow. Would it be as his counterpart or as his wife? Was that what this trip was really all about? Did the Colonel and her father have plans for her to marry Aarow one day and properly unite the two cities of the kingdom?

It made a lot of sense when spelled out like that. But did it make sense in her heart?

She looked across at Aarow, walking faithfully beside her. He felt her eyes upon him and looked back at her.

"Are you okay?" His brow crinkled as he scanned her face.

"I'm fine," she said, still pondering the idea of marrying this man one day and unable to deny that she liked the idea. The idea of being bonded to this strong handsome man who'd saved her life pulled her stomach into delicious knots. Although, she really did need to see an actual wedding first before she made up her mind about such things.

The terrain around them became greener with every step they took and soon they found themselves walking under a canopy of trees with soft grass beneath their feet. It was hard to get used to and Rani was grateful the terrain had transformed gradually, giving her a chance to get used to it little by little. It was so different to anything she'd seen before.

Stopping for a rest, they lay on the grass and Rani looked up, seeing the blue of the sky breaking through the leaves above. She'd once thought the Orbs of Time were the most beautiful thing she'd ever seen, but she knew now that wasn't true. As spectacular and mysterious as they were, they were no competition for the simple beauty of nature.

It was strange to think that right now, the sand would be continuing to fall through the orbs. For the first time, she thought she properly understood the concept of Evernow. Time never held still, which was why it was important to live every moment. Like right now, lying on the ground next to the man she loved with nothing and nobody trying to hurt her.

"Look," said Aarow pointing at a small bird, sitting on a branch. It wasn't a large eagle circling the desert looking for prey, but an innocent creature looking at them with pure curiosity and no motive whatsoever.

"It's so pretty," said Rani.

"There are more if you look," said Jinn, pointing to other trees. "There and there and...oh, look at that one. It's blue!"

"I wonder what other creatures are out here," said Rani, glancing around. There may not be coyotes, but surely other dangers existed.

"You're safe," said Aarow, sensing her fear as he passed her his waterskin for her to take a drink. "We won't let anything hurt you."

"How much further?" Rani asked. "I'm in no state to meet a future queen. Going by you three, I must look a sight."

Her three companions chuckled, although she was only half joking. They looked tired and filthy. Although, somehow Aarow was managing to look more rugged and less disheveled. A rough beard had started to sprout from his usually clean-shaven face and she decided it suited him.

"You look lovely," said Aarow, a comment that sent Jinn into fits of laughter.

"My friend, you have it bad," Jinn said. Then looking at Rani, he pulled his face into the most serious one he could muster. "Although, I admit you do look a whole lot better than my two friends here."

"I'm sure we'll all have a chance to freshen up before meeting the royal family," said Toran. "For their own sake as much as ours."

Aarow wrapped an arm around Rani's shoulder and she snuggled into him, drawing strength from the contact.

"You really do look lovely," he whispered in her ear, too quiet for Jinn to hear.

She smiled, knowing he meant it. In his eyes, she must certainly look lovely, which was surely a sign he loved her, just like he'd said on the sand dune. And if true love wasn't the basis for a future marriage, then she didn't know what was.

AAROW

THE EVERNOW

*A*arow felt like an imposter. Although, Rani was standing beside him and there was nothing about her that said she wasn't meant to be at this wedding. She had a regal presence about her and when he stood by her side, he felt like he belonged. It reminded him of the story about the princess who slept on the pea, not because Rani was like her, but because she wasn't. There was no need to set any tests to be certain she was a princess. It was in the way she held herself, whether she realized it or not.

She wore a dress made of lush red fabric, covering almost every part of her, except her hands and face. Unlike some of the other women here, who showed parts of their bodies that Aarow had been certain were meant to be kept hidden. Never mind. There was nothing about this kingdom that was like it was back home. What the women here chose to wear was the least of his concerns.

Rani may be the most modestly dressed guest at this wedding, however, she was the only one who held Aarow's eye. He'd told her twice already that she looked beautiful, and she'd smiled politely, not seeming to quite know what to do with his compliments. Perhaps she'd grow used to them in time, as she had with his kisses.

There were hundreds of people in attendance, all standing around a timber structure he'd been told was called a gazebo. It was covered in trails of delicate flowers and was the center point of this paradisiacal garden. Bunches of blooms had been picked and placed in vases around the gazebo and colored glass jars filled with fragrant oils had been strung from the timber beams, swinging in the gentle breeze.

Aarow had never imagined the world contained such a place like this. It couldn't be more different to The Sands of Naar, with trees, flowers, wildlife and a climate that didn't feel like it was trying to roast you alive or tear you to shreds with the relentless wind. In this kingdom, you could sit beneath the sun's rays and enjoy the feeling of the gentle warming of your skin.

They'd been received with great excitement at the apothecary by a group of women who'd been working in the garden. They were taken to the main house where baths laced with soothing oils were drawn and soft beds had been made, the quilts covered in petals and dried bunches of lavender strung from the bedposts to help them sleep.

Rani got her wish and had been able to freshen up before meeting their hostess, Jasmine, the future queen of Wintergreen. Not that Aarow felt Rani had needed to worry. Jasmine and her brother hadn't seemed to be the sort of people who cared in the least about appearances and despite Rani refusing to believe him, he'd honestly thought she looked lovely every moment of their long journey here.

Jasmine had been extremely hospitable, ensuring their every need had been met. She seemed excited at their arrival, explaining that the Queen and Prince of Forte Cadence had arrived at the palace with their young daughter and were being looked after by Jasmine's future husband, Prince Ari. She spoke fondly of them and Aarow looked forward to making their acquaintance and sitting down to speak at length with them after the wedding. Apparently, Queen Rose had whispered for their safe arrival and Aarow was keen to learn more about what exactly this meant.

Sadly, the other kingdoms had failed to respond to their invitations, not ready to acknowledge that people could achieve so much more when they worked together, than they could alone.

The Board had proven how badly this kind of thinking could also go wrong and Aarow was aware they needed to proceed with caution. He'd heard Rani talking to Jasmine about this and Jasmine was keen for them to share their experiences with Queen Rose. Apparently, she'd only just set up some kind of board of her own to help rule her kingdom. There was no doubt there were many lessons they could learn from each other to ensure mistakes of the past weren't made again.

Aarow watched the groom waiting in the gazebo for the arrival of his bride. He hadn't yet been introduced to Prince Ari. A tall, handsome man who stood with a straight back and a look of confidence in his dark eyes. He was flanked by a younger man who looked like a younger version of himself.

"I didn't know the prince had a son," Aarow whispered to Rani.

His whisper hadn't been quiet enough and a woman behind him tapped him on the shoulder and told him that the young man was the prince's nephew.

"Uncanny resemblance," said Aarow.

"Indeed." The woman nodded politely.

Aarow's attention was stolen by the grand entrance of the King and Queen of Wintergreen, dressed in their royal finery as they walked down a carpet of petals that'd been laid out on the grass to make an aisle. The King was a handsome man, tall like his son, yet his face was lined with years of worry. The Queen seemed a nervous sort, clinging to her husband's arm like she wouldn't be able to stand without his support. Aarow knew they'd once had a daughter and had been told the Queen had never gotten over losing her. This rumor appeared to be true. Then he saw her look up at her son and grandson in the gazebo and her face filled with renewed joy.

They were followed down the aisle by Queen Rose and Prince Jeremiah, with their young daughter asleep in her father's arms. Rose had her hand placed gently on Jeremiah's back, although it didn't seem like she was using him to hold her up. This couple exuded strength and a feeling of being evenly matched as rulers of Forte Cadence. They were certainly good role models for how Aarow would like to rule his own kingdom with Rani by his side.

Now that everyone was in place, an orchestra to the side of the gazebo began to play a melodic tune and several of the congregation sang quietly. The song was about having luck, which seemed appropriate on such a day.

The people turned their heads to see Jasmine walking through the garden toward the gazebo on the arm of her brother. He was quite a bit younger than her, yet held her arm nobly, taking his job of giving her away very seriously. Jasmine had already explained to them that their parents had died from the plague but hadn't seemed to want to go into any further details. It was clearly a sore subject and Aarow hadn't pushed her any further. If anyone could understand what it was like to lose a parent, it was him.

Aarow looked at Rani, who was taking in the scene with wide eyes and he hoped she was wondering if one day this wedding would be them. He still hadn't raised the subject with her, not wanting to scare her away, however, he suspected he was being overly cautious. Rani hadn't seemed to be scared by anything that'd happened between them so far. Perhaps that was because he was carefully judging the pace between them, rather than her being ready to embrace all that came her way.

Jasmine came closer and Aarow was unable to help himself from smiling at how beautiful she looked. She wore a dress, delicate purple in color, and had flowers in her dark waves of hair, forming a floral crown. More flowers had been looped into chains and she wore them as her jewels around her neck and wrists. She also held a bunch of wildflowers, many of which Aarow recognized from this very garden. She looked like some kind of fairy princess, her beauty magnified by the kindness Aarow had learned was in her heart.

Prince Ari was understandably transfixed by his bride, and Aarow put a gentle hand on the small of Rani's back, unable to help wishing they could trade places with Jasmine and her prince right now.

Although, everything about this wedding said Wintergreen. When he and Rani got married, it would be in the desert. Perhaps they could get married on the top of a dune and take off on an animal hide immediately afterward. He smiled to himself, certain that Rani would have other ideas about that.

Jasmine reached the gazebo and turned to her brother who kissed her on the cheek and let go of her hand, the special bond between them clear to all.

The Prince's nephew shook his hand, then went down the stairs. He patted Jasmine's brother on the back, took Jasmine's arm and escorted her up the stairs to her groom, also kissing her on the cheek before leaving them alone. It was a series of small gestures, all of which would have been punishable by death in the Capital before the revolution, yet it was impossible to imagine this ceremony without them.

Prince Ari took Jasmine's hands in his and she smiled up at him. It was like the hundreds of people who surrounded the gazebo were no longer there. It was just the two of them, joining themselves in marriage but also taking on the far greater responsibility of ruling the kingdom in the future.

"What do you think?" Aarow whispered to Rani, desperate to know what her wide eyes were making of all of this.

"It's amazing. Are all weddings like this?"

"They don't have all this," he said, waving his hands around at the flowers and the people in fancy clothes. "But most of them have that." He pointed to the two people in the gazebo, very much in love.

"It's pure love," said Rani, catching his gaze.

He bent forward and kissed her gently on her cheek. "It is."

And as Jasmine and Prince Ari spoke their vows, promising to be together always, Aarow and Rani watched on, making vows of their own in their hearts.

Aarow didn't know the answer to any of their problems. Or the best way to rule a kingdom. All he knew was that love was a far more powerful force than hate. Which meant that love would ultimately rule them all.

AFTER THE EVERNOW

The woman walked across the hot sand, remembering the time long ago when she'd stumbled and fallen, begging her departed ancestors to ready the heavens for her arrival.

But she'd been rescued, reborn into a new life in the Colony. It was a second chance at life although, in many ways, it'd felt like her first.

A gust of wind sent sharp grains of red sand flying toward her and she wrapped her face with her veil.

Her hands were drawn to her belly as if by a magnetic force and she remembered the baby that'd been taken from her. A daughter who was returned to her so many years later, just as beautiful as she'd been when she'd been torn from her outstretched hands.

This daughter of hers had grown without a single touch from another human, until she rebelled and ran into the desert, unaware she was following the same footsteps of her mother.

The woman startled as someone came up behind her. But when he wrapped his arms around her shoulders, she knew it was her husband. She knew the smell of him. She knew the feel of him. How appropriate that he was here with her now, just as he'd been when she'd thought all had been lost.

It'd been many moons since she'd last seen him and she'd been waiting, just as she'd waited for her daughter.

He pulled her close and she pressed her face against his chest to protect herself from the sting of the sand. She'd grown up having never been touched like this. She'd never been fed by her mother or held by her father. Never been embraced by a lover or struck by an enemy. She'd never been picked up when she fell. She'd lived a life untouched.

All that had changed when she was reborn. And it was to the desert that she came to call her gratitude to the sky. The place that nearly stole her life was the place she came to pay her respects.

"Am I dead?" she called over the wind, using the words she'd first said to her husband so long ago, as she struggled to believe he'd returned home at last.

"No," her husband shouted back. "We've never been more alive."

THE END
Ready to discover the next kingdom?
Check out Book 4, The Guardians of Evernow!
http://mybook.to/hcguardians

THE GUARDIANS OF EVERNOW

BOOK 4 THE KINGDOMS OF EVERNOW

Will he sacrifice everything,

for the one who sacrificed it all?

River is a Guardian, bred for courage and trained to fight. Her duty is to serve her King and her future was scripted long ago—marry a male Guardian and strengthen the bloodline of the next generation. But when the King decides his own bloodline must be strengthened, River's bestowed the honor of marrying his son, and her future slips even further out of her grasp.

Tate is a Prince whose heart is as kind as River's is strong. He'd rather protect the vulnerable and care for his reclusive sister than rule a kingdom. But he knows the time has come for him to step up. Marrying without love isn't something he wishes for either, but he has no choice if he's to take the throne and ensure the kingdom will live in peace.

But someone else has their eye on the throne... Someone who knows all about the tonics that are the key to the Guardians' strength, and he'll stop at nothing to bring the kingdom down so he can rule them all. Setting out on a path of destruction, he makes a cunning plan to marry the Princess and remove anyone standing in his way.

River and Prince Tate must work together as team to save the kingdom. As Guardians mysteriously die, boundaries are pushed and the threat of an invasion looms, they'll discover if their marriage is built on more than just convenience. Is it possible that it's also built on love?

With a story that will feed your imagination, the fourth book in the spellbinding *The Kingdoms of Evernow* series is a must-read by award-winning author, Heidi Catherine.

Grab your copy now!

http://mybook.to/hcguardians

ALSO BY HEIDI CATHERINE

The Kingdoms of Evernow
Five kingdoms. Five senses.
One secret that will change them all.
The Kingdoms of Evernow (Prequel)
The Whisperers of Evernow
The Alchemists of Evernow
The Empress of Evernow
The Guardians of Evernow
The Angels of Evernow

The Soulweaver series
Two girls. Two lives. One soul.
The Soulweaver
The Truthseeker
The Shadowmaker

The Sovereign Code
Humans saved bees from extinction...
and created the deadliest threat we've seen yet
Harvest Day
Hive Mind
Queen Hunt
Venom Rising
Sting Wars

Elemental Games

Elemental powers. Deadly games. No escape.

Elemental Games

Elemental Uprising

Elemental Wars

Elemental Solution

The Thaw Chronicles

Four tests. Seven days. Nine teens.

Only the chosen shall breed.

Burning (Prequel)

Rising

Breaking

Falling

Reckoning

Extant

Exist

Exile

Expose

Tournaments of Thaw

Conquer the Thaw

The Oasis Trials

The Oasis Deception

The Last Oasis

WANT TO STAY IN TOUCH?

Heidi loves to connect with readers, so please say hello on social media, leave a review on Amazon or Goodreads, or visit her at www. heidicatherine.com

facebook.com/HeidiCatherineAuthor
instagram.com/HeidiCatherine
tiktok.com/@heidicatherineauthor
amazon.com/author/heidicatherine

ABOUT THE AUTHOR

Heidi writes fantasy and dystopian novels, which gives her a chance to escape into worlds vastly different to her own life in the burbs. While she quite enjoys killing her characters (especially the awful ones), she promises she's far better behaved in real life. Other than writing and reading, Heidi's current obsessions include watching far too much reality TV with the excuse that it's research for her books.